A HAII

CLAUDE HOUGHTON OLDFIELD
and was educated at Dulwich
ant and worked in the Admira\.., ... world war, rejected
for active service because of poor eyesight. In 1920 he married a
West End actress, Dulcie Benson, and they lived in a cottage in the
Chiltern Hills. To a writers' directory, Houghton gave his hobbies
as reading in bed, riding, visiting Devon and abroad, and talking to
people different from himself. He added: "I like dawn, and the dead
of night, in great cities." He disliked fuss, noise, crowds, rows, and
being misquoted, or being told how much he owed "to some writer
I've never read."

Houghton's earliest writing was poetry and drama before turning to prose fiction with his first novel, *Neighbours*, in 1926. In the
1930s, Houghton published several well-received novels that met
with solid sales and respectable reviews, including *I Am Jonathan
Scrivener* (1930), easily his most popular and best-known work, *Chaos
Is Come Again* (1932), *Julian Grant Loses His Way* (1933), *This Was Ivor
Trent* (1935), *Strangers* (1938), and *Hudson Rejoins the Herd* (1939).
Although he published nearly a dozen more novels throughout the
1940s and 1950s, most critics feel his later works are less significant
than his novels of the '30s.

Houghton was a prolific correspondent, generous in devoting his
time to answering letters and signing copies for readers who enjoyed
his books. One of these was novelist Henry Miller, who never met
Houghton but began an impassioned epistolary exchange with
him after being profoundly moved by his works. Houghton's other
admirers included his contemporaries P. G. Wodehouse, Clemence
Dane, and Hugh Walpole. Houghton died in 1961.

By Claude Houghton

The Kingdoms of the Spirit (1924)
Neighbours (1926)*
The Riddle of Helena (1927)
Crisis (1929)
I Am Jonathan Scrivener (1930)*
A Hair Divides (1930)*
Chaos Is Come Again (1932)*
Julian Grant Loses His Way (1933)*
Three Fantastic Tales (1934)
This Was Ivor Trent (1935)*
The Beast (1936)
Christina (1936)
Strangers (1938)
Hudson Rejoins the Herd (1939)
All Change, Humanity! (1942)
The Man Who Could Still Laugh (1943)
Six Lives and a Book (1943)
Passport to Paradise (1944)
Transformation Scene (1946)
The Quarrel (1948)
Birthmark (1950)
The Enigma of Conrad Stone (1952)
At the End of a Road (1953)
The Clock Ticks (1954)
More Lives Than One (1957)

A HAIR DIVIDES

CLAUDE HOUGHTON

A Hair, they say, divides the False and True
                                Omar Khayyám

VALANCOURT BOOKS

A Hair Divides by Claude Houghton
First published London: Thornton Butterworth, 1930
First Valancourt Books edition 2015

Published by Valancourt Books, Richmond, Virginia
http://www.valancourtbooks.com

ISBN 978-1-943910-00-7 (trade paperback)
Also available as an electronic book.

All Valancourt Books publications are printed on acid free paper that
meets all ANSI standards for archival quality paper.

Set in Dante MT 10.5/12.6

Author's Note: This is a work of fiction, and all characters in the book
are drawn from the author's imagination. Care has been taken to avoid
the use of names or titles belonging to living persons, and if any such
names or titles have been used, this has been done inadvertently and
no reference to such person or persons is intended.

A HAIR DIVIDES

CHAPTER I

One evening in October 1910 Gordon Rutherford entered a café near Regent Street and after exchanging greetings with several acquaintances, he chose a table at which a stranger was seated. The conversation which ensued was the beginning of a friendship which developed rapidly and which ended incalculably. The name of the stranger was Martin Feversham. . . .

To evoke the atmosphere of London in 1910 demands imagination: it is necessary to forget so much in order to remember it.

A city, like an individual, is revealed by what it accepts as commonplace, and the London of 1910 regarded wealth, dominion, and security, as normal and natural – the undisputed and inalienable birthright of England. The twentieth century did not exist yet – it was only a fiction of the calendar – its true birth was 1914. In 1910 London was sentimental, romantic, and glamorous; it was exclusive and aristocratic. No vast nondescript hordes wandered about its streets: Bond Street was a club rather than a thoroughfare, and Piccadilly was the pulse of the world. By night the West End was dominated by the well-dressed and the well-born. A social hierarchy existed, and cheap restaurants had not yet risen in marble might. Everything was different. There were ballets at the Empire and the Alhambra and masculine young men used to wait impatiently at the stage doors after the performances. The theatres were not in the hands of speculators but were controlled by people connected with the stage, and picture palaces were dark, draughty booths patronized only by lovers. There were music halls, and popular songs were not imported from America.

There was no traffic problem – only the rich had cars – the streets were comparatively safe, it was possible to speak and be heard, and the air was not blue with fumes of motors. Nash's Regent Street still stood and innumerable songs celebrated the glories of the narrow and vulgar Strand. Women had neither legs nor votes.

Politically, there were Conservatives and Liberals – the Labour Party was still regarded somewhat as a joke in rather doubtful taste. Unemployment was practically negligible. The Irish Members frequently infused the vitality of the music hall into the staid atmosphere of the House of Commons. Otherwise, all was quiet on the home front. Lloyd George's "big bold Budget," and the reform of the House of Lords, were regarded as thrills.

People had manners in those days and money was not the sole topic of conversation. The world had been made almost safe for Victorianism. Everything proved it: popular heroes were either soldiers or sailors, not film stars; colour schemes were unknown, for the Russian Ballet had not arrived yet; houses and minds were lumber-rooms full of heavy furniture; and decent people still trembled at the mention of Oscar Wilde's name.

Commercially, England was triumphant. It was true that there were sinister hints of big scale strikes, and it was irritating that the Germans worked so hard and were so efficient but then – what could you expect? – they were not gentlemen. Income tax was about a shilling in the pound, but certain financial wizards prophesied disaster when the budget reached nearly a hundred million. Also certain eminent experts confidently predicted that the provision of twenty million a year for Old Age Pensions would reduce the country to bankruptcy. Meanwhile, England luxuriated in splendid isolation, and sport was the supreme activity of every right minded man.

As to religion, the Church of England was an immutable reality like wealth and security. You belonged to it in precisely the same way as you belonged to the Conservative Party. In fact, the Church of England had been defined as the

Conservative Party at prayer. If you did not belong to both organizations, you placed yourself irredeemably. That was all. Everything had been settled, and the criticism of some things – and the discussion of others – simply wasn't done. It was bad form and if anyone raised his voice in protest, he was immediately silenced. Plays – which have recently racked modern audiences with agonies of boredom – were rigorously suppressed by the Censor. Superficially, Respectability reigned.

An age was moving slowly to its death and London was beautiful with the elusive beauty of autumn. It was individual, intimate; it did not obliterate you – on the contrary, you owned it. It was seductive; it collaborated with your moods and desires; it had glamour, mystery; and it whispered its secrets to its lovers.

There were Bohemians in those days – they could afford it and it gave them a thrill. Actually, they were intensely romantic but they believed themselves to be ruthless, iconoclastic, and revolutionary. They dressed extravagantly and paraded their emotions. Some of them believed in Art for Art's sake to such an extent that a mirror was an adequate audience. It was the fashion to be decadent and therefore Baudelaire and Verlaine were gods. To be great – then as now – only three things were necessary: – to affect the vices of the illustrious; to scorn the financially successful; and to evince a passionate admiration for the obscure and the unknown. That formula – then as now – provided many mediocrities with an illusion, and rendered hard work superfluous.

There were certain night clubs and cafés at which these Bohemians were always to be found. The presence of one or two well-known artists was sufficient to convince ambitious youth that it had entered the promised land. It was in a café of this type that Rutherford met Feversham. . . .

For some moments after taking a seat Rutherford read the evening paper, then glancing round in search of distraction he became interested in the man at his table. He was sketching the head of a girl, who was talking animatedly a few yards away, and Rutherford immediately noticed the sensitive beauty of his hands. There was a negligent grace in Feversham's whole attitude, his left elbow rested on the table while his hand supported his head, and Rutherford became aware of an attraction in this stranger which defied analysis. He began to study him. Feversham was about twenty-three, tall, fair, with that slender type of athletic figure which inevitably suggests speed. His clear-cut, attractive features were lit by fine, intelligent eyes, intensely blue, which gave the whole of their attention to the object with which they were concerned. Tolerance and humour characterized a gay challenging mouth.

Feversham looked up, encountered Rutherford's gaze, and flicked his sketch across the table.

"There! What do you think of that?"

"It's much more desirable than its original," Rutherford replied almost with a sneer.

"You don't like Betty? She's not a bad sort – generous to the pitch of genius and an excellent model. Look here! I'll show you something."

He leant over and recovered his sketch, then picking up his pencil he altered the drawing with a few deft strokes till an entirely different portrait appeared. It was the face of a girl with dark, heavy hair, enigmatic eyes slightly aslant, rather high cheek-bones and powerfully moulded features. It was an arresting face. Under the mask of youth was potential power. Rutherford stared at it for some moments before he exclaimed:

"Good Lord! Who is she?"

Feversham laughed. "She's a girl I met two or three months ago. She comes to London to-morrow. I think she's hypnotized me. The best in another woman's face seems a prophecy of hers. That's dangerous, because it borders on obsession – and obsession is of the devil. Have a drink, or are you waiting for someone?"

He ordered drinks, then began to ruin the sketch with a few idle strokes.

Rutherford lit a cigarette then said to Feversham: "You're an artist, of course."

"No, not exclusively," he replied. "How can you know what

you are when you're under twenty-five? I can draw and it interests me, but I'm far from convinced that I want to give my life
to it. At the moment I'm amusing myself by writing."

Rutherford smiled rather patronizingly then said with
emphasis:

"If you want to do anything in the writing way, you'll have
to put all you've got into it."

"Ah, I see you're a writer," Feversham replied with a smile.
"I half-thought you were directly I saw you."

He spoke lightly as if the matter were not of supreme importance, a fact which irritated Rutherford, then he glanced
round the room.

The café was crowded by now and a blue cloud of tobacco
smoke hung over the animated groups at the tables. It was
clearly the aim of most of the people present to attract attention either by the extravagance of their gestures or by the
eccentricity of their appearance. Some of the men fiercely
proclaimed their Bohemianism by wearing corduroy coats,
huge black hats, and ferocious beards. They smoked enormous pipes in a reckless manner while enunciating theories
to brightly-arrayed models. Others, however, renounced the
age entirely and were immaculate in strapped trousers, stocks,
fobs, and elegant side-whiskers. One or two others, reputed
poets, evidently wished to indicate sartorially their convic-
tion that humanity was about to return to a primitive life of
Arcadian simplicity. These pioneers were hatless, low-necked,
and wore sandals. They were usually in the company of young
women whose profession induced a supreme sophistication.
The remainder of the company consisted of entirely respectable people, chiefly from the suburbs, who felt that a visit to the
Regal Café was an inexpensive way of seeing Life at close quarters. After all, on occasions, it was possible to catch a glimpse
of a well-known painter or sculptor – throned at a table and
surrounded by an adoring court. This glimpse enabled one to
say subsequently to an appropriate audience: "I saw Muratti
the other night. What a vital personality – so *dynamic*."

Feversham's glance flitted over this assembly. He nodded

to several people and it was evident that he knew a number of the more eccentric specimens. When he had completed his inventory, he turned to Rutherford:

"London would be impossible for a bird of passage like me if it weren't for a place like this. I've only been here a month, and I've made a hundred acquaintances already. They're a queer lot, but they're interesting, don't you think?"

But there was something in this broad, tolerant attitude which irritated Rutherford. Feversham was clearly not unduly impressed by his surroundings. This fact, and the strange independence implied in his whole bearing, jarred on Rutherford.

"It's difficult for me to say," he replied rather coldly. "You see, I belong to these people."

"Not a bit of it!" Feversham exclaimed confidently. "No more than I do. Your hair is rather long, I admit, but every line in your face and figure shows that you don't belong to this crowd. Three quarters of these people will never get anywhere. They haven't the will. You have – your mouth, your chin, and your hands all prove it."

Rutherford moved uneasily. This diagnosis partly flattered him and partly offended him, but to discuss it further might reveal his actual ambitions to this stranger whose unaided penetration was sufficiently embarrassing. An incident occurred, however, which relieved him of the necessity for continuing the subject.

A girl of about twenty stopped and spoke to Feversham. She was very slight and had a soft, appealing voice. She glanced over at Rutherford who nodded curtly and immediately picked up his paper.

"Hullo, Martin," she said, resting a hand on his shoulder.

"Hullo, Kits," he replied. "Haven't seen you for a week. Where have you been?"

"Ill," she announced laconically.

"That won't do. It's time we dined together again. I'll come round at about seven to-morrow. Is that all right?"

"I'll be ready," she replied and went to join a group at a table near by.

"That child has pluck," commented Feversham. "Actress when she can get a job and a model when she can't. There's the spirit of a Titan in that little body."

"Oh, she's all right," Rutherford admitted grudgingly, "but I get tired of her eternal dreams and ambitions."

He was about to continue when the great Wolheim emerged from a group and came up to Feversham. Now, Wolheim was a celebrity – a sculptor of considerable eminence – and consequently one of the idols of the café. A number of people would have given five years of life to be seen at his table, and Rutherford was not a little proud of the fact that he could claim his acquaintance. Unfortunately, however, Wolheim sometimes forgot him. The present occasion furnished another example of this defect of memory for, although Rutherford looked up with a smile, Wolheim seemed to be aware only of Feversham. He was a huge man with a shock of curly black hair and flashing eyes. His voice was deep and resonant and he spoke slowly with a strong foreign accent.

"And how is Mister Feversham?"

"I'm all right, Wolfie. You flourishing?"

"You haf deserted me. Yes? Well, kom soon and bring ze beautiful Sondra in addision."

They exchanged a few more sentences then the great man went his way. Neither spoke for a minute. Rutherford was amazed by the discovery that his companion's reception of the renowned Wolheim differed in no way from that he had given to the unknown little actress. As he would have been immensely flattered if the famous sculptor had shown him such attention, Feversham's attitude impressed him profoundly. There was something mysterious about this stranger who was several years younger than he was, and who, nevertheless, made him feel crude and inadequate.

Any observer, however, would have remarked the contrast between the two men. Build, features, dress – each and all were different. Rutherford with his broad, heavy shoulders, set determined face, and untidy suit obviously saw life in different terms from the slender, fair-haired Feversham whose clothes possessed that negligent but debonair aspect which no tailor can confer.

They chatted for another quarter of an hour and discovered that they had a number of acquaintances in common, then Rutherford suggested that they should dine together. He had a great belief in his powers of penetration and was convinced that if he spent an hour or two with Feversham he would discover the secret of his attraction.

Certain tables at the end of the large room were reserved for patrons who wished to dine in the café and they moved over to one of these. They drank a good deal of wine and, consequently, by the time coffee arrived, they were in that mood which – for men under thirty – inevitably involves an exchange of confidences. It was perhaps significant that Feversham was the first to put his cards on the table.

"I can see that you think I'm a queer bird," he began, "so I'll tell you about myself, if you like. Personally, I like people to emerge gradually rather than to be instantly revealed."

"A person must have a background," Rutherford objected, "otherwise he exists in a void."

"Perhaps you're right," Feversham replied, "but the background which can be reduced to words is only a very superficial one. Anyway, here goes! I was born in America. My parents were English but they both died when I was quite young. The only remaining relative I possessed was an aunt. A remarkable woman – I have only recently discovered how remarkable she was. When I was seventeen I went to France and Germany to finish my education. I returned to America when I was nearly twenty, to find my aunt seriously ill. She died within a year and I found myself alone in the world."

He broke off, lit a cigarette, and helped himself to another cup of coffee. Rutherford was surprised to discover the extent of his interest in every detail concerning this man of whose existence he had been ignorant two hours ago.

"When things had been straightened out," Feversham continued, "I found that I had about seven thousand pounds. I decided to invest them in myself."

"In yourself!" Rutherford exclaimed. "What does that mean – exactly?"

"This, my dear fellow. I know quite well that I have capabilities in a number of ways. Well, most men bind themselves irrevocably to some profession at the age of twenty, knowing precious little about it, and usually discover when it's too late that they hate it like the devil. I was under no immediate necessity to earn a living. I decided to knock around and discover what I wanted to do. So I've spread my money out – it's in banks in New York, Paris, Berlin, and here. I don't worry because long before it's exhausted I'm certain I'll be financially independent. Meanwhile, I travel about from one city to another and I find life an amazing adventure."

He laughed gaily and flicked the ash from his cigarette. Rutherford was staring at him moodily: attraction and repulsion being equally represented in his expression. He was fascinated yet, simultaneously, he was aware of a feeling of jealousy and a desire to find a label for this man who was outside all his categories. He wanted to assert himself, to compel Feversham's admiration, to impress him in some way, but to his great irritation he felt awkward and uninteresting. Frequently with him the desire to shine made performance impossible, but he had never felt so impotent as on the present occasion. The knowledge that it was now necessary to give some details about himself – and that his narrative would be less individual than Feversham's – only increased his feeling of inferiority.

Feversham began to talk on impersonal subjects, however, as if to indicate that Rutherford could confide in him or not, as he chose, but – paradoxically – this attitude increased Rutherford's annoyance more than a series of questions would have done.

"Well, I'm placed somewhat differently," he began heavily, "and I'm under no delusions as to what my job is – I'm committed to writing. It was on that issue that I practically quarrelled with my family. They are pretty typical, well-to-do, English people – no imagination of any kind. My brother is their hero. You know the type – good at games, handsome, and brainless. Naturally we were packed off to the same public school to which my father had duly been sent in his day. Equally inevitably, we went up to Cambridge. Look here!" he suddenly burst out angrily, "does all this bore you?"

"*Bore* me!" exclaimed Feversham genuinely astonished. "Why on earth should it? Everything interests me. Go on!"

Rutherford reddened then after a pause continued:

"Well, my brother got his Blue for rugby and became the family idol. I loathed Cambridge. Anyway, to cut a dull story short, I came into a hundred a year or so when I was twenty-one, and I cleared out. There was a hell of a scene with my father because he wanted me to go into his business. He makes a lot of money out of it and was incapable of realizing that I didn't care a damn about money. I was only interested in writing. Anyway, I cleared out and I see precious little of any of them."

For some reason, Feversham's comment took Rutherford completely by surprise, although it was appropriate to the context.

"I see," he said slowly, then added: "What have you written?"

"Oh, I can't point to a row of volumes published at my own expense like half the poseurs in this place," Rutherford blurted out angrily.

"But you said they were your people."

"No – not exactly – you don't understand. Some of them are – the genuine ones."

"People like Wolheim?" Feversham inquired.

"Yes, quite," Rutherford muttered. "I've written stories and articles and so on. I've a volume of verse nearly ready." He paused, then added impressively: "And I'm half-way through a novel."

"I see," said Feversham lightly. "I feel you probably will write something worth while one day. And by that I mean that you'll write something which only you could write."

"You think so?" The tone in which the question was asked

revealed the importance he attached to Feversham's opinion.

"I'm certain of it. It's a pity you quarrelled with your family. I've a theory that an adequate technique overcomes all problems of that kind."

"You only think that because you haven't a family," Rutherford cut in with a sneer.

"Quite possibly. All the same, I feel there's something wrong with that type of rebellion which immediately takes a violent outward form. Half the people in this place are below the conventions they deny so passionately."

"And you think I'm like them," Rutherford said angrily.

"Not in the least. I've told you that I think you'll do work worth doing." Then he added with a smile: "That is – you'll prove to your father that he was wrong."

But further confidences were impossible, for acquaintances in common, two men and a woman, joined them and a long argument developed as to the exact importance of Wolheim's work. As each participant used different terms, without any attempt at definition, the discussion was not very productive. It was followed by another on Socialism which in due course was succeeded by another on free love. Various people joined the group, chatted for a while, then disappeared. It was nearly midnight when Feversham and Rutherford rose and left the café together.

They stood at the entrance talking for a few minutes then Feversham turned to his companion and asked:

"By the way, what is your name?"

Rutherford stared at him. He had forgotten that he only knew Feversham's name because Wolheim had mentioned it.

"My name!" he exclaimed. "Oh, of course, you don't know it. It's Rutherford – Gordon Rutherford. Yours is Feversham, isn't it?"

"Yes. Martin Feversham. Is your brother the Rutherford who may play rugby for England?"

"*Yes, he is.*" The emphasis revealed intense irritability. "Why the devil do you take the slightest interest in that fact?"

"I'm interested in everything to a point," Feversham replied.

"Well, I expect I'll run into you again some time. That's better than making a set arrangement, don't you think? I nearly always let Destiny arrange my social encounters. Good-night. It's been interesting."

CHAPTER II

I

Rutherford lived in a couple of rooms in Bloomsbury which in those days had no intellectual or social pretensions but, on the contrary, was infested by cheap boarding houses and squalid apartments. It was the haunt of the homeless and consequently, in genteel circles, it was regarded as not quite respectable. Innumerable barrel organs used to emit senti-mental complaints, or whisper rustily of some vague, unde-fined region where hearts were golden and skies were blue. Fogs had a remarkable partiality for the district and during the winter Bloomsbury was a desert of dripping desolation. In the sunshine, the grimy stucco houses regarded each other disconsolately, and each Sunday in turn produced its heavy odour of beef and cabbage – and a silence that could be felt. Time crawled away like a wounded snake.

We judge everything, however, by the ends we have in view and, to Rutherford, Bloomsbury was but a stretch of a shin-ing thoroughfare which led to success and freedom. He did not see the squalor of the district, and if he ever compared the dinginess of his two rooms with the disciplined comfort of the home he had abandoned, he only did so in order to evoke the luxury of self-congratulation. He was free, and each day he was progressing towards a greater freedom. That was the supreme fact and it blinded his eyes to all minor disadvantages. Here, in these rooms, he could believe in himself, he could dream dreams and see visions, without being under the necessity of justifying them to those who regarded all such activities as sterile and ridiculous. It was because he had failed so signally to impress his father and brother with the elevated nature of his ideals and ambitions that he had gone his own way and broken finally with the tradition to which they adhered so inflexibly. The rupture had affected the two parties very differently. At first, his family had regarded his defection with amused tolerance, confident that it represented merely a passing phase, but as the years produced no sign of the prodigal's return they had long since written him off mentally as a failure. Rutherford, on the other hand, was still possessed by a spirit of passionate bitterness and an angry determination to compel them to recognize his superiority. His feeling of antagonism, which almost amounted to a desire for revenge, did not extend to his mother, as he recognized that she merely echoed opinions, having none of her own. But although his father and brother were symbols of everything he despised yet he was unable to ignore them and – deep in him – he knew that no matter what measure of success he might achieve, it would lack validity for him unless it compelled their respect. He would not admit this paradox, but it existed and it influenced not only his actions but the very structure of his hopes. Again and again he tried to persuade himself that he was indifferent to them, and to all they represented, but his victories were only logical ones and consequently did not affect his feelings. He despised their criticisms but hungered for their admiration.

Rutherford was the type of enthusiast who mistakes intolerance for singleness of purpose. He could only believe fully in the importance of his writing by denying any value whatever to certain other activities which were more highly esteemed and more generously rewarded. It was this vein of fanaticism in his nature which restricted him to an intensely personal world of narrow allegiances and fierce animosities. His mind was permanently in a state of civil warfare, consequently he was often ignorant of the real motive behind his passionate invectives. Jealousy is frequently the unsuspected origin of much righteous indignation, and usually when we condemn others from an altitude of moral fervour it only means that we are angry with them for refusing to recognize our importance.

Rutherford was neither popular nor the reverse with the easy-going Bohemian set in which he moved, and certainly no one had had the interest, or the insight, to penetrate beneath the well-fitting mask which he presented to the world. But, for Feversham, this mask simply did not exist, and, therefore, Rutherford's meeting with him was in the nature of an epoch in his life. He was dimly aware of this during their first conversation but before a week had elapsed, during which they met frequently, he was convinced that he was concerned with someone of quite a different order from his usual associates.

The temperamental contrast between the two men was quite as pronounced as the physical one. Rutherford's outlook on life was as clearly defined as a chessboard, and every move he made was in relation to a pre-determined strategical plan. To succeed as a writer was the supreme objective to which all else was subordinate and he applied himself to this end with mathematical precision. His days were marches – Feversham's were explorations. Rutherford never surrendered himself to an impulse – Feversham was incapable of arbitrary action.

"You're so definite about everything," Feversham remarked one evening when Rutherford was in his room. "Your outlook is like Euclid's definition of a straight line – length without breadth."

"You'll get nowhere if you don't know where you want to arrive," Rutherford retorted sullenly.

"You may be right, but nevertheless I think Napoleon was nearer the mark when he said: 'He will not go far who knows from the first where he is going.' You've no sense of Destiny – and I've too much."

Rutherford did not reply. He looked round Feversham's room and contrasted it with his own. It was attractive and intimate and he wondered by what miracle Feversham had discovered it. He was familiar with the common run of apartments in and near Chelsea and knew, therefore, that a room like this was wholly exceptional.

"I suppose you furnished this place?" he asked, seeking an explanation of the mystery.

"No, I haven't a stick of furniture in the world. I took it as it was. It's true I bought that picture and fitted up those curtains – otherwise it was waiting for me."

"Well, it must be pretty expensive."

"I don't think so," Feversham replied. He mentioned a figure which was a few shillings less than Rutherford paid, then he began to look for a book which they had discussed earlier and in which he wanted to find a certain passage.

Rutherford lit a cigarette. It annoyed him that Feversham had a more attractive room at a cheaper rent than he had. If the room had been more expensive than his, he would simply have regarded Feversham as a fool to waste his money but, as things were, it seemed yet another indication to him of Feversham's innate superiority – a superiority of which he was apparently quite unconscious, yet one which manifested itself in every detail. Rutherford was irritated and intrigued, but what disturbed him more fundamentally was the fact that Feversham was clearly aware of certain traits in his character of which others were ignorant. The remarks about his outlook were an example. Rutherford had told him nothing concerning his secret plans for attaining his ambition, yet Feversham was aware of his motives and methods as no one else had been. Not only was this so but his whole manner when discussing him seemed to suggest that he was only enunciating a few self-evident platitudes. To be instantly understood in this careless and comprehensive manner was a new experience for Rutherford and it disturbed him. It made him feel less important, less secure, and a sudden sense of resentment woke in him when he realized that at each meeting he became more transparent while Feversham remained mysterious.

"Look here," he blurted out suddenly, "all that stuff you said just now about my outlook being like Euclid's definition of a straight line – how do you know anything about it?"

"But it's true, isn't it?"

"Well, what the devil does it matter whether it's true or not?" Rutherford asked after a pause. "How can you be so cock-sure about it?"

"I don't understand you," Feversham replied slowly. "Surely the only important thing is whether it's true or not. *How* I know doesn't matter, does it?"

"Yes, it does," said Rutherford stubbornly. "In the first place, I don't admit it's true and, anyhow, I'd like your reasons."

"I haven't any, my dear fellow. I just *see* some things and feel they are true. If you say that what I said was nonsense, then I was wrong and you must forgive me. I spoke so confidently because I felt so certain."

Rutherford did not answer. If the conversation developed, either he would have to assert that Feversham had been wrong; or he would have to admit that he was right – in which case, his outburst would appear ridiculous. He was rescued from his dilemma, however, by Feversham, whose quick transitions from one subject to another had frequently surprised him. The present example was opportune and he welcomed it.

"Oh, I meant to tell you," Feversham exclaimed, "Sondra's arrived. I saw her yesterday."

"Sondra!" Suddenly he remembered the face of the girl Feversham had drawn during their first conversation at the Regal Café. "Sondra," he repeated. "Is that the girl you sketched at the Regal? You remember? You altered the sketch you had made of the girl near us till it was someone entirely different."

"Yes, that's Sondra." He looked over at Rutherford with a smile. "That's a case in point! You *knew* directly I mentioned Sondra's name that she was the original of the second sketch. Well, how did you know? You had no evidence."

He passed a photograph to Rutherford, then continued: "You felt it was Sondra – you were certain – and you were quite right. I forgot that I hadn't told you her name. I expected her to arrive a week ago but she only turned up yesterday."

Rutherford did not reply. He was studying the photograph minutely. His relations with women had been restricted to the rather crude level of the set to which he belonged and having had too much experience on a superficial level, he made the fundamental error of regarding himself as an expert. It follows that his contempt for women was in reality contempt for himself – the distortion being effected by his pride. But the face which now confronted him stirred his imagination, and he was forced to realize that it was far removed from the faces of those *vivandière* women who had provided him with a sequence of easy triumphs. Here were purpose, resolution: a vitality unaware of its own intensity, demanding much, seeking, accepting. It is only necessary to glance at certain faces in order to see the hint of an unusual destiny and it was this potentiality which separated Sondra from the women of Rutherford's circle. Immediately he was conscious of the gulf between her and them. As he studied the photograph he was aware for a second of a feeling of pity. Even if this emotion had not been immediately succeeded by a darker one, he would have been unable to detect its origin. Possibly he recognized unconsciously that she was isolated, and to be isolated – by gifts, temperament, or beauty – is to be precariously poised in a world such as this. There are neither altitudes nor abysses for pavement people. Perhaps that is the reason why it has been said that the devil is nearer to God – by the whole height from which he fell – than the average man.

"I see she interests you," said Feversham. "I'm glad – I thought she would, and I want you to meet her. We'll all dine together some time when we can arrange it."

"Have you known her long?" Rutherford asked as he handed back the photograph somewhat reluctantly.

"No, not a bit of it! I met her on the boat when I came to Europe three months ago. She was alone, so was I. She was born in America but educated over here – just as I was. That formed one link right away. Her mother is an Italian and her father a Scotsman – he's a very well known doctor in New York. She was on her way to visit some old school friends and we saw a good deal of each other in Berlin and then, later, in Paris. She'll be in London for about a month before she goes home. That's about all I can tell you and, personally, I think the photograph reveals much more."

He moved impetuously over to Rutherford, sat on the arm

of his chair, and held out the photograph for his inspection.

"She attracted me directly I saw her," he went on. "Amid the blur of a thousand faces sometimes there emerges one face that holds you, and you feel that to exchange one glance with its owner is more significant than all the conversations you've ever had. In that glance you are conscious of a great possibility. I felt like that when I saw Sondra." He paused for a minute then went on: "She might so easily have been just a pretty, well-educated girl of about twenty. But I don't want to tell you about her – I want you to discover her for yourself – and don't imagine that she's showy or brilliant, because she isn't."

Rutherford did not reply. His dark eyes gleamed as they stared fixedly at the photograph and he seemed to have forgotten Feversham despite his proximity.

After a long pause the latter went on: "Of course, I may simply be infatuated by her. I can only say this: she seemed to me to be one of those rare beings who are born complete. Do you know what I mean? Most people are born empty, but manage to get something or other knocked into them as they go through life. Others – a tiny minority – are born complete. They've one job and one only: to discover their wealth and then to find something good enough to invest it in. I believe she's that type. But I may only be theorizing, and the truth may simply be that the rhythm of her figure has enslaved me."

Rutherford looked up at him quickly but Feversham rose with a laugh, went back to the bookcase, and continued his search for the volume which eluded him.

"Well, when shall we dine together?" Rutherford asked. He was determined to secure a definite arrangement. "What about Saturday night?"

"Yes, all right. I'll bring Sondra along. You choose the restaurant, but make it a quiet one. We can always go on somewhere afterwards, but we'd better settle the restaurant first."

"*The Goya?*" Rutherford suggested.

"Yes, I want to try it. Shall we have a fourth? No? Perhaps you're right. Somewhere about seven-thirty."

They talked on various subjects for another hour but Rutherford was abstracted and dull. Just before he went, he asked casually:

"By the way, what is Sondra's surname?"

"Nesbitt. I may see you somewhere before Saturday. You can find your way down? Right! Good-night."

II

The Goya was a restaurant on the fringe of Soho, recently opened by a Frenchman and his wife, where Rutherford frequently dined with one or other of his women friends. It consisted of one room on the ground floor and had not yet been discovered by the general public. The proprietor, Adolphe, was decorative in appearance, romantic by temperament, and eager to attract the patronage of writers and painters – but his wife, Thérèse, had her own opinion as to the financial prudence of such a policy. For the time being, however, she yielded to him, and thus it was that the walls of the restaurant boasted several examples of the painter's art – each picture, it was rumoured, representing payment in kind for a considerable number of dinners.

The restaurant was dimly lit, contained about a dozen tables, and was frequented chiefly by couples. The *table d'hôte* dinner consisted of five courses at a cost of one-and-sixpence and although each course was necessarily diminutive, the illusion was produced that you were getting an enormous amount for your money. A barrel organ in the narrow street outside usually deputized for an orchestra and a shop round the corner provided wine for those diners who were flourishing, or thought they were. Adolphe and Thérèse lived on the floor above, while the rooms at the top of the house were let to mysterious and frequently changing tenants – one or other of whom usually strode through the restaurant during the evening, arousing the curiosity of the diners by his ferocious mien and unorthodox appearance. The most remunerative trade, however, was done with the theatre opposite as it was the custom of several of the artists employed there to have dinners sent to their dressing-rooms, notably on matinée days.

As Rutherford walked down Shaftesbury Avenue on his way to *The Goya*, he felt unusually pleased with himself. He had heard that morning that one of his short stories had been accepted by a magazine and although, theoretically, he had an immense scorn for the magazine in question – it had frequently rejected his work – his outlook on it and the world in general was altered appreciably by this success. Although he had long since passed the stage of being thrilled by seeing his work in print, nevertheless, any recognition of his ability confirmed his belief in his powers and gave a more definite contour to his hopes. Consequently he walked along in a world of his own and ignored the posters which announced, with vertical jubilance, the latest exploit of the suffragettes.

He entered *The Goya*, nodded to Adolphe, and chose a table in the corner. It was nearly a quarter past seven. He lit a cigarette and muttered a curse on the head of a person outside who was performing on the bagpipes with alcoholic enthusiasm. Damn the idiot! He wanted to surrender himself to this rare mood which possessed him, a mood which flattered his vanity and whispered of triumphs to come, and he also wanted to decide what attitude he should adopt to this girl, Sondra, whose photograph had made such a strange appeal to him. One thing was certain: he'd let her know that he wasn't a dilettante like Feversham. . . . What a fool Adolphe was not to stop those confounded bagpipes!

A few minutes later Feversham entered with Sondra. They were both in the highest spirits, obviously delighted with everything in general and the restaurant in particular. But this light-hearted gaiety jarred on Rutherford, who was still feeling successful and important, as it indicated from the outset that he was regarded simply as a collaborator in the proceedings and not their centre. It never occurred to him that his irritation was caused by the fact that his companions had assumed that their mood would be his – just as he had assumed that his would be theirs.

But Sondra exceeded his expectations. He had not imagined that the powerfully moulded features under the dark heavy hair would be so vivacious, any more than he had expected that the light in the deep wide-set eyes would be so gay. She had a magnetism which individualized even the details of her clothes and by its alchemy transmuted her most trivial remark. Directly he saw her he was ashamed to remember how proud he had been of certain recent successes with women, and a grim determination to impress her took possession of him.

Feversham went over to make Adolphe's acquaintance and Rutherford turned to Sondra.

"Feversham's told me a lot about you," he began. "Will you be in London long?"

"No, only a month, I'm afraid." Her voice was low and vibrant. "But it's marvellous to be here alone. My aunt loathes London so she's staying in Paris, but we shall return to New York together in about a month."

"Well, we must give you a good time. I know a fair number of interesting people – I think you'll find Wolheim's crowd pretty amusing."

"We just met him in Paris," she replied, "but, of course, you know him really well. I don't know what's the matter with Martin to-night – he's behaving like a lunatic. You've only met him recently, haven't you?"

"Yes, quite recently," he assented quickly. He did not want to discuss Feversham.

"Can you make head or tail of him?" she asked with a smile.

"I don't know that I've thought about him very much," he replied after a pause. "He seems to enjoy knocking about and having a good time. I suppose he'll settle to something one day."

"But it's obvious!" she exclaimed, looking up at him mystified. "You've only to see him to know that he's going to be a success at something. The only question is – *what*?"

"Oh, yes, quite," he admitted quickly. "What I really meant was that he told me that he was flirting with the idea of writing and, as I told him, he'd have to put all he'd got into that if he wanted to make anything of it. I've written for some years and know what it involves. Why, even to write a short story – I've just had another accepted by *The Globe* – makes pretty considerable demands."

She did not reply and he felt uncomfortable. He had dragged in his own affairs so inartistically that he felt humiliated and angry. Fortunately, however, Feversham returned and they settled themselves at the table.

"Come on," Feversham began, "let's start this phantom dinner. I've argued with Adolphe that he can't make a profit at the price but he thinks he can – which is proof positive that we'll be horribly robbed if we have coffee." He turned to Rutherford. "Don't be deceived by Sondra. I thought at first she was just a pretty innocent girl who needed protection, but I soon discovered that she has the insight of the devil. She's much more dangerous than the suffragettes – they only chain themselves up, but she chains *you* up in no time."

"All nonsense!" she exclaimed. "You're intoxicated with yourself to-night, Martin. You've never been quite like this before."

"You're just getting to know me," he replied. "Now, I've just thought of a brilliant idea. What do you think of this? We'll all meet here twenty years hence and see what we've made of it. Do you both agree? We'll come to this very table and compare notes."

He broke off, then with a gesture summoned Adolphe. The smiling Frenchman came over to their table.

"We want to book a table," Feversham announced.

"*Oui, monsieur?*"

"Yes, a table. Have you a pencil? Good! A table for three, at seven-thirty – twenty years hence. Now, have you got that?"

Adolphe wrote down the particulars with due solemnity.

"Now, tell me this," Feversham went on. "Will the dinner still be one-and-six?"

"It is unlikely, monsieur. Already, my wife wish to make it two shilling. *Bon Dieu!* Twenty years! Anything could happen."

"Then it soon will be," said Feversham grimly. "Well, never mind – we shall be here on this date twenty years from to-night. You will see two men of great distinction enter with a lady of extraordinary beauty."

"Then it will be exactly as it was to-night, monsieur," exclaimed Adolphe with a graceful gesture and a little bow to Sondra. After which verbal felicity he retired.

"There's a diplomatist wasted," Feversham announced. "Anyway, we'll all meet here and see what we've done with life."

"Or what it's done to us," Rutherford interposed, hoping to bring the conversation to a more philosophical level.

But Feversham's gaiety was not to be dethroned. He began to give eloquent descriptions of what they would be like in twenty years and he invested each portrait with such a wealth of imaginative detail that he produced the illusion that he was discussing actual people. Then, seizing the menu, he drew three sketches in rapid succession depicting each one of them twenty years hence. "There you are!" he exclaimed triumphantly. "We've only to live and we shall look like these."

The three of them leant over and studied the drawings till their heads were almost touching. It was brilliant work. He had accentuated the potentiality in each of his subjects with the result that the drawings revealed three highly individualized, interesting people, yet there was enough emphasis of present defects to give a critical significance to his pictorial prophecies. Then, seizing the pencil again, he drew Adolphe as he would be in twenty years time. A stern, tight-lipped, cynical French-man seemed to leap from the paper. Underneath the sketch he wrote: "Adolphe – when the dinner is three-and-six."

Sondra took up the menu and studied the drawings in silence, then she exclaimed:

"Martin! They're incredibly clever! But why haven't you given me a hat?"

"A *hat*. Do you think I'm a lunatic! Good heavens, I can prophesy what you will look like, but it would puzzle the devil to know what you will *wear*. Why, hats may be even bigger in

1930 than they are now. I don't want those sketches to date – they're for posterity."

"They aren't – they're for me," she announced as she put them away. "I'd no idea you could draw like that."

"When we know everything about each other, my dear, it will be nearly as marvellous as the present process of discovery." He turned to Rutherford: "I shall pay for the dinner tonight, and you'll pay for the one twenty years hence. I've a flair for finance, you see."

"Obviously," Rutherford replied, then added: "So much so, in fact, that despite your gift for drawing I shouldn't be a bit surprised if you end up as a big business man."

"Neither should I," Feversham agreed.

"A business man!" Rutherford exclaimed in a tone of immense contempt. "Why, I was only joking. Surely you couldn't sink to that."

"Easily," said Feversham lightly. "It might even be an ascent for me. I've no prejudices. It must be quite interesting to have an enormous organization under your control – a huge instrument ready to react to your will."

"And grind down your workpeople in the approved manner?" Rutherford inquired.

"Probably – and yet they might be worse off without you. Anyway, everything is a possibility for me. I'll know soon. If it's drawing, I'll put all I've got into it. If it's business, I'll have such a factory as never was. And if it's a woman, she'll be my sun, my moon, and my stars. Sondra's laughing. That's a bad sign because she listens to what you don't say – and never misses a single silence."

On several occasions Rutherford tried to twist the conversation to a more serious level in order to parade his ideas and theories on an imposing background, but although Feversham yielded him the centre of the stage with the utmost readiness, he succeeded in being merely dull and egotistical. After one or two attempts to dominate the conversation, he relapsed into a moody silence – indicating by his whole attitude that he was concerned with issues so fundamental that words were quite inadequate to express them. Feversham and Sondra, however, rattled on, illuminating each subject they discussed with flashes of wit and insight, although apparently they were merely fencing with each other in a mood of lyrical extravagance. In spite of himself, Rutherford was fascinated by them and, at moments, forgot his own ambitions and enjoyed himself immensely.

Dinner being over, Feversham summoned Adolphe, paid the bill, reminded him that the table was booked for the same date in 1930, and a moment later they all left the restaurant. It was a dark night, swept by a gusty wind. The swinging signs over the shops creaked, and the stars were hard, clear, metallic points of light. It was one of those nights which create a sense of space and freedom – a night which awakes the desire to do something unprecedented and unimaginable.

Feversham responded to this vibration and turned to the others:

"It's a night to sail up the Milky Way, or to swim in the waters under the earth, but – as we can't do either – we shall end up at a night club. That's the modern substitute for adventure. Everything is measured or charted nowadays, so we amuse ourselves by running away from ourselves. What luck! There's a hansom."

He hailed the driver enthusiastically. "Jump in," he cried to the others. "There'll be no hansoms soon – they are relics of a dead age. In you get!"

It was a tight fit but they managed to get in somehow. Feversham explained to the driver, through the trap, exactly where they wanted to go. After which they all surrendered themselves to gliding movement and the rhythmical beat of the horse's hoofs.

In due course they reached *The Dive*. It was a cellar in a cul-de-sac off Regent Street, run as a club by a rather grimy gentleman named Bliss, but known as "Blotto", who had failed in every other type of activity. *The Dive*, however, was a success although the atmosphere was awful, the floor almost impossible for dancing, and the meals quite unbelievably bad. But there was the bar. Now, there is one remarkable fact concerning drunkards which is frequently over-looked by the more serious students of sociology. It is this: many drinkers are most particular as to *where* they get drunk. This explains why many a dingy hole with no apparent attractions does an enormous trade while palatial public houses in its vicinity are ignored. The bar of *The Dive* was a magnet for several drunkards of almost European eminence. They sat like a semi-circle of idols, drinking for hour after hour, gazing into vacancy with glazed eyes. Everyone ignored them, but the continued existence of the club depended on them.

Bliss greeted the new arrivals deferentially. His face was quite yellow but as he slept on the premises it was no mean achievement to be alive at all.

"Hullo, Blotto," said Feversham. "You all right? Good! Anyone here?"

"It's rather early," Bliss replied. This was his inevitable reply to the question just asked. Every evening he gave this answer at least fifty times. In his outlook, it was "rather early" until day had dawned.

"But it means there's more room to dance," he added in the same mechanical tone. After which he returned to the bar.

"What an odd man!" exclaimed Sondra.

"He's become a gramophone record. And yet, I don't know," Feversham went on, "if he could write the story of his life no one would believe it – Blotto, least of all. Come on, let's go in."

They entered the chief room – a large low-pitched apartment with red walls crudely ornamented with nudes in white chalk. At the far end was a piano and near it, on a table, stood a gramophone. When the pianist was exhausted, the gramophone served as understudy. Ranged round the walls were a number of most uncomfortable benches where people sat and watched the dancers. There were a few small tables dotted about where endless conversations, punctuated by drinks, took place between bearded men and shrill-voiced women. One or two men trying to look unsophisticated were obviously detectives.

The newcomers attracted a good deal of attention. The pianist, a weedy youth with a strand of hair in each eye, made a desperate attempt to infuse some vitality into his playing, annihilating time in the process. One or two of the men, after an expert scrutiny of Sondra, began to talk more loudly. Bliss emerged from nowhere and asked if they were hungry, alleging that he could supply steaks of quite superlative excellence.

"You dance with Rutherford, Sondra, and I'll watch you."

"I don't dance," Rutherford cut in. He had always regarded that activity as below him, but now he regretted that he was not a brilliant dancer. "So you dance," he went on. "I shall be all right."

He sat at one of the tables while Sondra danced with Feversham. Many watched them as they glided about the room but no one so intently as Rutherford. Emotionally, he was in a state of chaos. His meeting with Sondra had made his relations with Feversham even more complex and at the moment he did not know whether he admired or hated him. It seemed to him that Sondra also possessed just that elusive quality which distinguished Feversham. As he watched them, he tried to discover what it was which separated them not only from their surroundings but from all the other people he knew. They seemed to accept everything without surrendering themselves, thereby giving the impression that their present activities were merely episodes in which they were not involved fundamentally. *They* were passengers through this room, whereas many of those who watched them were fixtures.

Rutherford noticed an old man, fantastically attired, who had not ceased to stare at Sondra since she entered. And, for the first time, Rutherford realized how tragic a figure is an old Bohemian. . . . Yet Rutherford had been so proud of this world – he had fought and struggled to belong to it by right of conquest – had surrendered so much for it, defended it so passionately against the sneers of his family. And now, these two strangers, whom he had met so casually, had only to appear in order to make him realize how dull, squalid, and stupid it was.

How different they were from the others! The lines of their

bodies, the poise of their heads, their voices, their gestures, their hands, all proclaimed it. They were isolated and yet they could enter into this Bohemia more intimately than he could. This was the paradox which baffled him. How heavy and dull he had been at dinner, and how afraid he was of enjoying himself lest he should seem commonplace!

Sondra and Feversham danced so perfectly together that it was difficult to believe that they were separate beings. There was a new light in Rutherford's eyes as he watched her. For the first time, where a woman was concerned, he felt a desire to ask rather than a determination to take. He had passed completely under the spell of her fascination, and although one side of him desired her in the same way as he had desired many women, this emotion was qualified by a feeling of humility which was a new and unexpected experience for him.

A friend attempted to join him but he indicated curtly that he was with a party, so the man went over to the bar. The incident was symbolic of Rutherford's sudden dissatisfaction with his way of life. He found his old associates uninteresting. The man he had just dismissed was a journalist whom he had numbered among his more important friends and it surprised and disturbed him to discover how suddenly he had become indifferent to him. He'd have to stop this nonsense! After all, Feversham and Sondra were only visitors – they would vanish in a few weeks and he would probably never see them again. It was ridiculous to allow his interest in them to undermine the foundations of his life in London, and yet he had a premonition that his friendship with them was in no sense an episode, but that on the contrary it was destined radically to alter the familiar frontiers of his world. The whole of his logical nature rebelled against this feeling but he had experienced it during his first conversation with Feversham and it had invested every detail of their relations with a curious significance.

The Dive began to fill up rapidly and, to Rutherford's annoyance, a number of people joined them, with the result that he felt one of a crowd and the intimacy of the evening was ruined. He was jealous of these new friends of his and did not wish to share them with others, but Feversham's vitality and Sondra's beauty soon made them the centre of an ever-widening circle. Rutherford sat silent, scowling at these hangers-on. After all, what an ill-bred noisy lot of idiots they were with their ridiculous clothes and absurd affectations! What interest could Sondra and Feversham possibly find in such people?

A quarter of an hour later he rose suddenly and went over to Feversham. "I think this is pretty dull, don't you? Shall we go?"

Feversham looked over at Sondra but was unable to attract her attention. "Oh, we'll stay a bit longer," he replied. "Sondra seems to find it amusing. Well, if you're off, look me up soon. We must show Sondra all the freaks before she goes back."

Rutherford went over to her and said good-bye in a possessive manner, adding that he had arranged with Feversham that they should all meet again very soon.

He walked back to his rooms through the windswept darkness, dissatisfied with himself, and disturbed by the feeling that he had reached a frontier where his old life ended and a new one began.

CHAPTER III

I

An avalanche can be caused by the fall of a pebble – and a life can be revolutionized by an apparently trivial incident. Rutherford's meeting with Feversham is an example. It is an error, however, to believe that the visible cause is the true one. The origin of things lies deeper than their first manifestation. Where events bear an organic relation to one another, they represent a Destiny; and it is idle to isolate the first event and to regard it as the cause of the subsequent ones. We should remember that the Explained is not the Known – any more than the Unknown is merely the Unexplained.

Rutherford, however, imagined that his meeting with

Feversham was purely fortuitous and consequently it seemed
to him that its results were as capricious as their origin. It did
not occur to him that anything which moves us profoundly –
be it a person, or be it a book – is an aspect of ourselves hitherto unrecognized. To him, Feversham was simply a disturbing
element which had diverted the current of his thoughts and
created unexpected problems in his emotional life. He did not
realize that Feversham, quite unconsciously, was making him
aware of certain of his own possibilities. He blamed him for the
revolution he was experiencing and at moments felt a passionate sense of grievance against this stranger who had turned his
world upside down. The advent of Sondra only increased these
perplexities.

Normally, Rutherford's days were governed by an inflex-
ible formula. He worked all the morning, walked for an hour
or two after lunch, read or worked again till six o'clock when
he went to one or other of his haunts in search of company.
But during the period immediately succeeding the dinner at
The Goya, he abandoned this programme entirely. He spent
whole days with Sondra and Feversham, either together or
separately, only returning to his rooms to sleep. His association with Sondra soon necessitated a fundamental adjustment
in his outlook on women and he discovered to his surprise that
he now regretted his lack of certain qualities – such as cour-
tesy and consideration – which previously he had regarded as
sentimental and superfluous. His social technique was inadequate to his present task; competition was keen; and before
many days had passed he felt grateful to Sondra for giving any
of her time to him. The spell of her fascination was potent
enough to effect this miracle.

Nevertheless, during this period, he frequently experienced
angry moods of dark rebellion, moods in which his whole
nature revolted against this surrender, and when this dæmonic
spirit possessed him he not only hated Feversham but tried
to elaborate a scheme by which he could humble Sondra and
bend her to his will. He was terribly afraid of being deceived
– and therefore anything which seemed superior to himself

was suspect in his outlook. Thus it was that he could not yield wholly to the appeal of these new friends of his. He kept pulling himself up in order to review the situation in the terms of his old values and, whenever he did this, his thoughts centred wholly round one question – what were the actual relations between Sondra and Feversham?

One side of him wanted to believe that they were more intimate than they appeared although, paradoxically, even to admit this as a possibility fanned all his latent jealousy of Feversham into an ardent flame. Yet, on balance, he wanted to believe it. If they were lovers, then – fundamentally – they were like all the other people he knew, and the issue between him and Feversham was a clearly defined one and one which he could understand. If he could convince himself of their intimacy, then he would be able to dismiss a number of his perplexities as irrelevant. He found it difficult to believe that their apparent relations were the actual ones, for he was incapable of imagining such a companionship between a girl as beautiful as Sondra and a man as attractive as Feversham. He knew that she frequently visited Feversham in his rooms and Rutherford's outlook on such matters was largely that of the King's Proctor – who holds grimly to the axiom that immorality automatically occurs whenever circumstances render it possible. And yet he was not certain.

On more than one occasion he had been tempted to ask Feversham for his views concerning women but something had always restrained him. He noticed that when the conversation turned to that subject – which it did with monotonous and awful regularity in their set – Feversham soon became bored by the exploits, real or imaginary, of his companions. Yet it was obvious that the society of women was essential to him and that he was very popular with them. Only once had he given Rutherford a hint of his views on the subject. It was after a conversation in the Regal Café which had lasted for two hours and consisted wholly of a series of anecdotes, reminiscences, and adventures, all relating to sex. When they were alone Feversham turned to him and said:

"It's a damnable conspiracy, isn't it?"

"I don't know what you mean," Rutherford had replied.

"Certain? Think for a minute. What's the truth about these men who've been talking for hours about sex? It's let them down. But instead of admitting it, each one of them boasts, lies, and imagines he's a devil of a fellow. Each one hypnotizes himself by hypnotizing the others, and each will continue to waste time and vitality on a fraud. The fact that they find it necessary to talk about it, proves it."

"Do you suggest universal celibacy?" asked Rutherford with a sneer.

"You know that the whole thing isn't worth a damn unless there's real affection behind it, and you know that if there were it couldn't be discussed like that. You never discuss what you really possess."

Something in Feversham's tone implied that he had nothing more to say and the subject was abandoned. But this fragment – which might have told Rutherford a good deal – revealed nothing to him. In fact he regarded it as an indication that Feversham was not prepared to be frank with him.

But the question of Feversham's relations with Sondra was only one of the many problems which confronted Rutherford. Apart from her, Feversham was an enigma to him. His plastic nature was a revelation to Rutherford, who was critical by temperament and incapable of surrendering himself to anything outside the range of his own ambition. He regarded people and problems as a background for his own ideas, whereas Feversham yielded the whole of himself to anything which interested him. He gave the best of himself to everyone with the result that people who were normally dull or affected became transformed, and Rutherford was surprised to discover that a number of his acquaintances, whom he regarded as bores, seemed to acquire vitality and distinction in Feversham's presence.

Feversham was free and everything relating to him was representative of that freedom. He was bound to no place, to no person, and to no vocation. In the same way as his physical appearance suggested speed, so his circumstances rendered movement always a possibility. Above all, he was free mentally and Rutherford did not realize that this freedom existed because Feversham was not the slave either of pride or vanity. He had staked no claim and consequently he had nothing to defend. He was not haunted by the fear of making himself ridiculous. He was not trying eternally to prove his own importance to himself. He wasted none of his vitality on negative criticism and, unlike the set in which he moved, he did not label and dismiss as negligible whole fields of human activity. He had no fixed ideas. He once explained to Rutherford that a fixed idea was a fossilized idea. Science, religion, politics, all interested him, whereas for Rutherford and his associates Art was the only activity for supermen.

Now, if Feversham had not been an artist, he would have had no influence over Rutherford. But the latter knew that Feversham's gift for drawing was quite exceptional and that therefore he could make a reputation if he chose to do so. But Rutherford was shortly to discover that, as a writer, Feversham possessed abilities none the less remarkable because he attached no importance whatever to them. In fact it was this discovery which introduced an entirely new factor into their relations.

II

Rutherford introduced his new friends to all his haunts with one exception – the Sphinx Salon run by Madame de Fontin.

Madame de Fontin was remarkable physically and in many ways. She was forty-five and enormous; she had black very frizzy hair, great flashing eyes and a prominent nose. She was extremely vivacious and playful – she devised pet names for all her friends – and she lived in a large house near Notting Hill Gate. It was rumoured that she had had several husbands but it was certain that she had a very large income. Also she painted. She painted portrait after portrait with fearful fecundity and the walls of her huge drawing-room on the first floor were hung with examples of her work in massive gold frames. But her Sunday suppers were excellent and many a Bohemian managed to eat enough at one of them to enable him to fast till the following Wednesday morning without the slightest discomfort.

It was not easy to obtain admittance to the Sphinx Salon. Madame de Fontin's soul loathed the commercial and therefore it was her desire to become the centre of a group of devotees to Art for its own sake. Money was never mentioned at her Sunday evenings and only those who tried to borrow from her really discovered how deep was her contempt for lucre, and how absolute was her belief that poverty was essential to the evolution of a great artist. Indeed she dare not interfere with this dispensation of Providence. Applicants for loans left her no heavier in pocket but immensely elevated in spirit. Certain good-looking and very young men found the way to her purse but each in turn had to have his portrait painted, an ordeal which necessitated a number of very intimate interviews, and not one of them was ever quite the same afterwards. It was the portraits of these victims which adorned the enormous drawing-room and there were rumours that soon the apartment would have to be enlarged.

Anyone deemed worthy of admission to this hothouse received a chastely inscribed card headed THE SPHINX SALON. Underneath, the Aims of the *salon* were set forth with typographical extravagancies excusable in the circumstances. One Aim was to provide an intellectual and spiritual retreat for those whose ideals set them apart from the herd. Another Aim was to encourage the *young* writer, artist, painter. It was pointed out that in the hands of the young were the Banners of the Future – although they might be invisible. Between each Aim was a small sphinx, printed in red, which was very effective and which restrained the reader's impetuosity. The third Aim was to form a dynamic centre of artistic and cultural influence which would shed beneficent beams above surrounding midnight. After the Aims, came a few dignified warnings, printed in block letters. The chief of these was to the effect that no member of the *salon* must employ the privilege of admission for base commercial ends. The reader was reminded that the gift of creation was fire from on high and that an artist's work was its own reward. Finally, there was a Definition of Art, with a sphinx on guard at each corner, which was impressive, inspired, and incomprehensible.

It follows that the initiates who assembled in the great drawing-room on Sunday evenings were a motley assembly. It was a strange fact – and one which received every variety of cynical comment – that very few women under fifty were present. No girl had ever received a direct invitation from Madame de Fontin. Girls were brought occasionally by certain bold spirits but to continue in this practice was to incur the wrath of Madame and consequently to jeopardize one's place at the supper table. Young men therefore predominated and – despite the elevated nature of the Aims of the Sphinx Salon – they were as disillusioned and as cynical as a crowd of ruined speculators.

One Sunday evening, about a fortnight after his introduction to Sondra, the great doors of the drawing-room were flung open and Rutherford's name was announced. Madame immediately left an animated group and greeted him effusively. She was dressed in a gossamer and transparent robe and was adorned with many flashing jewels.

"And how is my rugged bear?" she inquired.

The rugged bear said he was all right, whereupon she continued:

"I believe my rugged bear is lusting after the flesh-pots of Egypt. I saw his name on a dreadful magazine the other day."

Rutherford escaped and joined a young man in romantic clothes who was one of the hundred leaders of a new advanced Art movement. This gentleman, Ashley Alston, greeted him with the minimum of vitality, then said in a whisper:

"The Gorgon has become a symbolist. Look at her clothes. She is a mountain caressed by a cloud." After a pause he went on: "Have you seen Eric? He is worthy of study. The Gorgon has asked to paint his portrait. He is Fear incarnate."

Rutherford looked round the room. Thirty or forty people were present, split up into little groups, and a babel of conversation and tobacco smoke rose on all sides. He left Alston and, keeping an eye on his hostess, made a tour of the room, pausing at different groups in order to discover what topic was under discussion.

In an alcove near the window, two elderly men and three rather dowdy women were discussing Murder. Rutherford gathered that they were all looking forward to Crippen's execution with a good deal of impatience. That unfortunate man's appeal had recently been dismissed and – as one of the men jubilantly remarked – nothing could save him now. They began to discuss the case, which had thrilled all England, with that intimate knowledge of every detail which can only be obtained by prolonged study of the Sunday newspapers. Rutherford, feeling extremely irritated, left them and joined a noisy group in the vicinity which contained two young men and three pretty girls who had been smuggled in somehow.

Musical comedy was the theme under debate. *The Quaker Girl* had just been produced and was receiving every type of superlative admiration except from one young lady who, though admitting it was "sweet," was not quite certain whether it was quite as marvellous as *Our Miss Gibbs*. Whereupon one of the young men, whose knowledge of musical comedy was clearly encyclopædic, announced that he had heard a rumour that *The Waltz Dream* was going to be revived with Miss Lily Elsie. A statement which produced ecstatic cries of delirious joy.

Rutherford glided to another group of three portly men in evening dress who were evidently engaged in a conversation of great gravity.

"We've reached a pretty pass in this country, I must say. Here's this blackguard Redmond about to tear down the British Constitution with American dollars. A nice thing! An Irishman to become Dictator of the British Empire!"

"They're calling him Dollarver Cromwell," replied one of the others. "I don't know what we're coming to – what with this so-called reform of the House of Lords and Cabinet Ministers having to be protected from these mad suffragettes! I'd shoot the lot if I had my way."

"Well, I blame Lloyd George for everything," said the third mournfully. "This Budget of his is the thin end of the wedge. You mark my words – it's the thin end of the wedge."

Rutherford crept away unnoticed. It was easy enough to stand near one group and listen to the conversation of the one next to it. After a swift survey, he made his way to a crowd of several men who were talking excitedly. One or two of them were in evening dress and the remainder were very decorative and artistic.

They were discussing the Post Impressionist exhibition which had recently opened at the Grafton Galleries. The names of Gauguin, Cézanne, and Van Gogh kept shooting up like rockets. A fierce argument was in progress and when a little man with a monocle quietly asserted that Henri Matisse's "Woman with Green Eyes" was a masterpiece, the atmosphere became volcanic.

"A masterpiece!" shouted a fat man with a red face and disappearing eyes. "A masterpiece! Listen to me. I've been looking at pictures for thirty years, so you'll admit that I ought to know something about 'em."

"You ought," replied the little man.

"Very well then," said the other, evidently satisfied with this comment. "You give a child some paint and a brush and a bit of canvas and it will produce a better result than that greeneyed monster."

He broke into a roar which shook the room and attracted Madame de Fontin who bore down on them like a cruiser approaching a fleet of sailing vessels.

"Now, now!" she cried, waving an admonishing forefinger. "Why is my menagerie roaring?"

Without waiting for a reply she began to rave about Strauss's *Salomé*, having been to a rehearsal of that work at Covent Garden. After which the conversation turned to Tolstoy's disappearance and rumoured death, thence – by a swift transition – it passed to the reception accorded to Pinero's play, *The Thunderbolt*, which had just been produced in New York. A dramatic critic, who had been silent till now, announced heavily that he entirely agreed with the leading American critics who had characterized the play as "too unpleasant."

Rutherford wandered off in search of a drink. The company to-night was not typical – normally it consisted of the brighter lights of the Regal Café. He put this point to Ashley Alston, who knew instinctively the moment a drink was obtainable, and consequently was now at ease in a corner which he called The Bar.

"Yes, they're a different crowd to-night," he admitted. "The Gorgon has two sides to her nature, although she has only one to her figure. These are some of her respectable friends. If you come to tea on a Sunday afternoon, you will discover that she knows a number of solid God-fearing people. Thank the Lord for drink!" he exclaimed as he took another, then added: "Eric's gone home. He's going to commit suicide."

Rutherford began to feel desperately bored, and his state was not improved by an announcement, gushingly made by his hostess, to the effect that a Madame Marsa – who had either just made her debut at Milan or was about to do so – would sing to them. Whereupon a large woman sang a song in a voice of such natural power that all attempts to train it had clearly proved unavailing. The applause had scarcely died away when the doors were flung open and more names were announced.

Rutherford did not hear them, with the result that a moment later he was amazed to see Feversham and Sondra and a man he did not know being greeted by Madame de Fontin. He was wondering who the stranger could be when Alston enlightened him:

"Hullo!" the latter exclaimed. "That's Murdock with a damned pretty girl as usual. You know Percy Murdock, don't you?"

Rutherford did not know him by sight, but everyone knew that Murdock was a well-known novelist. Could *he* have brought Sondra and Feversham? If so, why on earth had not Feversham told him that he knew Murdock? He stared at the group in the centre of the room with angry eyes. His position was not an enviable one as he had told Feversham the day before that he had an important engagement for Sunday evening. Now it would look as if he had not wanted to introduce him to the splendours of the Sphinx Salon. It infuriated Rutherford to see the rapturous welcome which Madame was giving to Murdock, although he had reason to know that whenever anyone of the smallest distinction appeared, his hostess immediately forgot her devotion to the unknown but aspiring. He was surprised, however, that Sondra was so well received but naturally he could not know that Madame de Fontin had just discovered that Sondra was leaving for New York very shortly.

Feeling ill at ease, he crossed to the group and spoke to Feversham.

"So you know my rugged bear!" exclaimed Madame lyrically. "How *delightful*! Sometimes my bear is surly but he's always rugged and I believe I shall teach him to dance one day in spite of everything."

With murder in his heart, Rutherford made a hurried explanation to Feversham, telling him that his man had let him down and that he had come on here at the last minute. Feversham, who had evidently forgotten that Rutherford had said he was engaged for that evening, introduced him to Murdock. A minute later their hostess left them.

"I haven't seen you here before," Rutherford said to Murdock.

"I come very seldom," the novelist replied. "I can't imagine why an intelligent woman goes in for this rot but I come to look at it sometimes."

"Intelligent!" exclaimed Rutherford.

"Certainly – underneath. Apart from her painting, and being girlish, and running this restaurant, she's not a bit of a fool. It's significant that you can be frank with her. She asked me once how long her *salon* would last and I told her that it would last just as long as she continued to provide supper. She was not in the least annoyed. She has some object in view – I can't imagine what it can be but I'm certain it exists."

A few minutes later they went in to supper and everyone began to brighten up. Carefully prepared epigrams were produced and exploded like crackers. Half-a-dozen of the Regal Café contingent arrived just as supper was announced and added considerably to the noise and gaiety of the proceedings. Complete strangers began to talk to one another with enthusiasm while scientific Bohemians silently stuffed themselves.

After supper Ashley Alston became more friendly to Rutherford than he had ever been and then asked him to introduce him to Sondra. But people began to dance and Rutherford could not get near her. It seemed to him that her arrival had altered the vibration of the room and that now everyone, with the exception of himself, was having a very good time. People clustered round her and Feversham like moths.

Just before midnight Madame de Fontin informed Sondra that she had noticed how divinely she danced with that irresistible Mr. Feversham and suggested that they should give an exhibition dance for the education of the others. The performance was duly given to the enjoyment of everyone, except Madame Marsa who expected to be asked to sing again. Still everyone had forgotten all about her by now and when Sondra and Feversham's exhibition was over, Madame de Fontin announced that there was no doubt whatever that dancing was the poetry of motion.

"How like my naughty bear," she said a moment later, "not to tell his keeper that he had such attractive and accomplished friends. Who else are you hiding, I wonder?"

Rutherford escaped and at last managed to speak to Sondra. Murdock had left and Sondra explained that they had met him for the first time that afternoon and that he had brought them to the Sphinx Salon thinking that it might amuse them.

"Have you been here often?" she asked.

"Yes, pretty often." He lowered his voice. "It's dull, but

sometimes one meets useful people here. But I loathe the old woman of course like the devil."

"She's good-natured," Sondra replied, "and very generous."

The more respectable began to go soon after one, but Madame would not hear of Sondra's departure although Feversham suggested that it was time they were off. Instead of which punch was produced and the remaining guests gathered round the fire and exchanged witticisms.

"Now, Mr. Feversham, I'm sure you're dreadfully clever at something," Madame de Fontin began when at last the three of them had risen to go. "And you must tell me what it is. Percy told me that you are a brilliant draughtsman but I believe you're clever at all sorts of things."

"I'm experimenting," Feversham explained. "I draw a bit, I write a bit, I——"

"I *knew* you wrote!" Madame cried triumphantly. "I have intuitions about people. You know what I mean? *Directly* I saw you I knew that you wrote. Now, what do you write?"

Feversham laughed. "I've been amusing myself with a play. I've just drafted it."

"A play!" Rutherford almost shouted the words. "You never told me you were writing a play."

"It's of no importance. Why should I bother you about my amateur efforts? You've enough to do with your own work. Besides——"

"Besides," Sondra cut in, "Martin loves having secrets from everyone."

"How did you know that?" he asked.

"But it's true, isn't it?"

"It's perfectly true," he admitted. "It's great fun to keep something absolutely to yourself. It doesn't matter if it's an entirely ordinary thing. It's yours – wholly – if no one else knows about it."

"I thought you were subtle," said Madame, "and I knew we had something in common. I keep quite a number of things entirely to myself. That's why I'm never lonely when I'm all by myself."

But Rutherford kept referring to the play till at last Feversham promised to show him the manuscript. It was evident that he regarded the whole subject quite lightly but Rutherford was insistent.

"You will probably think very little of it," Feversham said finally. "On the other hand you might suggest some improvements."

It was nearly three o'clock when they left and Madame de Fontin would not let them go until she had extracted a promise that they would visit her anyhow once more before they left England.

CHAPTER IV

I

Rutherford's sitting-room was lit only by a lamp which threw a vivid patch of light on to his desk. It was eight o'clock. All day it had rained heavily and now the world outside was a blur of desolation emphasized by the flickering lights of the street lamps. No sound rose up to him from the deserted street as he paced monotonously up and down the room with hands clasped behind his back and every thought intent on the problem which had so urgently presented itself.

At last he paused by the desk and picked up a manuscript which lay in the circle of light. It was the play Feversham had written and had been left at Rutherford's rooms by hand early that morning. A new light gleamed in his eyes as he turned over the pages, read a passage here and there, then glanced at a sheet of notes in his own handwriting. Suddenly an idea occurred to him; he sat down hurriedly, scrawled a few lines in feverish haste, then rose and began to walk up and down again like a sentinel.

When Feversham had told Madame de Fontin that he had written a play, Rutherford was convinced that it would be simply the work of an amateur, in which, at the best, there would be more promise than achievement. He had wanted this to be so and it was therefore in a patronizing spirit that he had begun to read the play soon after eleven o'clock that morning. But, from the outset, it captured him. He forgot its author, himself, his surroundings – everything – except the drama which leapt into life from the closely written pages – a drama in which he felt so intimately involved that it was only when he reached the end that he remembered Feversham.

The play was called *The Death of John Brand* and was concerned with the murder of a man in such circumstances that it was believed that he had committed suicide. Even his wife was convinced and all his friends evolved conflicting theories to account for his action. The device at the end of the play by which the murderer was detected was a triumph of ingenuity, as it was completely unexpected, yet – when revealed – it was accepted as inevitable. The characterization and dialogue amazed Rutherford. It seemed to him that the characters were realized by the author from within and that their lines belonged to them as intimately as their physical characteristics, with the result that Rutherford in reading the play experienced the rare illusion that he was watching and hearing living people – not artificially manipulated puppets. The humour did not consist of smart lines laboriously manufactured by the author and arbitrarily imposed on his characters. It was organic not mechanical. The whole play, which might so easily have been merely an exploitation of a given situation, was character drama projected on a sensational background.

Rutherford's enthusiasm, however, soon yielded to jealousy. It infuriated him to remember that this was the work of a man who attached no particular importance to it, a man to whom it was an experiment – a flirtation with one of his many possibilities. It seemed to Rutherford that whereas he had had to fight and struggle for every petty triumph he had ever known, Feversham had only to attempt in order to achieve. During his second reading of the play his jealousy became so intense that it was little removed from hatred.

He even conceived the plan of returning the manuscript

with a disparaging remark in the hope that Feversham would accept his verdict, regard the play as a failure, and put it on one side. But another idea occurred to him and one which gradually usurped the whole of his mind.

Why should not his name appear as part author? Feversham had suggested that he might be able to improve the play and although the words had been spoken half in jest could not this opening be utilized to his advantage? This was the subject which occupied Rutherford's thoughts as he continued to pace up and down the room. The sheet of notes in his handwriting represented the criticisms by means of which he hoped to justify his claim to recognition but they were all superficial in character and soon he was forced to realize that he would have to evolve a suggestion of fundamental importance in order to gain his end.

Another half hour passed but left him no nearer the solution of his problem. He lit a cigarette, sat down by the desk, and stared fixedly in front of him. Was it really essential to tax his ingenuity to this extent? Would it not serve equally well to advance a criticism, in which he did not really believe, simply in order to provide a basis for hours of argument? Surely it was enough to create the impression that he had made a valid contribution.

He decided to risk it. It was only necessary now to select a criticism which would provoke active opposition, endless discussion would ensue, and the result would be that his name would appear on the final script as part author.

Eventually he decided to challenge Feversham's assumption that a man could be shot at close quarters in such circumstances that the murderer could escape, and others be convinced that the dead man had committed suicide. He decided to maintain that this was an impossibility, hoping that prolonged discussion would hypnotize Feversham into the belief that he had made a real contribution to the play.

All former perplexities ceased to exist for him as he continued to elaborate this plan. His ambitions were now involved and everything else became secondary. He did not give a thought to Sondra and he was no longer concerned with Feversham as a man. Feversham became simply a short cut by which he could reach his goal more quickly, and he was determined to make the most expeditious use of this unexpected opportunity. He recognized that the play was unorthodox and original, quite outside the rut of commercially manufactured plays which followed one another with automatic regularity. Nevertheless he was convinced that even if it were not a success financially, it was certain to attract attention. Also he was sure that if his name appeared as part author, he would instantly achieve that background which he had always lacked and which he regarded as essential. He felt excited and exhilarated. After the disturbing perplexities of the last few weeks, it was a relief to be aware of a clearly-defined objective in his relations with Feversham and he decided to concentrate on it to the exclusion of everything else. Of only one thing was he doubtful – the most effective attitude to adopt with Feversham. He had always found him an incalculable person and in the present issue it was vital not to blunder and reveal his motives. He became more confident, however, when he remembered that in discussing literary work he would be on his own ground, and it was also fortunate that Feversham regarded the play in such a nonchalant manner.

Rutherford convinced himself that he would be able to dominate the situation, then just as nine was striking he went out to dine. . . .

The next morning he called at Feversham's rooms, hoping to spend a couple of hours discussing the play, but to his annoyance he found that Feversham had an appointment and could only spare him a few minutes. Also, although it was clear that Feversham was glad that he liked the play, it was equally clear that he did not welcome the suggestion that an appointment should be made at which every aspect of it should be discussed in detail. This attitude annoyed Rutherford profoundly, but as he did not want to reveal the full extent of his enthusiasm, he had to mask his irritation. It is not easy to be obsessed by a subject and yet convey an impression of comparative indifference.

Rutherford wanted Feversham to continue to underestimate his work and at the same time he wanted him to spend hours discussing it. To achieve both desires demanded a genius for diplomacy which Rutherford did not possess.

Just before Feversham left to keep his appointment, he said to Rutherford:

"Well, look here, it comes to this: you really think there is something in it. Is that so?"

"I think something could be made of it," he replied judicially, "but it will need a lot of working up. I've a lot of ideas to put to you and I don't mind spending a lot of time on it but naturally it's necessary to discuss things with you."

"The devil of it is," Feversham began apologetically, "I shan't be in London much longer. Sondra sails in a fortnight and I propose to go back to Paris about then. Anyway, let's have an hour on it in the morning. Do you mind coming here? Good! I'll expect you at about this time."

Rutherford left, disappointed, but based great hopes on their next interview. The following day, however, Feversham agreed so readily to all the minor alterations he suggested that he was seriously alarmed. He had hoped that each point would be vigorously contested, so that – in retrospect – it would appear that his contribution had been a considerable one. As it was, in the space of an hour Feversham had admitted all his minor suggestions, consequently Rutherford was obliged to mention his main criticism which he had hoped to reserve till much later. After a long preamble, therefore, which bored Feversham as he considered it unnecessary, Rutherford at last announced that in his opinion the man in the play could not be murdered in the manner described. He stated that it was impossible for a man to be shot at close quarters in such a way that others could reasonably assume that he had committed suicide. He was about to enlarge on this theme at great length when Feversham interrupted him.

"Wait a minute. You may be right but, if you are, then there's no point in arguing because the whole play is based on the fact that it *is* possible. If it isn't, then the thing is a failure.

You can't remove the foundation and expect the edifice based on it to remain standing."

"But there's probably an alternative treatment," Rutherford suggested.

"Have you got one?"

"Well – no – not exactly – not yet," he stammered. "I've an idea but it's not definite enough to discuss yet. I'm working on it continually."

"But why should you? Besides, frankly, I think the present treatment is all right. Anyway, I'm prepared to risk it. I'm certain two men could be struggling, one shoot the other, then clear out after arranging things in such a manner that others would be convinced that the dead man had destroyed himself. Remember this too: each of his friends regarded him as capable of suicide, so they were not so surprised as they otherwise might have been. I'll show you what I mean about the mechanical part of the business. It may make it clearer."

He rose and explained to Rutherford by gestures his conception of the struggle between the two men and how the murderer utilized a sudden opening to shoot his adversary.

"You see, it's simple enough," he said as he returned to his seat. "Why the murderer could even have made out that it was an accident – if he had been caught red-handed."

But Rutherford wasn't watching or listening. He felt that his plan was collapsing. He had imagined that Feversham's vanity would have been piqued by his criticisms and that therefore his defence would have been more ardent. Instead of which he had taken the line that if the treatment of the murder in the play could not be justified, then the whole thing came to the ground and – as Rutherford had no alternative – his position was a very awkward one.

"Let's think it over for a day or two," he said at last, "then meet again and discuss it thoroughly. In the meantime, I don't mind putting everything on one side. I'll strike an alternative, I'm certain. A lot can be made of the play and I'm prepared to put all I've got into it."

"But why should *you* bother about it?" asked Feversham.

"Well, if you remember, you said last Sunday that we might work together on it, and I think that already I've improved it somewhat. Anyway, you've accepted several of my suggestions."

"But if you go on like this, Rutherford," Feversham exclaimed, "you'll be part author." He began to laugh but noticing that his companion remained grimly serious, he stopped abruptly, then added: "Well, you think it over. I think that, on main issues, the thing is all right as it stands. But I'm not going to let you work on the play for nothing – you must come in on this adventure. *The Death of John Brand* by Gordon Rutherford and Martin Feversham. Sounds most imposing, doesn't it? We'll make our fortunes yet. I must be off to meet Sondra. Sure you won't come?"

"No, thanks," Rutherford replied. "I'm giving the rest of the day to John Brand."

A few minutes later he started to walk back to Bloomsbury. He had succeeded, yet he felt neither elated nor grateful. He was jealous of Feversham and disgusted with himself: jealous – because Feversham's generosity was another example of his consciousness of power; disgusted – because he was getting his name to another man's work by a fake. The situation compelled a comparison between Feversham and himself which forced him to realize his own inferiority. He hated him, and he did not know that this hatred was a projection of his own humiliation. His pride was pierced to the quick and, therefore, he was eager to justify himself in order to regain his habitual self-satisfaction. He began to walk quickly, striving desperately to discover an indictment of Feversham which would enable him to regard himself in a more favourable light.

We are often unaware of the nature and intensity of our emotions until an event occurs upon which they converge and thereby attain precision and perspective. The incident of the play served as such a centre and consequently all the vague and obscure animosities which Feversham's personality had awakened in Rutherford instantly became defined. Hence his hatred of Feversham became conscious and he immediately felt an urgent need to justify it logically. With this end in view, he began to survey the last few weeks in detail and soon succeeded in convincing himself that Feversham had deliberately thrust him into the background on each and every possible occasion – with the result that now whenever he ran into any of his friends it was apparent that they were interested in him only because he was a link with Feversham. Madame de Fontin was the most recent example. He had heard from her that morning imploring him to persuade Mr. Feversham to bring Miss Nesbitt to see her again before they left London. The note had concluded with the sentence: "Of course, I expect you, anyhow" – which had irritated him more than if there had been no reference to him of any kind. He had been a fool, but he was beginning to see things more clearly. He had introduced Feversham to everyone and now no one wanted him. And Feversham wasn't the innocent he pretended to be – not by a damned long way! He had used him; he was using everyone, to gratify some hidden ambition of his own. Hadn't Sondra said, last Sunday, that he was secretive? Sondra! Her image rose before him and his thoughts centred in her. Of course she was his mistress! What a fool he had been ever to have the smallest doubt on that subject! What! Was he to believe all that nonsense about her being an American, educated in Europe, who had returned to visit some old school friends, and was sailing for New York almost immediately? He must have been mad to listen to all those fairy stories. What a damned pack of nonsense! He'd been hypnotized by Feversham to such an extent that he had accepted any rubbish he chose to tell him. Why, she was always visiting him in his rooms! They had used him as cover and that was why Feversham had always been eager that he should spend a lot of time with them. Good God! What a fool he had been!

He continued to walk rapidly through the dark, louring November day, consumed by these thoughts and convinced that they represented the facts. A deep smouldering anger possessed him from which new discoveries kept darting up like devouring flames. He began to see it all! He'd been cheated, exploited, and bluffed out of his chance with Sondra. He had been deceived by Feversham's hypocrisy and so he had idealized her, treated her as a great lady, been grateful to her for seeing him! And all the time he had wanted her like hell, as he had never wanted any other woman, and she was Feversham's mistress! Only anger prevented him from laughing at his stupidity. He had been fooled pretty successfully. Well, his eyes were open at last. He would use *them* now! Feversham first and then, later, Sondra. She was going to New York no more than he was. It was too rich that Feversham expected him to believe that his departure from London was unrelated to hers. Of course, they were going back to Paris together and, one of these days, *he* would run into her there. But he must lay his plans carefully – he had made enough mistakes. The play came first, everything else could wait.

Before he reached his rooms he had convinced himself that he had been badly treated and that his hatred was justified.

II

During the next few days he avoided seeing Sondra and Feversham together, alleging that he was too occupied with the play to spare the time, but he continued to pester Feversham with requests for interviews till he succeeded in boring him to such an extent that the latter regretted having shown Rutherford the manuscript of the play. Two or three discussions, moreover, showed conclusively that although Rutherford still maintained that a structural alteration was necessary, he could suggest no alternative treatment.

It was a Saturday afternoon. Unwillingly enough, Feversham had spent a couple of hours going over the same arguments till he was utterly weary with the whole subject. Consequently he was anxious to end the discussion, but Rutherford continued to repeat himself, and finally suggested rewriting the play in such a manner that Feversham burst out laughing.

"Why, my dear fellow, in my opinion that would rob it of

any value whatever." He paused and glanced over at Rutherford who was staring at him angrily.

"Look here," Feversham went on. "We can't go on like this – it might last for ever. It's clear that we can't agree, so I'd better be frank with you. I'm getting tired of the whole business. You may be right – the play may be no good as it stands – but I really can't go on discussing it eternally."

"Well, what do you suggest?" There was a rising note in Rutherford's voice which Feversham decided to ignore.

"I suggest this," he replied after a pause. "You think the murder incident is all wrong, and I hold that it's essential. You've suggested one alternative which frankly I think is hopeless. Well, let's agree to differ – and I'll let the play take its chance as originally written."

Rutherford leapt to his feet in a fury.

"And what about all the work I've put in?" he demanded.

"I said I'd let the play take its chance as originally written," Feversham reminded him.

"Oh, I daresay! You were keen enough on a good number of my suggestions!"

"It's pretty simple, Rutherford. Here are your suggestions – all of them." He handed him a sheet of notes. "I've not made a single alteration in the manuscript – it's exactly as I wrote it. If you destroy that sheet, your contribution will have disappeared."

"You expect me to believe that fairy story! I admit I've believed a good many that you've told me but there are limits. Your memory isn't a bad one and I expect a good deal of my work will find its way into the final script."

His face was red with anger and his eyes were blazing. Hatred so dominated him that it became articulate against his will.

"I see your game," he shouted. "My work is to be used as *I* have been used."

"What on earth do you mean?" asked Feversham with genuine astonishment.

"Oh, for God's sake, drop that innocent pose and behave

like a grown man! You've got all you can out of me on this play, so now you want to cut me out – just as you've got all you want out of me while you've been in London, so now you're going back to Paris. Do you think I believe all that nonsense about Sondra sailing for New York? She's going to Paris with you. She's your——"

He broke off abruptly. Feversham had risen and was looking at him with an expression which Rutherford had never seen before. He was entirely calm and it was obvious that he was not merely suppressing his anger. His glance met Rutherford's and the latter felt that his very thoughts were being read.

"I think we can leave Sondra out of this, don't you?" Feversham asked quietly.

"No, I don't! It would suit you to do so – just as it would suit you for me to believe that she's simply a friend of yours who sails for New York——"

"Don't be a fool, Rutherford," Feversham cut in. "She sails in a fortnight. Her cabin has been booked for weeks. Go down to the shipping office and find out for yourself, if you don't believe me. You've evidently a grievance of some kind——"

"I've several! But we'll stick to the play. I'm not going to have my work stolen."

Feversham indicated the sheet of notes in Rutherford's handwriting.

"There's your work, I tell you. I'm sorry about all this, but you'd better take this sheet and destroy it yourself."

"Which means you know the notes by heart," Rutherford sneered. "I quite believe that you want them destroyed."

There was a pause then Feversham said:

"Hadn't you better go?"

"You've arranged it all damned neatly. You came to London not knowing a soul, you picked me up, got to know all my friends, sucked my brains, then coolly suggest that I'd better clear out. All right! I'll go. But I'll get even on this somehow and I don't care who knows it. And if you use one word of my work, I'll show you up in a way you won't like."

"You know perfectly well that I won't use a word of it."

"Do I, by God! You've used me in every way. And you'll use my work so that I shan't be able to prove it. It was a damned bad day for me when I ran into you."

A moment later he left, banging the door behind him.

CHAPTER V

I

When Rutherford found himself in the street he began to walk rapidly, regardless of direction, as if strenuous physical activity were an inevitable reflection of his mental state. His thoughts lacked an objective in the same way as his haste lacked a destination. Thought after thought shot like a rocket across his brain, illuminating chaos before it flashed into obscurity. There was no relation between them because each was independent of his will, but he accepted this subservience knowing that he would suffer more acutely when he was forced to regard his quarrel with Feversham in perspective.

He reached a main road crowded with Saturday night shoppers in which rapid progress was impossible. At each corner garishly lit stalls displayed every variety of goods, while hoarse voiced vendors proclaimed their cheapness and excellence with untiring enthusiasm. The posters announced that complete football results and reports were now obtainable, and public houses bulged with jostling humanity. Salutations and jocular comments were bandied about on all sides, while boisterous youths, marvellously attired, hung about in groups and greeted each pretty girl with crude witticisms or whistles indicative of admiration.

In order to escape from this animated scene, which filled him with loathing and contempt for the whole of humanity, Rutherford entered a dingy café owned by an Italian and ordered some coffee. A barrel organ outside immediately began a selection from its repertoire consisting of ballads which had enjoyed great popularity during the Boer War and which now lacked several notes originally regarded as essential. Memory, unfailingly though unwillingly, filled the gaps.

Melancholy was possible in such an atmosphere but not anger, and by the time his coffee arrived Rutherford's mood had altered to the extent that his irritation was now directed wholly against himself, not Feversham. It was characteristic of him that having thrown away his chance of being associated with the play, he became more than ever convinced of its merits. He must be a madman! How had the quarrel occurred? It seemed to him that it had had no origin, but had leapt suddenly into being with all the intensity of a flame. Why had he pestered Feversham, insisted on discussions, when at their second interview it had been agreed that his name should appear as part author? If the quarrel had ensued as a result of Feversham's refusal to allow him to collaborate, it would have been understandable, but to have flung his victory away for no reason was an act of incredible folly. He could not believe he had been such a fool and what, exactly, had he said to Feversham in the heat of his anger? In much the same way as a drunkard returning to normality remembers the acts of his frenzy, so Rutherford recalled certain of the phrases he had flung at Feversham, with the result that he realized the extent of the gulf he had created between them.

He looked round the squalid café and a feeling of loneliness invaded him. All confidence in himself vanished. This was what his life would be; he would never succeed and so he would be doomed to spend his life in surroundings like these. Hitherto, hope had blinded him to their squalor, but perhaps a day would come when hope would disappear and he would be left with only his ambition gnawing ceaselessly within him. What then? Besides, had he ever possessed real confidence in himself? Had he not been obliged recently to silence a voice within him which whispered that he was nearly thirty and was still practically unknown as a writer? *Why* had he been so anxious to collaborate with Feversham? This was the question of which he was afraid but now it rose menacingly in his mind, demanding an answer.

He lit a cigarette and stared at the stained tablecloth. The quarrel he had had with his father years ago came into his mind. He remembered how indignantly he had refused to go into the business and how proudly he had announced his intention of becoming an author. How certain he had been that his father was a fool and how convinced his father had been that he was making a mistake which he would regret bitterly. Whatever happened, he would never admit to him that he had failed. Also, in no circumstances, would he ever endure again that slightly contemptuous air which his brother had always adopted towards him. If he were a failure, he would hide the fact from his family at all costs. It was strange that he should be thinking about them now – he had neither seen nor heard of any of them for over a year. They went their way, he went his, and they would not have entered his thoughts if his future had not ceased to be a map and become chaos. But now their warnings and prophecies were like owls hooting in the darkness of his mind, and in his dejection he became convinced that they had been right and that he had no talent whatever for the career he had chosen.

How the devil was he going to get through the evening? He couldn't stay here another second and listen to that damned barrel organ! He rose hastily, demanded his bill angrily, and went out through the swing door into the street. He walked a few yards then paused irresolute. A drunkard reeled out of a public house, singing a sentimental ditty which announced that "Mother's Portrait is Still on the Wall," then he clasped a lamp post affectionately and stared at the traffic with glazed eyes. Rutherford watched him almost enviously. He knew it was not in his nature to get drunk as a deliberate policy and for the first time in his life he regretted the fact. After all, it was one way of cheating time. The evening presented no problem to this poor devil, whereas *he* had no idea how to get through it. The thought of returning to his room repelled him, he knew the type of remorse which would rack him there. On balance, he had better go to the Regal Café and argue about some theory or other till it was time to go to bed. As he couldn't get physically drunk, he'd get mentally intoxicated. Different types required a different kind of dope – there was only a difference of degree between him and the drunkard embracing the lamp post.

But then it occurred to him that if he went to the Regal Café, he would be certain to run into Feversham. What effect had the quarrel had on *him*? Rutherford discovered that he had not the slightest idea and this fact made him recognize what an enigma Feversham was to him. It annoyed him that this man, who was several years younger than he was, remained such a mystery that he was unable even to guess what his present feelings were.

At this point, however, another aspect of the quarrel emerged, and one which caused Rutherford profound uneasiness. What would Feversham reveal to others? If he told them the facts, Rutherford knew the kind of reception they would receive from the set in which he moved. Everyone would side with Feversham with the result that soon there would be a conspiracy to humiliate him. He flushed at the thought that even now Feversham might be telling his story to the malicious delight of such people as Ashley Alston. It would be repeated, with every variety of spicy exaggeration, and might even form a theme for cynical mirth at one of Madame de Fontin's supper parties. Suppose that Feversham revealed in detail how he had tried to get his name to the play and how meagre his contribution had been! He would become a laughing-stock. He remembered how frequently and how eagerly in the past he had listened to tit-bits about one or other of his group and how he had not failed to embellish the original scandal in order to make its narration more amusing. He would have no logical grievance if they pilloried him, yet how every nerve in him winced at the possibility of ridicule!

He was tired, depressed, lonely. The animation and noise of the streets jarred on his nerves but, as anything was preferable to solitude, he continued to walk about aimlessly till it was ten o'clock when he returned to his rooms and went to bed.

For the next two days he went nowhere, but eventually he

was forced to seek company in order to escape from himself. His work had deserted him, he found it impossible to read, and each hour seemed a weight which crushed him. On the Tuesday night, therefore, he decided to go to *The Dive* in order to ascertain Feversham's version of their quarrel and how it had been received.

Hiding his nervousness under a swaggering exterior he entered *The Dive* at about seven o'clock, knowing that Feversham was unlikely to be there then. Except for the semi-circle of drinkers at the bar, the place was almost empty and after hanging about for half an hour he was about to go, when Ashley Alston appeared. He was his customary romantic self, complete with strapped trousers, stock, fob, and elegant side whiskers. He greeted Rutherford languidly, but the latter noted apprehensively that an ironic smile curled his thin, very red lips.

"Hullo, Gordon!" he exclaimed as he gave him a limp, damp hand. "You deserted the Gorgon on Sunday. Pity! You missed an elephant in orange chiffon. But I forgot – of course, you wouldn't be there."

"Why not?" Rutherford demanded.

"Because Feversham was, and I believe you have quarrelled with that talented gentleman – or is that only a rumour?"

"Yes, we've quarrelled," Rutherford said shortly. There was a long pause, then he added: "Possibly Feversham told you the details."

"He did *not*," Alston replied as he fixed a cigarette into an ebony holder, "and you won't either. You're both right – details are entirely superfluous."

As this statement mystified Rutherford completely, he smiled knowingly and offered Alston a drink, hoping to make him more communicative.

They sat down at one of the little tables. Someone started the gramophone and two girls began to dance. A red-faced man at the table next to Rutherford's was eating a steak with remarkable rapidity.

"I knew you two would quarrel," Alston announced wearily.

"It's dull to be always right but it has to be endured. Only a psychologist knows the meaning of the word boredom."

But Rutherford was not interested in Alston's aphorisms. He wanted to get the facts, if there were any to be had, in order to know the appropriate attitude to assume.

"Why did you think we should quarrel?" he asked.

"My dear fellow," Alston began patronizingly, "I should love to believe several things. For instance, I should love to believe in platonic love; in the integrity of politicians; and in the importance of the Empire. I should adore to believe in Wolheim half as much as he believes in himself – then I should know he was God. It would be marvellous to believe that the Gorgon has an immortal soul. But, above all, it would be charming to believe that two men could be friends with a girl as beautiful as Sondra – and not quarrel. Unfortunately, however, I realize that two lions could not lie down with that lamb."

Alston, pleased with this effort, ordered another drink for which he forgot to pay, then proceeded to give Rutherford a list of Sondra's physical attractions – which was exhaustive and not lacking in candour.

But Rutherford was not listening to him. It was an immense relief to know that Feversham had given no details of their quarrel, and it flattered his vanity that people believed that Sondra was the cause of it. He decided that he must ascertain whether the play had been mentioned, and whether Alston had discussed the quarrel with Sondra. But he knew that Alston was quick to detect any attempt to pump him, and consequently Rutherford recognized that diplomacy was necessary.

After another drink or two, however, Alston became expansive and it was easy to get him to discuss any subject.

"Well, naturally, I don't want to discuss the row," Rutherford began. "It's of no importance, really, as Feversham leaves London soon. Wonder what he will do eventually? Do you think he'll ever write anything?"

"Good Lord, no!" Alston exclaimed. "He'll never make the

mistake of testing his talents by creating anything. He'll marry a rich woman – and live and die an infant prodigy."

Rutherford sneered approvingly, then said carelessly: "Well, I've no doubt he's told Sondra his version of the row very carefully."

"As a fact, he hasn't," Alston replied. "I asked her. She doesn't lie directly, which is original of her, and she told me that she had no idea why you had quarrelled. That was a lie by implication, because she must know perfectly well that she was the cause of it."

Rutherford had discovered all he wanted to know and escaped as soon as he could. Feversham had revealed nothing except the bare fact, and everyone would accept Alston's theory concerning Sondra. Things had gone better than he had dared to hope – he had only to keep out of the way for a few days, then Feversham would go abroad and possibly would not return to London for two or three years. If only he had played his cards better in regard to the play! But it was no good regretting that stupidity eternally. Once Feversham had left London, he would be able to resume his normal life and in a couple of months he would have forgotten that such a person ever existed. The supreme fact was that he had not been made to appear ridiculous – and it was evident that Feversham was not proud of his share in the quarrel, or he would not have been so reticent about it.

II

By a blend of judgment and luck Rutherford not only succeeded in avoiding Feversham during the next week but he also contrived to visit his usual haunts and meet several of his friends. He found that Sondra was regarded as the cause of the quarrel and consequently his stock had gone up rather than the reverse. It was believed that Feversham feared him as a rival. And although Rutherford studiously omitted direct reference to the rupture, something in his manner deepened the existing impression that the quarrel had been a very bitter one.

So much so that on one occasion, when Rutherford was not present, Alston announced that whatever Feversham's feeling might be, there was no doubt whatever about Rutherford's hatred.

But there were two Rutherfords during this period – the public one and the private one. When he was alone, he was miserable, for he found to his dismay that all his old associates had become unutterably dull. Their artificiality and their eternal vanity bored him beyond endurance, and he was amazed that only a few weeks ago he had been proud of his association with these people. Compared with Feversham, the men were vulgar; and compared with Sondra, the women were insipid. Before a week had passed, Rutherford preferred to be alone and, with a view to ensuring solitude, he told his friends that he was leaving London for a considerable time as he had been commissioned to write a book which involved going abroad. More than once of late the idea of leaving England had occurred to him and, consequently, in announcing his immediate departure, he felt that he was only anticipating the fact. But, whether he went or whether he remained, it was essential to be alone in order to take stock of his position and make plans for the future.

He spent a week in his rooms – the longest and most depressing he had ever endured – then an event occurred which he did nothing to originate. . . .

All the morning a grey fog had shrouded London. Rutherford remained in his sitting-room till nearly twelve, listening to the muffled cries and shouts which rose to him from the street below, and feeling as isolated as if he were a prisoner in some forgotten fortress. He stood by the window staring down into the grey abyss. It seemed to him that the familiar world had been replaced by a fantastic one whose denizens were ghosts and demons intent on unimaginable ends.

Just as twelve was striking he put on his overcoat and pulling his hat well down over his eyes he went out of the room and out into the street, having decided that he might as well be in the fog as stand and stare at it. He walked for about ten minutes, discovering more than once that he was in the road when he imagined he was on the pavement, then turning a corner he collided with a man carrying a bag. He looked up, was about to mutter an apology, when he saw it was Feversham. For a second they stared at each other in amazement, then Feversham exclaimed:

"What luck! This is the most amazing thing that ever happened! Look here, we've been a couple of fools – let's shake hands and forget all about it." He held out his hand and after an almost imperceptible pause Rutherford took it.

"Good! That's the end of that," Feversham went on. "Running into you beats everything! I'll prove it to you later, but tell me this first – are you doing anything to-day?"

"Neither to-day, nor to-morrow, nor the day after," Rutherford replied. "I'm at the end of things."

"Then you could come away with me?" Feversham inquired.

"Come away with you," he repeated.

"Yes. We'll have lunch and I'll explain. There's a full hour before the train goes and I'm going to persuade you to join me on it. There's a restaurant just round the corner – let's get out of this fog as quickly as we can."

Rutherford followed him and they entered a small restaurant which was nearly empty. When they had given their order, Feversham turned to him gaily: "I'm free as air. I've given up my rooms and said good-bye to everyone. Sondra sailed for New York yesterday, but I hope to see her before long, as I propose to go there myself early next year. Anyhow, I go to Paris in a week and everyone imagines that I've gone there to-day."

"Well, what are you going to do in the meantime? You've given up your rooms, you say?"

Feversham nodded. "I'm going to my cottage in Cornwall for a week," he announced impressively.

He laughed at Rutherford's perplexity, then raced on: "You didn't know I owned a cottage? No one does. You remember I told you that I had secrets which I keep to myself? Well, the cottage is one of them."

"But why on earth rent a cottage at this time of the year?"

"Rent it! I own it. I bought it when I was in England two years ago. It's freehold, very ramshackle, and I got it for next to nothing. I discovered it on a walking tour and it's the most out-of-the-way, primitive affair that ever existed. There aren't even any curtains. I've only been to it twice and only for a day or two on each occasion."

The food arrived. When the waiter had disappeared Rutherford said:

"It's a damned good idea to have a place which no one knows anything about. Wish to God I'd got one! But it's a queer time of the year to go all the same."

"You're responsible," Feversham replied. "Don't look so surprised. I can't believe you're sitting there. I feel as if all this were a dream – you, the lunch, and the fog. I'm going because I've made up my mind to decide about the play finally so that I can forget all about it and get on to something else. That's why you've got to come with me. After all, you're the man who raised the criticisms."

"To Cornwall!"

"Yes, in an hour. Why not? All you need buy is a toothbrush. I can fix you up with sheer necessities. The place is rough, but you won't mind that. Then we can get the play into its final form and you can come back – or come over to Paris with me. Now, will you come?"

Rutherford hid his elation. He had recovered everything his stupidity had thrown away. A sense of adventure stirred in him.

"I've a damned good mind to!"

"That's settled then." Feversham consulted his watch. "We're all right for time, so I'll tell you my plans. I'm going to get a dinner-basket so that we can dine on the train, then we needn't bother about food till to-morrow. We can go over to the farm in the morning and lay in a stock. Hope you like walking because the farm is my nearest neighbour and it's a good five miles away. The cottage is a pretty desolate spot, I warn you, and, of course, there's no light except candles, and you have to get water from a well in the garden."

"I hope the water won't have frozen. There was the devil of a frost last night and it feels as if it will be worse to-night."

"It never freezes," Feversham reassured him. "The well is about a hundred feet deep and there's always water. You can't hear a sound in that cottage day or night. I believe you'll like it. Perhaps you'll buy it one day."

"I might; I'm sick enough of London."

They talked on for half an hour, then as they were leaving, Feversham said:

"It's understood that this is my trip. I'll get the tickets while you get a toothbrush. Where did I put that bag?"

"Is that all you've got?"

"Yes. I've left my other things in the station cloakroom. I'll pick them up when I come through on my way to Paris. You go to a chemist's, then meet me at the barrier. It's rather a bore, but we have to change on to a local line for the last part of the journey."

They separated for a few minutes then met by the barrier and made their way on to the platform.

"This will do!" Feversham exclaimed as he opened the door of a carriage.

"Going first? This trip will cost you a lot, I'm afraid."

"The play has got to pay for this," Feversham replied. "With any luck we'll have this carriage to ourselves. There aren't too many travelling. I suppose they're scared by the fog. I'll bet it's perfectly clear twenty miles outside London."

They put their feet on the seat opposite and began to smoke. A huge dinner-basket reposed on the rack next to a pile of newspapers.

"Why all those papers?" asked Rutherford.

"To light the fire with on arrival. I know there's plenty of logs in the place but I'm not so sure about newspapers. Anyhow, I've got heaps of candles in my bag so we'll have enough light. Everything will be all right if you don't mind roughing it pretty thoroughly."

The train started and after proceeding rather slowly for over an hour it emerged into brilliant sunshine.

Rutherford gazed at the fields which were white with frost, and could scarcely believe in his good fortune. He felt that London was already far behind and his old life with it. He surrendered himself to this sense of freedom and began dreaming of his future. Why shouldn't he go to Paris with Feversham? He could live there as cheaply as in London. He was sick of his rooms, his friends, everything. It would be delightful to escape from all familiar surroundings for a few months; to open himself to new impressions; and to begin that book he had planned, off and on, for months.

But Feversham's voice cut across his reverie:

"Did you wire your landlady that you'd be away for a few days?"

"No, I didn't bother. I'm often away for a night and I can send her a post card to-morrow. I suppose there's a pillar box somewhere, isn't there?"

"Yes, just beyond the farm. It's a good thing that everything is such a devil of a way from the cottage because it means that we have to get exercise. And, anyhow, it's better to discuss the play at night."

"The night's the time for it," Rutherford agreed.

Feversham began to discuss all sorts of subjects, passing from one to the other easily and divertingly. Rutherford watched him as he listened, noting the occasional gestures of his fine hands and the gay light in his blue eyes, till gradually a shadow began to lengthen across his mind. He was no longer jealous of Feversham as the author of the play, he was jealous of him for what he *was*. He seemed so responsive to life, so quick and eager, so receptive, that Rutherford understood only too clearly why he had discovered that people like Ashley Alston were colourless. They were narrow, fierce, egotistical people who never forgot themselves for a single moment, whereas Feversham lived, moved, and had his being, in the theme under discussion. The vibration he created was of a different order from that of others; it quickened intelligence and kindled imagination. With him, there was no gulf fixed between the important and the negligible – as there was in the outlook of those in Rutherford's set. He gave everything its appropriate value and consequently the commonplace ceased to be the ordinary. He possessed the supreme art of the conversationalist, which is to hypnotize the listener into believing that he is a collaborator.

Rutherford now understood fully why Feversham regarded the play so nonchalantly. There are people to whom achievement is part of their inheritance and Feversham was one of them. Rutherford was convinced that it belonged to him, that it was only a question of when and how greatly he would excel, and this knowledge kindled a jealousy wholly different from that he had experienced in regard to the play. Feversham's generosity in proposing that they should collaborate was only an example of his careless certainty in his own power. It was the largesse of a rich and vital nature. Rutherford would have bartered his chance of immortality to gain such confidence in himself; to have done with vacillation, questionings; and no longer to be the slave of appearances. As it was, a trivial success elated him and a petty reverse plunged him into gloom. He alternated between extremes and consequently he envied that central stability in Feversham which did not continually require a sign in order to convince itself that it existed.

The train sped on through the December landscape, the day was sinking, and distant lights in cottage and farmstead flashed a welcome, then vanished. At intervals a town seemed to leap into life out of the darkness, a glimpse was caught of brightly lit buildings and shadowy forms in a station, as the train roared through and plunged into the night again.

"We'll have to dine pretty early," Feversham remarked. "Once we leave this train, we shan't move like this by a long way."

"What time shall we arrive at the cottage?"

"About eleven. You see, it's five miles from the station. I suggest we sleep for an hour then we'll be fresh on arrival and can talk instead of going to bed."

They stretched themselves out and slept for over an hour, then they dined and discussed all the people they had left behind. London already seemed to belong to a different world, and Rutherford found it difficult to believe that only a few hours ago he had been in his sitting-room staring disconsolately down into the fog.

It was dark and very cold at the station at which they alighted to get their connection. About twenty others also changed and in a few minutes the local train appeared. It was one of those trains which seem so surprised at their appearance that they remain stationary for some time in order to obtain a sense of their own reality. However, Feversham and Rutherford secured a carriage to themselves, and in about twenty minutes the train started, apparently very unwillingly, for it crawled along with frequent jolts, followed by sudden enthusiasms, and pulled up with an air of finality at invisible stations which were entirely deserted and at which no one ever seemed to alight. The carriage was badly lit, cold, and draughty. Conversation flagged, then ceased. Every now and again one or other of them tried to peer through the misty windows into the darkness through which they were moving so slowly.

They were both extremely cold and generally uncomfortable when the train stopped abruptly at a station consisting of a miniature platform and a light. Feversham rubbed the window, stared out, and exclaimed:

"Here we are!"

Three men got out with them who made their way quickly to a waiting cart and drove off immediately. The station master, who was also the porter, was too engaged on his major duties to collect any tickets. The night was intensely cold and dark, moonless and starless, and the ground was as hard as iron.

"I can't see a thing," Rutherford muttered as they emerged from the ill-lit station.

"It doesn't matter," Feversham replied. "There's only one road – those men drove one way and we go the other. It will take us over an hour but we'll get warm walking – thank heaven!"

They began their journey, glad to be on the move. They spoke little as they strode along, carrying Feversham's bag alternately. Their footsteps rang out on the frosty air, and they did not pass a single human being on their long tramp through the darkness.

III

"It's somewhere near here," said Feversham. "I was a fool not to bring a torch. Yes, this is it – I remember now. We leave the road here and we'll be at the cottage in a few minutes."

They walked on in silence, then Feversham exclaimed:

"At last – and about time too!"

"I can't see anything," Rutherford replied.

"Wait a minute and don't move because there's a step. Strike a match, will you?"

Rutherford discovered the vague outline of a cottage. A moment later Feversham had opened the door and they went in.

"Better not move or you'll fall over something," Feversham warned him. "I'll soon light some candles. It feels damp and a bit eerie, doesn't it?"

He lit candle after candle and the room came to life. It was broad and low-pitched and contained only essentials in the way of furniture.

"Is this all there is?" Rutherford asked.

"Only this and a loft. Might as well have a dozen candles going. There! That's more like it!" He pointed to some ashes in the grate. "There's the remains of the fire I lit over a year ago. Give me one of those papers. I've plenty of logs and by a miracle there's some firewood. You sit down and I'll soon have a fire going."

In a few minutes he had kindled a blazing fire which, with the candlelight, made the room seem very desirable after the cold darkness.

"Well, Rutherford, what do you think of it? It's not too bad, is it? And the nearest human being is five miles away. Think of that, and be thankful. We'll get our supplies to-morrow so we can forget humanity to-night. I've always brought food when I've been here before, but then I only stayed for a day or two and this time I want to stay a week."

Rutherford lit a pipe and pulled his chair nearer the fire.

"I think it's a brilliant scheme," he began, "to have a place like this and to tell no one about it. I wish I had a secret refuge – I'd spend a lot of time in it."

"Well, no one except you knows of this place. I made an oath to keep it a secret when I bought it. A queer old man used to live here and when he died his son didn't want it, as he was going to the Colonies, so he sold it to me for a song. But it's pretty ramshackle, if you examine it closely, and it will cost me something very soon, because if I don't have the roof attended to, it will fall in!"

After a pause he went on:

"Would you like some coffee? I've brought some, and I can easily get some water from the well. There's a pail in the loft with a coil of rope attached to it. The rope is rather a bore because there's so much of it that it's the devil's own job if it gets tangled. Or shall we have coffee later?"

"Later, I think. We can't move from the fire just yet."

They sat and smoked in silence. Feversham stared at the flames and Rutherford watched him. What a jolly sort of life he led! How full of change and adventure! How rich in vivid contrasts! To-night – this isolated cottage in Cornwall; a week hence – Paris. And early next year, probably New York. He was independent in every way; he picked up friends as and when he wanted them; he could see Sondra again whenever the mood took him. But, above all, he was independent because he relied on none of these things. They were only the settings to his life. He created his conditions; others were the slaves of theirs.

Rutherford contrasted Feversham's life with his Own, and again jealousy dominated him. Feversham moved so lightly through the world; had neither family nor relatives – whose very silence could be a subtle form of criticism. He had no doubts, no misgivings; he accepted the adventure of life; grasped at nothing, and was given everything.

They began to talk about the play. It was Feversham who introduced the subject for, by this time, Rutherford took little interest in it. He knew that he had no contribution to make and he knew that, if eventually the play were a success, everyone would guess that it was Feversham's work. But it was necessary to maintain the conversation, so he repeated the arguments he had expressed a dozen times, criticizing the manner in which the man in the play was murdered.

"Yes, I know how you feel about it," Feversham said at last, "but I do want to convince you that the present treatment is all right."

They went on arguing for another five minutes and Rutherford found that all his old animosity returned as he continued to repeat criticisms in which he did not believe. It was difficult to keep his temper. Feversham lit a pipe and listened to him patiently, then he exclaimed impetuously:

"Look here! I've got it! I'll convince you yet. I know I've shown you the sudden movement the man makes when they're struggling, but I've got a better idea. We'll *rehearse* the struggle. And – yes, by Jove – there's a revolver in the loft. The old man had it because the place is so isolated and the son gave it to me. Wait a minute and I'll get it. There's nothing like realism."

A moment later he produced the revolver. "Here – you take this. Wait a minute, I don't want this pipe. Now, you catch hold of me. That's right. And I'm holding you like this. Ready?"

A sudden hatred possessed Rutherford. What a farce it all was! He knew that Feversham's treatment was all right and it annoyed and humiliated him to be proved wrong. He began to tremble with anger.

"Are you all right?" Feversham asked. "Good! Now, you're holding me tightly with your left hand, and I'm struggling to get free. Now, *this* is the sudden movement I've tried to explain."

He swung round quickly. Although he had shown the action to Rutherford before, the latter had not been paying attention and so it was completely unexpected. Rutherford made a sudden movement with his right hand, there was a loud report, and Feversham fell to the floor.

He stood motionless for a minute, deafened by the noise, and unable to collect his thoughts.

"Feversham!"

No sound, no movement.

"*Feversham.*"

He fell to his knees, but he was afraid to touch him. A fearful thought hung like an icicle in his brain. He could hear the ticking of the watch on Feversham's wrist.

"Feversham! Don't – don't! You're frightening me – you're frightening me, I tell you!"

A log cracked in the fire, causing his heart to beat even more rapidly.

A minute passed, then another. He knelt motionless, still holding the revolver in his right hand. He was watching a tableau in a dream of terror – he was certain of it. Feversham was not lying there: he was not kneeling by him – it was impossible, impossible!

Dead. The word was like the stab of a dagger. *Dead?* The man who had laughed and joked in the train – the man who loved life so wholly – the man with the gay, intensely blue eyes! He began to laugh. It was terrible laughter which he did not recognize as his own. It frightened him. Only madmen laughed like that.

"Feversham. . . . Feversham . . . *for the love of God!*"

No sound, no movement.

He rose slowly and walked on tip-toe to the table. *Dead* – the word had no meaning for him, it merely circled round his brain. The flame of one of the candles began to flicker and he stared at it fascinated. *He* had lit those candles: bought them, packed them in his bag, put them in their present positions – and now? . . .

Then, as if the floodgates of fear had been suddenly

opened, he saw the horror of his situation in this room with Feversham dead on the floor. He put the revolver on the table as if it had turned to flame. Thought after thought leapt into feverish, fearful life.

They had quarrelled – everyone had known that their quarrel had been a bitter one! He had made no effort to conceal his hatred. Alston knew of it, they *all* knew of it. His manner had proclaimed it to everyone. They would think he was a ——. The word shaped itself, slowly, relentlessly. First it took a shape in his brain, then a sound – *Murderer*. They would think he was a murderer. He began to tremble and an icy perspiration broke out on his forehead. But – it was ridiculous – murderers weren't people like him. They couldn't be – they were quite different – different in every way. And yet if someone came into the room now, mightn't they think, wouldn't they think——?

It was incredible, fantastic! He would be able to explain. Yes, he would keep quite calm and explain all about the quarrel, and then go on to describe how they had been rehearsing a struggle in a play they were writing together. Then——. But it seemed that a voice in his brain suddenly began to mock him. It took up the theme of his argument, distorted it, made it ridiculous. He seemed to hear it say:

"Oh, yes, of course, people would believe that after a bitter quarrel you came down here with him. You met in the fog, didn't you? Quite! And made up your quarrel for no reason whatever, and he never referred to the way in which you had insulted him and Sondra? Quite natural and probable, of course. In fact he suddenly discovered that he liked you so much that he asked you to go away with him. What a beautiful nature he must have had! And you went – and no one knew anything about it. And, on arrival, you began to rehearse a death struggle in the play. And there happened to be a revolver in the loft which *he* suggested that you – his enemy – should hold while you struggled with him. Yes, just so – of course, we believe you. And he didn't look to see whether it was loaded? No! And neither did you? Exactly – why should you?"

A moan broke from him and he collapsed into a chair, with his arms across the table and his head buried in them. The minutes ticked away but he did not move.

Gradually it seemed to him that another voice in his brain began to reason with him – a cold logical voice, quite different from the one which had mocked him.

"You must keep calm," it said to him. "It's your only chance. There's another way of looking at all this. No one knows that he owns this cottage. He's given up his rooms; he's said good-bye to his friends; Sondra has sailed for New York. Everyone thinks he's in Paris. Perhaps things aren't so black as they look. He has no family and no relatives. He's simply a bird of passage. Didn't he tell you that his money is in banks in various places? Ask yourself this question – *who would miss him?*

He sat upright and stared in front of him like a man in a trance. After all, who *would* miss him? People in London thought he was in Paris. Any friends he had in Paris would think he was still in London. He was never anywhere for long and he only knew a handful of Bohemians in each city who were far too concerned with themselves to remember him when they ceased to see him. Even if they did, they'd assume that he'd gone to New York. Why, only to-day he had told him that he proposed to go there early next year.

What was he to do? One thing was certain: the truth would send him to the scaffold. No one would believe the truth if he told it. The truth was powerless to save him.

He must think, he must *think*. It was madness to let the seconds slip away. No one knew that he had come to Cornwall with him. London had been shrouded in fog and they had travelled down alone. No one had seen them alight at the local station – he still had his ticket in his pocket – and they had passed no one on the long walk to the cottage. There was no evidence of any kind to show that he had been with him to-day.

Suddenly he remembered the report of the revolver. *That* might be evidence against him! He crept to the door on tiptoe, opened it noiselessly and listened. The silence seemed one vast accusation.

He closed the door and crossed to the fireplace, averting his eyes from the motionless form on the floor. The cold, logical voice in his brain began to repeat one sentence with monotonous insistence: *"You have only to get rid of the body."*

As he listened to it, a strength equal to the desperate situation was born in him and he began to think with a strange clarity which he had never experienced before. He was no longer afraid. A cold, relentless logic possessed and instructed him. One object, and one only, was paramount – to save himself. He *must* get rid of the body, then he could return to London, and no one would be able to prove that he had ever visited the cottage with Feversham.

He found that he was thinking of the well in the garden. Something kept saying to him: "There is a deep well in the garden." He must find the courage to do this thing, or he would be lost. He clenched his fists, stood motionless for a minute, then went to the door, opened it, and crept into the garden on tiptoe. He groped about for some time but at last he found the well and removed the heavy board which covered it. Then he returned to the room, his nerve and muscles braced to their task.

Feversham had been shot through the heart and had not bled externally. Rutherford dragged him with difficulty into the darkness, remembering as he did so that the ground was like iron and that, therefore, there would be no footmarks. He was sweating although the cold was intense. Then with sudden resolution he pushed the body into the well. The sound of a splash rose up to him from the abyss. He replaced the board and returned to the room.

It seemed terribly empty. Feversham's pipe was on the table – it was still warm. He threw it into the fire, then looked round the room, anxious to remove every trace of their visit. He picked up the revolver, stowed it in Feversham's bag, then climbed into the loft and covered the bag with some rubbish which the former owner had evidently left there. The fire was getting low, he could leave it to burn itself out, then it might easily be the remains of the fire Feversham had lit over a year ago. He stuffed the newspapers into a pocket in his overcoat, then he glanced at the door and was relieved to see that the key was still in it.

How calm and collected he was! He seemed to be watching himself as he moved about the room, studying every object carefully. Only the candles remained. He put them out one by one and as he extinguished each, he put it into the empty pocket of his overcoat. Finally only one was left burning. He looked round for the last time and saw that the manuscript of the play was still on the table. He picked it up, folded it, and put it into his breast pocket, then crossed to the remaining candle.

He was afraid to extinguish it. A mad unreasoning fear of being left alone in the dark room paralysed him. His icy calmness deserted him as quickly as it had been born and he began to tremble violently. He *dare* not put out that last candle! He was afraid to extinguish it, although it seemed like an eye watching him. It was ridiculous that he could tremble at the thought of a dark room after the horror he had just performed so coolly and remorselessly.

With sudden resolution he extinguished the little flame. Darkness, save for the faint glimmer of the fire. He thrust the candle into his pocket and was about to leave when a curious desire to know the time came to him. He crossed to the fire and looked at his watch. It was twelve-thirty. Then he crept to the door, went out, locked it noiselessly behind him and stole away into the darkness, with the key clutched tightly in his hand.

IV

An insane desire to run seized him – to run on and on, away from the cottage, into the darkness. But by sheer will power he forced himself to walk slowly, and every now and again he stopped and listened intently. There was not a sound: the silence had become his accomplice.

He thrust the key into his trouser pocket then went on, gradually increasing his pace, utterly ignorant of direction,

intent on leaving the cottage behind him as rapidly as possible. Only an hour and a half ago they had entered it together!
He wanted to laugh when he remembered that. Ninety minutes! The whole conception of time became supremely ludi-
crous and he would never be able to tell anyone how absurd
it was. . . . Then, letter by letter, a word began to spell itself
across his brain: M-U-R-D-E-R-E-R. That was the word people
would use. His head became flame and his heart became ice.
Phantom thoughts flitted like bats through his mind. But it
was ridiculous, fantastic, that anyone could believe that he
had murdered Feversham. He wanted to shout, to proclaim
his innocence aloud, so that the sound of his passionate denial
would bring the blood back to his heart.

Suddenly, quite near to him, an owl hooted. He stood and
swayed like a drunken man, then reeled on, determined to
increase the distance between him and the cottage at all costs.
Also he knew that he must control himself, his life depended
on it. He must banish every thought – every memory – which
made him tremble. . . . Ninety minutes ago! And now Feversham was dead and he was a murderer. How easily the word
slid into his mind! But it was an accident – of course, it was an
accident – yet he had acted as if he had killed him deliberately.
Everyone would believe him guilty. The truth was useless to
him now: he had rejected it finally and for ever, and so it ceased
to have any relevance. "If you were innocent, why did you act
as if you were guilty?" There was no answer to that question.

From the depths of an invisible wood came a cry like a
scream. He clutched the air with frantic hands, then began to
run headlong into the darkness, certain that someone was following him, till at last, breathless and half mad with fear, he
sank to the ground.

It was several minutes before he was calm enough to rise
and continue his journey. On and on into the darkness he
went, terrified by the noise his footsteps made as they rang out
on the frosty air.

Now, with subtle irony, a voice within him began to suggest how the truth would have served him if only he had

trusted to it. If he had immediately reported Feversham's
death to the police, that act alone would have been eloquent
testimony to his innocence. Then there was the manuscript
of the play – it would prove that there *was* such a scene as the
one they had rehearsed. He would have been able to explain
how the accident occurred and if people did not believe his
story, they would be unable to prove that it was a lie. Then,
surely, it would not have been difficult to obtain evidence that
they had travelled down together – he still had his ticket in his
possession – and that would have shown that there must have
been a sudden reconciliation between them. The truth *would*
have saved him! He had allowed a moment of panic to capture
and dominate him till he had become its slave and acted under
its dictation. But it was all too late now – he had rejected the
truth, set himself for ever outside its shelter, and, therefore,
he might just as well have murdered Feversham so far as the
opinions of others were concerned.

Murder! He repeated the word to himself striving to realize its implications. Yes, of course, murderers were hanged.
A judge pronounced them guilty and they were taken from
the dock to a cell where they waited for death – three weeks,
wasn't it? – watched day and night by warders. Then early one
morning they were hanged – and Society felt more secure.
And probably several of these murderers were like him – men
maddened by fear or passion who had committed some act
of nameless folly and so brought themselves under the pitiless
machine of the law.

He remembered a recent case. For months the papers had
been full of the arrest and trial of a wretched man called Crippen. He had been executed about a fortnight ago. He remembered that group of people at Madame de Fontin's who had
discussed him and how pleased they were that his appeal had
failed, and how relieved they were that nothing could save him
now. All the incidents of the case came back to him: the hysterical headlines in the papers; the gloating over each loathsome
detail; the minute description of the doomed man's appearance. He, too, had regarded him as a leper, a being different in

kind from himself, a person with whom in no circumstances whatever could *he* have anything in common. Was the evidence against Crippen more overwhelming than the evidence against him? Had there been something which Crippen could not urge in his own defence, knowing that an action dictated by panic had removed him from its aid? Supposing Crippen had only meant to give that woman a sleeping draught and had accidentally given her an overdose! Suppose that this had happened and then he had lost his head and had decided to get rid of the body! Who would have believed him if he had told the truth at his trial? And yet it would have been the truth. Might not anyone be innocent – as *he* was innocent – no matter how damning were the facts marshalled against him?

Good God! What a hair-line it was between security and the abyss! Yesterday, he had been safe, convinced that whatever happened he would never encounter certain experiences, never be subjected to certain ordeals. They belonged to a different world – they happened only to people quite unlike himself – he could afford to ignore even the possibility of their approach. That was yesterday, and to-day he was a man whom the world would judge and condemn as a murderer.

On he strode, hour after hour, with no conception of direction, haunted by the insane fear that he might be tracing an immense circle and that when the light came he would find himself outside that cottage from which he had fled in terror.

Dawn. First a faint glow in the sky, and the dim emergence of things, then day unfolded like a swelling symphony of light and song. He paused near a wood threaded by the silvery music of an unseen waterfall. Overhead a bird sang rapturously. And the beauty of earth was agony to him.

He knew that he must nerve himself to encounter the eyes of men and he tried to forget that the dawn was flooding the cottage with light and that birds were singing in that garden where his secret was hidden from the world. He walked on for another hour, unmindful of fatigue and hunger, till he reached a small town and learnt that a train left for London in an hour. He sat in an empty waiting-room at the station, staring in front of him, unable to believe in the actuality of what had happened.

At last the train appeared. He was unable to find an empty carriage and had to endure the comments of a farmer who travelled with him till he reached the station at which he had to join the London train. The express appeared in a quarter of an hour and he managed to secure an empty compartment. He flung himself along the seat and immediately fell into a sleep of utter exhaustion.

Hour after hour passed but he slept on and had to be roused by a porter when the train reached Paddington.

CHAPTER VI

"You can't go no further than this, sir."

Rutherford stared up at the porter in great perplexity, then the man added:

"Any luggage in the van?"

He rose with difficulty, being stiff after his long sleep, and reached for his hat which he had thrown on to the rack.

"There's no luggage," he muttered, buttoning up his overcoat and still scarcely aware of his surroundings. A moment later he left the carriage and walked unsteadily down the platform, greatly to the disappointment of the porter who had cherished a secret hope that the dishevelled passenger was thoroughly intoxicated and, therefore, good for a generous tip.

The lights, the crowd, the noise and bustle of the platform bewildered him but he continued to move automatically towards the barrier, guided by the moving column of people who were discussing the whereabouts of luggage or the most expeditious ways of reaching destinations.

"Tickets please!"

The tone was peremptory and Rutherford started. A collector was eyeing him impatiently and he began to fumble in his pockets, greatly to the exasperation of those who were waiting behind him.

"Stand aside, please. Don't keep others waiting."

He fell out of the queue and began a more systematic search, noting that there was a key in his trouser pocket and vaguely wondering what it was doing there. At last he discovered the ticket, handed it to the collector, and passed through the barrier.

In the station proper there was no specific movement of people to which he could subordinate himself. Consequently after wandering aimlessly for a minute he stopped and stared about him as if he were a friendless foreigner who was ignorant of the language. An enterprising porter approached him:

"Looking for the cloak-room, sir?"

Rutherford shook his head and the man disappeared. A feeling of resentment stirred in him. Why the devil couldn't they leave him alone! He'd ask for the cloak-room if he wanted it. Officious, interfering idiots!

Suddenly he started – *the cloak-room*. Swift as a tidal wave, Memory towered above him – then engulfed him. Feversham ... the cottage ... murder ... Paddington .... the cloak-room! Good God, Feversham's things were in that cloak room! He had left them there, intending to pick them up when he came through on his way to Paris. Why had he forgotten till now? Was he menaced by the existence of those things in the cloak-room? But he was incapable of concentration. He found that he was living again through the horror of those ninety minutes in the cottage, striving to convince himself that it was a dream, and that at any minute he would wake to find that his martyrdom was at an end. Then, incontinently, he discovered that a greater sense of security came to him when he remembered that it was night. The cottage and garden were hidden – they were buried in silence. A traveller could pass by them and remain unaware of their existence. How dark and cold the garden had been when he had dragged – but he must not think of that. It was madness to think of it. ...

It seemed to him that people were staring at him. So he decided to leave the station and wander about till he could make up his mind what he should do next. In a few minutes he reached the street. It was a fine night, clear and cold. The lights in the shop windows and on the moving vehicles gleamed like jewels; posters fluttered in the wind at every corner, and newsboys shouted the day's sensation with an enthusiasm which repetition failed to diminish. But, to Rutherford, all this animation appeared remote and unreal – the feverish activity of another world – utterly divorced from him and, therefore, without relevance. It seemed like a scene from a pantomime into which he had strayed, and the fantastic thought came to him that at any minute it would vanish and he would find himself alone in a dark and silent place.

Then he discovered his hunger, and immediately the desire for food became paramount. He crossed the street rapidly, regardless of the traffic, made his way to a restaurant facing him, and was about to enter when he noticed that the face of a waiter – who was looking at him through one of the glass squares in the door – was vaguely familiar. In a flash he remembered! It was the restaurant at which he had lunched with Feversham! He swung round and began to run down a side street, hunted by an invisible pack of phantom fears. But a few minutes later, everything was forgotten in the desire for food which again dominated him.

He stopped, looked round in desperation, then saw that there was a coffee stall on the corner only a hundred yards away. He hastened to it, ordered some sandwiches, then climbed on to one of the two high stools provided for the accommodation of those patrons who were not in a hurry. A jovial, red-faced man began to cut the sandwiches while he whistled gaily.

" 'Tain't so long to Christmas," he announced. "Soon be 'anging the stockings up."

Rutherford grunted and the man continued:

"One of my nippers 'e sez to me the other day: 'Dad,' 'e sez, 'is there really a bloke called Father Christmas?' Only six, mind you, but sharp! – sharp as a needle. 'Not 'arf there ain't,' I sez, 'what next!' You see it was this way: I've always told the kid that there *is* Father Christmas, so I had to keep it up like. Might as well be 'anged for a sheep as a lamb."

Rutherford moved uneasily on his stool. What was the fool saying? Yes, of course, once men were hanged for stealing a sheep. A sheep was worth more than a man in those days. But he *must* say something – the man was looking at him.

"How do you find things?" he muttered at last.

"Mustn't grumble," the man replied briskly. "What I sez is this," he announced with a sweeping gesture which culminated in depositing the sandwiches in front of Rutherford, "what I sez is *this*: if a man can keep himself and his wife and kids decent, 'e ain't got no cause to grumble. Can't all live in Buckingham Palace, can we? I often say to my missus: our ship will never come 'ome if you're always a-looking for it. Corfee?"

Rutherford nodded. He was eating ravenously but the idea of hot coffee was irresistible. The man turned round to attend to the urn. Coffee! *Feversham* had offered him coffee last night! He had told him that he had some in his bag. It was still in the place where he had packed it, but – now – the bag was in the loft covered with rubbish. Why did he remember these details? Why did——

"Yes, it's a rum trade this, and no mistake," the man began as if in reply to a question. "You meet all sorts – good and bad, rich and poor – never know who you're servin'. When I'm slack I sometimes try to guess what sort of a bloke my customer is. Everyone knows me round 'ere: the copper, the cabmen, they all know Joe. You're pretty 'ungry, I reckon."

"Yes," Rutherford stammered. He was about to continue when fortunately another customer appeared and Joe had to attend to him.

Rutherford tried to eat more slowly in order to render himself less conspicuous and, with a view to diverting his thoughts, he began to study the equipment over which Joe presided. He noticed that, near the urn, was a small mirror which, doubtless, enabled Joe to assure himself at intervals of the propriety of his appearance. By tilting his stool slightly, Rutherford managed to obtain a glimpse of himself, but almost immediately he returned to his original position with alacrity. He had seen a haggard face with deep black circles under the eyes and a heavy growth of dark stubble on the chin. A haunted face had looked at him from the little mirror.

He slid off the stool. "Here, what do I owe you?" he demanded. He handed Joe the requisite amount and began to walk away quickly.

"There's a rum 'un and no mistake," Joe announced to the remaining customer. "Ain't 'ad a meal for a month, if you ask me. Fair wolfed them sandwiches, 'e did, and they ain't too thin neither."

"You're right there, mate. They're about as thick as my 'ead on a Sunday mornin'."

Rutherford hurried down streets, the names of which conveyed nothing to him. Now that his hunger was appeased his brain became extraordinarily active. There was no longer a veil between him and the horror of his predicament. But what should he do? Where should he go? His *life* depended on not making a false move. He had found strength last night to do what was necessary and he must find it again, or he would become hysterical and betray himself. He decided to go to his rooms as quickly as possible. It was essential to be alone, to think, to plan carefully, and then to act.

He walked more quickly, eventually reaching a street which he recognized. A few minutes later he boarded a 'bus and was soon in Bloomsbury. He looked up at the house where he lodged, being anxious to encounter no one, then he let himself in silently and glanced automatically at the table in the hall to see if there was anything for him. He picked up a letter, then climbed noiselessly to the top of the house and entered his sitting-room. He slit open the envelope and learnt that another of his stories had been accepted and that the editor would always be glad to consider any future work he cared to submit to him. A bitter smile curled his lip as the letter slipped from his hand to the floor. Stories! He could write a story such as he had never written – a story of darkness, terror, madness.

Stories! He glanced at his desk and remembered the countless hours he had worked at it. Would he ever write another word? Once, writing had been everything to him; now, it was nothing. He had one object and one only – to save himself. To live, simply to live – that was enough.

There was a packet of cigarettes on his desk and he seized it eagerly. He had not smoked since he had fled from the cottage and he lit a cigarette in feverish haste then inhaled the smoke deeply. The night was before him. He was not tired after his long sleep in the train, so he decided to smoke and evolve a plan.

He began to take off his overcoat and discovered the candles in the pocket. He must get rid of them and, later, he must dispose of the key. He lit a fire, using some of the candles to make it blaze more quickly, then took the manuscript of the play out of his breast pocket and locked it in a drawer containing some of his private papers. A sense of assurance came to him when he remembered that for several hours he would be alone. He could sit by the fire and smoke and gradually he would see what was the wisest course to adopt. There was no point in repeating to himself that he was innocent – others would hold him guilty and it was their opinion which counted. In fact, it would be wiser to regard himself as a murderer, then the necessity for caution and cunning would always be uppermost.

He began to review the reasoning of that cold logical voice which had instructed him last night. Was there a flaw in it? *Would* anyone miss Feversham? Everyone thought he was in Paris and as the weeks passed and no word came from him, would anyone give him a thought? Rutherford remembered others who had strayed into his set and vanished, no one ever referred to them – they were entirely forgotten. People would imagine that Feversham had gone to New York, if they thought about him at all. And, in any event, no one knew that he owned that isolated cottage in Cornwall, so no one would seek him there. No, he was safe – he was certain he was safe – if only his nerve held and he did not betray himself.

An hour passed but he still sat huddled in his armchair by

the fire, smoking cigarette after cigarette, and going over all that had occurred since he had gone out into the fog yesterday. He began to reconstruct his actions since his arrival at Paddington. Immediately he became uneasy. What a fool he had been to sleep so deeply that a porter had had to rouse him! Had the man noticed anything? Then that other porter who had asked if he wanted the cloak-room. Had he looked scared when the man had put the question to him? God! How important all these trivialities became in retrospect! Then the waiter in that accursed restaurant. He was the one person in the whole of London whom it was essential to avoid. *He* had seen him with Feversham! Had he recognized him to-night? What evil destiny had led him to that damned restaurant? What a fool to have wandered about like a sleep walker when he should have had a plan and put it into execution with every faculty alive and alert! And what about that talkative idiot at the coffee stall? He *must* have noticed how ravenously he ate those sandwiches. Also, his appearance advertised the fact that he had not been to bed for twenty-four hours. He seemed to have committed the maximum number of possible mistakes in the minimum space of time.

But the desire to believe in his safety was so imperative that soon his thoughts became its slaves and he, therefore, decided that he was exaggerating the importance of these incidents. He began to regard them from a different angle. The two porters were of no significance: the first probably thought he was drunk, and the second was merely touting for a job. As to the waiter, he would have forgotten him entirely – he only remembered the amount of his tips. It was a good thing that he had looked so haggard and had been unshaven as that made recognition even less likely. The coffee stall man was used to odd people of every kind and would have forgotten him five minutes after his departure. No, he was safe – there was no doubt whatever about that – he had acted with courage and resolution and he had only to keep a tight grip on himself and no one would ever be able to prove that he had seen Feversham yesterday.

He settled himself more comfortably in the armchair, stretched his legs nearer to the fire, and lit another cigarette. Thank God, Sondra had sailed! What incredible fortune that Feversham had never told anyone that he owned that cottage....

Suddenly a new thought darted into his mind – a wild disturbing thought which made him spring to his feet in a frenzy of fear.

Perhaps Feversham had been lying. What guarantee was there, except the statement, that no one knew of the existence of the cottage? He might have been posing in order to make himself more interesting. And what proof was there that he had neither family nor relatives? Feversham might be a romantic who delighted in parading his personality on the background of the unusual. It was a common enough failing and Rutherford knew several temperamental people who evaded the prosaic facts about their lives by the invention of ingenious fictions. Perhaps Feversham was this type. Possibly Sondra was still in London and knew perfectly well that Feversham had gone to that cottage in Cornwall!

Fear swept him like a whirlwind. He must leave London as soon as possible and hide himself till all risk of detection had passed. He ought to go immediately. He must think, he must *think*. He must tell his landlady some convincing lie to explain his sudden departure, or should he go at once and write to her from abroad? No, that wouldn't do. He must not act precipitately, he must avoid even the possibility of arousing suspicion. But if Sondra were still in London, she might *call*. The thought of facing her made him tremble. Probably Feversham had only said she had sailed in order to make any further reference to her unnecessary. He might have felt that, in spite of their reconciliation, it was impossible to discuss her. *Why* had this possibility only occurred to him now? Why——

He heard footsteps slowly ascending the stairs. He stood quite still, his heart beating violently. Slowly and laboriously they came nearer and nearer. It *couldn't* be anyone coming to see him! He dare not face another human being to-night!

He had not the strength, his nerves were in shreds. "God Almighty!" he muttered, "I can't – I can't!"

There was a knock at the door. He made no reply and a moment later the door opened a few inches.

"Can I come in?"

It was his landlady. He made a noise which she interpreted as a welcome and, therefore, came slowly into the room.

She was a large woman, not over tidy in appearance, whose manner suggested that the innumerable tasks she had already performed were nothing by comparison with those which still awaited her. An atmosphere of grievance pervaded her. She belonged to that class who never complain but who, nevertheless, are a living complaint. She had a habit of looking round her in a lugubrious manner, then moving her head up and down as if to indicate that experience had accustomed her to battle, murder, and sudden death, and that she did not complain. Her favourite remark in adverse circumstances never varied: "It's just as I thought," she would say. "Everything is even worse than I expected." Also she sniffed frequently and eloquently, and the corners of her mouth drooped permanently.

"Thought you must be in as I saw your letter was gone."

Rutherford did not reply and she took a step nearer the fire.

"You weren't in last night then?"

"No. I – I was ill."

"Ah!" she exclaimed with immense satisfaction. "It's them there fogs. Dratted things, they are. I had one of me seizures last night. It got me right across here." She made a generous gesture which comprised the majority of her ample anatomy. "A nip of neat brandy is what you want. It steadies the colic."

A pregnant pause followed, then she sniffed scornfully, having remembered that a gent who had never left his liquor unlocked once in a period of three years, was not likely to prove susceptible to a hint.

"I thought you must have been taken poorly, that's why I come up."

"I stayed the night in Chelsea," he said in a low voice. "I felt ill and shivery."

"Diphtheria, I shouldn't wonder. I can see you're sickening for something. Mrs. Mullins' little girl is crool bad." She looked round mournfully. "Well we all get our ups and downs – and some more than others."

This last sentence was a great favourite and usually formed the prologue to her pet theory which explained that the true aristocracy of England was hidden; that one day it would be discovered; and that *then* there would be a dramatic change in her circumstances. But on this occasion she did not penetrate into these dark mysteries but merely continued to assure Rutherford that he was seriously ill. Then she informed him that she would look after him and that her experience of fatal illnesses was very considerable.

An idea occurred to him.

"Wait a minute, Mrs. Oliver. I know I'm not at all well and it's extremely awkward. I'll explain the position." He paused then went on: "I'm going to have a drink and you'd better have one too."

Mrs. Oliver immediately became motherly – also, she sat down without waiting for a formal invitation. Rutherford unlocked a cupboard, produced a bottle of whisky, and poured out two generous tots. Mrs. Oliver watched him perform this rite with due solemnity, then announced briefly:

"I'll take it 'ot."

He filled a small kettle and put it on the fire. There was silence for a minute or two, then he began to talk rapidly.

"I'll have to spend a couple of days in bed. I simply cannot afford to be ill. It's like this: I've got a good offer, but it means going abroad almost immediately. And I don't know how long I shall be away."

"Something in the writing business?"

"Yes, I've been commissioned to write a book."

"Pity it ain't something serious, but we all have to do what we can – while we're in our *present* circumstances."

"Precisely. Well, I'd like to pay for the room for a month in advance then, later, I'll send you a line and let you know my plans." He paused, then added: "Now, the important point is this——"

"The kettle's boiling," she announced, greatly to Rutherford's irritation, but he mixed the drinks and handed her a steaming tumbler.

"The point is this: it's absolutely essential that I remain undisturbed or I shan't be well enough to get away. So if anyone calls, perhaps you'll say that I left London two days ago."

"You count on me," Mrs. Oliver assured him. "You'll be wanting your meals, of course, and another bottle of whisky, I daresay."

"Yes, yes," he agreed quickly. "And you understand that this job I've got may involve a long absence but, as I say, I'll pay you a month in advance and when I return to London, naturally I shall come here. And now I think I'd better turn in."

She chatted for a few minutes then disappeared and he began to pace the room restlessly. . . . Two days in this accursed room! Still, it was the best arrangement he could have made. He could count on her to say he had left London two days ago. She loved lying – even for others. What superlative luck that he had told his friends that he was going away! It was unlikely that anyone would call and no one would miss him. He must endure the next two days and then he'd go to Paris. He would write to his family from there. Once out of England, away from everything which reminded him of Feversham, he would be all right. . . .

But the next two days were a martyrdom. He had to mask his feverish impatience when Mrs. Oliver brought him the morning or evening papers. He had to pretend to listen to her when he was quivering with eagerness to look at the headlines. For whole hours together he was possessed by fear. Detection meant death. This stark fact dominated his mind and he realized more fully every minute the jeopardy in which he had placed himself by the decision that the truth was impotent to save him. The truth now would sound like a gruesome and fantastic lie. Innocent people do not act like murderers. . . .

The horror of those hours in the squalid sitting-room! The cry of a newspaper boy ... a glimpse from the window of a stranger looking up at the house ... the terror of his own imaginings! It seemed to him that he died a death every hour, and when he managed to sleep his dreams were more fearful than his thoughts. He would wake, sweating with fear, wondering if he had cried out in his sleep.

At last the two days passed. He had decided to travel by night. He said good-bye to Mrs. Oliver assuring her that he had entirely recovered and that he would write to her before long.

He arrived at the station just before the departure of the boat train. The desire to leave England had become a passion and every trivial delay seemed an eternity. At last he reached Dover and soon he was gliding through the darkness towards France.

When he was half-way to Calais, he threw the key of the cottage into the Channel.

CHAPTER VII

On arriving in Paris Rutherford took a small studio in Montmartre where he spent two or three days in a state of collapse. He only avoided a serious breakdown by eating practically nothing and sleeping for the greater part of the day in addition to the whole of the night. Dreams ceased to trouble him and, when he was awake, he scarcely realized where he was or what had happened to him. Eventually this exhaustion was succeeded by a condition of lethargy in which he could neither think nor feel but remained for hour after hour staring in front of him, incapable of action.

He had no plans and no desires: he was content to remain numbed, mentally and emotionally, knowing that the return of vitality would inevitably involve a quickening of memory. Even the thought of his danger failed to rouse him. It had become remote, one shadow among the many which haunted him, and he felt indifferent to all things except the continuation of this timeless state in which nothing was urgent or real.

He went out only at night to visit a small café, frequented chiefly by workmen, where he obtained his daily meal which usually consisted of rolls and coffee. On the first few occasions he noticed nothing but gradually he found that the unfamiliarity of his surroundings – the café itself, the language, the gestures of those near him – seemed an ally in his war against memory and, simultaneously, a sense of security deepened in him. How wise he had been to leave London where every street had its associations and where every acquaintance was a menace! Sometimes the Regal Café rose vividly before him. He remembered that night he had entered it at his usual time, sat down and glanced at the paper, then become interested in a man sketching at his table. Had that occurred only six weeks ago? The whole structure of his mind trembled as he attempted to realize this impossibility. Feversham was dead and he was a fugitive in Paris. These were facts yet, paradoxically, they deprived every other fact of substance. They had happened so anything could happen – madness, suicide, confession. All were equally possible, and equally meaningless.

But when a few days had passed he recognized the danger of surrendering himself to this inertia. Since his arrival he had not seen a single English newspaper. He hastened to obtain one and glanced apprehensively at the headlines. Nothing! He was safe!

A General Election was raging and Tory propaganda featured the perfidy of Redmond, who was hailed as the Dictator of the British Empire, with every satirical and sarcastic comment which journalistic ingenuity could devise. It appeared that in addition to the unprecedented crime of using his political position to the best advantage of his cause, Redmond was guilty of the more heinous enormity of destroying Christmas Trade. Now, anyone who interferes with the commercial orgy of Christmas is regarded with a ferocity of which un-christian people are incapable. If the most popular Sovereign who had ever reigned in England were to die in the early part of December, he would live in the memory of his people merely as the man who had destroyed the Christmas trade. It follows that the papers of this period were adorned with numerous cartoons, one of which depicted an enormous Father Christmas prostrate in the snow, transfixed by an assassin's dagger on the handle of which fluttered the inscription: "Killed – by Redmond's Orders." Otherwise the papers contained references to numerous defaulting secretaries of Slate Clubs, and commented at length on forthcoming pantomimes, giving details of the leading players in the various productions.

Rutherford glanced at all this with scant attention. The supreme fact was that nothing had been discovered and that therefore he was safe. But the sight of an English paper was sufficient to convince him that in no circumstances could he return to England for a very considerable time, and it was therefore necessary to write to his family and friends in order to prepare them for a prolonged absence.

The letter to his people was a simple affair. He wrote a brief note to his mother explaining that he had been commissioned to write a book which necessitated extensive travel and that it would be a long time before he returned to London. He added that he could not give an address but suggested that she should write *poste restante* Paris and that he would pick the letter up eventually. He felt more at ease when this letter had been dispatched.

But the other letter required more consideration. He decided that it was desirable to send it to someone who occupied such a central position in his set that it would be unnecessary to communicate with anyone else. After some deliberation he selected Madame de Fontin – she knew all his friends and had a passion for details. The decision to write to her was made fairly easily but the composition of the letter proved to be a task of great difficulty, especially as Rutherford was convinced that it was not only necessary to convey an atmosphere of high spirits but also to make some reference to Feversham. After many drafts the final letter read as follows:

"Chère Madame,

"I have been in Paris for a fortnight. I meant to write before but I have been extremely busy and when you receive this I shall have left for Italy where I shall be for a month before I go to Spain.

"I am wildly excited and never felt better in my life. I have had some luck with my work in America and so have enough money to concentrate on my new book for a long time without worrying. All of which is very fortunate as travel is essential if I am to make a good job of it. Also I have been commissioned to write a book. I told Alston and some of the others just before I left London that this seemed likely to come off, but eventually it was fixed up more quickly than even I anticipated.

"My only regret is that I shall not see any of you for a long time – anyhow for some months and probably a year. Will you tell the others this? I simply have no time for letters at the moment.

"I was sorry not to come to you that Sunday – you remember you wrote to me? Frankly, I did not want to run into Feversham. You probably heard that we had a disagreement and I thought it might be awkward. I suppose he is about to leave London – if he hasn't actually left? I came here almost immediately after our stupid misunderstanding and so have heard nothing of him.

"I am eager and anxious to get to work and I am glad to be in Paris. I had been in London too long and if it had not been for your Sunday evenings, I should have ended by hating the place.

"I can't send an address yet but I will let you have a line later on.

"Please remember me to everyone.

"Yours sincerely,

*"*GORDON RUTHERFORD.*"*

It was with great reluctance that he wrote and posted this letter but, having decided that it was necessary to let people know that he would be away for a long time, he took the opportunity of lying as to the date of his departure from London. If anything were discovered and he was challenged, the date on which he had left for Paris would be all important. He had had this in mind when he had paid his landlady the month's rent in advance and had worded the receipt, which she had signed, in such a manner that it appeared that he had vacated his rooms some days earlier than the actual date. He was determined to make the utmost use of the fact that for a week before his reconciliation with Feversham he had seen literally no one – and consequently there was every reason why people should believe that he had come to Paris several days before the date of his actual arrival. Of course his landlady knew when he had left, but her memory was so defective that by now she would accept the evidence of the receipt as conclusive. If he could also make Madame de Fontin and his friends believe that he had come to Paris very soon after his quarrel with Feversham, so much the better. Also it was desirable to suggest that he was in good spirits and to refer to Feversham as, by so doing, he was creating psychological evidence in his favour which might prove useful if suspicion ever fell on him.

When he had posted the letter he reviewed his financial position and discovered that he had very little money. He had spent a good deal with Feversham and Sondra, consequently even before the payment to Mrs. Oliver and the expense of his journey to Paris, things had been rather difficult. After a good deal of planning, he wrote to his bank instructing them to sell his securities and place the proceeds to his credit at their branch in Paris. For the time being he would have to live on capital but, apart from this, he was anxious to sever all relations with England. He would re-invest the money in France, after paying the minor debts he owed in London, then in a few months he would be forgotten.

But another and a greater problem confronted him – the problem of time. Writing was an impossibility because his imagination was paralysed, and although he believed that this impotence would prove to be only temporary nevertheless each day had to be endured – and soon became unendurable. Like many writers, Rutherford welcomed solitude but was afraid of loneliness, and directly his work deserted him he passed from one state to the other in a stride. In normal circumstances this could be remedied by the stimulating companionship of a book or a friend but, as things were, reading failed to distract him and he shrank from all human contacts. Loneliness is agony to a man at war with Thought and Memory. Before many days had passed Rutherford realized that if he did not apply himself to some activity he would sink into melancholia and possibly into madness.

At last, almost in desperation, he began to study French systematically and with great application. He imposed a rigorous régime upon himself and allowed nothing to interfere with it. He rose at the same hour each morning, worked till luncheon – when he prepared a meal – read for an hour, then continued his studies till seven o'clock. He never went out till it was dark and always dined at some obscure café where it was unlikely that he would encounter any English people. It was only necessary to avoid certain places in order to ensure not running into anyone he knew. The days went by. He was as solitary as if he had been on a desert island and although he often spoke to strangers – with a view to improving his French – he became intimate with no one.

A month passed. Every other day he glanced at an English newspaper. Nothing! His hand no longer trembled as he scanned the headlines. He had found a way of cheating time, thought, even memory, and he clung to the routine he had devised with an increasing faith in its efficacy. Each night after dinner he wandered for hours through an unknown Paris, frequently losing himself, and he always returned to his studio so physically tired that he slept soundly till late the next morning. He had a powerful will and he exerted it to the full, refusing to allow his thoughts to concern themselves with the tragedy which had driven him into exile. His unfamiliar environment helped him and each day he was at pains to create memories, however trivial, with which to supplant those of which he was afraid. He even hypnotized himself into believing that he had always been a student of languages; that he had lived in this studio for years; and that his daily habits were those of a lifetime. He divorced himself from the past and refused to think of the future. Each hour of the day had its prescribed activity and he focused all his attention upon it with such success that soon the days began to succeed each other rapidly. He did not know one from the other and before long he could not have given the name of the month with any certainty as to its accuracy. Time only exists for social beings. Which one of us – living alone, writing and receiving no letters, and ignoring the newspapers – would know or care whether it was Monday or Tuesday, December or January? But Rutherford always knew whether it was two o'clock or three o'clock, for each day was an enemy, and therefore it was necessary to be vigilant. He had to sentinel the citadel he had built in the void.

To subject oneself to the discipline of a routine, as an end in itself, is to deaden every faculty. One ceases to be an organism and becomes a mechanism. Before many weeks had passed Rutherford experienced whole days during which he forgot Feversham entirely, and gradually the unreality of that night in the cottage aided him in the extermination of his memories. It had seemed like a dream and he learnt to regard it as a dream. His imagination became atrophied and as a result his fear diminished. We all experience fear to the extent that we are imaginative. Moreover, almost imperceptibly, a new element entered his thoughts on the increasingly rare occasions when Feversham came into his mind. He began to congratulate himself on the courage and resolution with which he had acted. How easy it would have been to have lost all control and to have committed one of those absurdities which people in such circumstances usually do commit! He had avoided every pitfall and taken the only road which led to safety. He had been successful not only in the sphere of action but also in dealing with the psychological problem of outwitting the spectres of memory. He had conquered two worlds.

He consulted the English papers less frequently and after a while he ceased to bother about them for weeks together. One thing was certain: Feversham had not lied when he said that no one knew that he owned a cottage in Cornwall. . . .

The weeks became months, and the months glided away. A year passed. Nothing! He was safe!

PART II

LONDON 1930

CHAPTER VIII

I

Rutherford remained in Paris for two years after the death of Feversham and during the whole of this period he devoted all his energy to the study of languages. By 1913 he looked several years older than his age: there was that tensity in his features which frequently characterizes those who lead lives of great isolation, and he stooped slightly as if the weight of his broad shoulders were a burden. The fixed expression in his dark eyes was more pronounced.

For some time now he had realized that his fears regarding Feversham had been unnecessary. He had been hypnotized by the common belief that it is impossible for anyone to disappear without inquiries being immediately instigated, but he now recognized that this belief is founded on the assumption that everyone is an integral part of the social fabric. An occupation, or the ownership of property, cements a man to his fellows, but where he has neither – and nevertheless is financially independent – it is nobody's concern where he is, and if he ceases to be seen he is soon forgotten. Who would have missed Feversham? He had been born in America, educated in Europe, and had no relatives. He travelled constantly from city to city making only Bohemian acquaintances. His money was lodged in various banks and the fact that these balances remained unclaimed would excite no more comment than his failure to recover the luggage he had left in the cloakroom at Paddington. His Bohemian acquaintances would either have forgotten him or would think he had returned to New York. As Rutherford now saw it, the only remarkable feature in the whole situation was that Feversham had told no one of his ownership of that cottage in Cornwall.

But even his silence on this subject was not so surprising as it appeared. Feversham had admitted at Madame de Fontin's that there was a vein of secrecy in his nature. Sondra had detected it and he had admitted it. The cottage therefore was simply one example of this idiosyncrasy and possibly there were others. If Rutherford had not quarrelled with Feversham, and subsequently been reconciled, he would never have known of its existence.

The supreme fact however was that the cottage had kept his secret and that it would continue to keep it. It amazed Rutherford to remember that he did not know the appearance of its exterior, or the size of the garden surrounding it. He had come through the night, to it and had stolen away from it in the darkness. He knew that it was dilapidated for Feversham had told him that if the roof were not attended to shortly it would collapse. Probably it had caved in long ago and now the cottage was almost a ruin surrounded by a garden full of weeds. Who would inquire as to its owner? Neither rates nor taxes are payable on uninhabited property, consequently there would be no official inquiries. As to local curiosity, Feversham had only been to the place twice previous to their fatal visit and on each occasion he had taken what food he needed with him, so in all probability he was unknown even to the people who lived in the farmhouse five miles distant. Nothing had been discovered and nothing would ever come to light. The years would pass and gradually the whole structure would become half-hidden by undergrowth. And if, eventually, someone patched it up and took possession, would they investigate the well? And if they did, would they discover anything? It was very deep. Feversham had told him that the water never froze. Conceivably there was twenty feet of water permanently at the bottom, or possibly the well was served by an underground stream.

All these considerations, however, now possessed only a

secondary interest for Rutherford. It would be impossible to associate him with any discovery. He was forgotten, as Feversham was forgotten, and not a shred of evidence existed by which it could be proved that they had ever visited the cottage together. He was safe, and his safety was due to the fact that he had had the courage to recognize that the truth could not save him. Rutherford was convinced on this point. He had acted as if he had murdered Feversham and his present security was the result.

In retrospect, it all became clear to him. There had been only one risk – Feversham might have lied to him. It was certain now that he had told him the truth and consequently there was little to fear. In fact, during his second year in Paris he ceased to think about him but, somewhat to his surprise, he found that his thoughts became increasingly occupied with Sondra. In the first place, he was convinced that he ought to write to her. On more than one occasion he began a letter but each sentence seemed so artificial that he was afraid to continue. Yet he knew that it was essential to write. He had asked for her address soon after their first meeting because he wanted to send her a short story of his when it appeared in print. If she heard nothing from him, she would naturally assume that he regarded his quarrel with Feversham as a quarrel with her. But, apart from this, tactical considerations made a communication necessary. It was conceivable that she would return to London and visit the friends she had made on her former visit. Immediately, interest in Feversham would be revived and naturally Sondra would ask what had happened to him and Rutherford. People would begin to wonder why he had remained abroad. A skilful letter to Sondra would remove all these potential dangers, but he could not write it. Each attempt was less convincing than the last. He detected a sinister motive behind the simplest sentence, and any attempt at humour had a fraudulent note. But, deeper than all this, he *dared* not mention Feversham to Sondra. It had been difficult enough to refer to him in the letter he had written to Madame de Fontin soon after his arrival in Paris, but to Sondra it was impossible. Eventually he was forced to abandon the idea of writing, but he did so with great reluctance.

But his preoccupation with Sondra was not restricted to the plane of strategy. During his second year in Paris he had several affairs, of the type in which he had indulged in the old days in London, but they had failed to distract him. Formerly, they had seemed an adventure; now, they were merely squalid. Promiscuity is only possible where no standard exists: Sondra had supplied a standard, and judged by it other women were uninteresting. Strangely enough, this discovery quickened his former resentment against Feversham, for it seemed to him that, by his death, Feversham had separated him from Sondra permanently.

But there was even a greater problem than Sondra. His gift for writing had deserted him entirely. Again and again he attempted to write a story but his creative faculty was dead and he could only sit and stare at the manuscript paper for hour after hour. Directly he attempted any imaginative work, the history of his relations with Feversham unfolded itself incident by incident before his eyes. It was as if his mind became a stage on which scene by scene the drama of Feversham was enacted. He witnessed the swift tragic evolution of their friendship from their first meeting in the Regal Café to that night of terror in the cottage. How could he create fiction when scenes like these haunted his memory? Anything less actual, less vivid, less tragic was vague and unreal – lacking significance and devoid of emotional vitality. How could he manufacture some mechanical plot when he had known drama of this intensity? There was only one story he could write – the history of Feversham – and he could write it with a power beyond the compass of authors far more gifted than himself, for he had known and lived the agony and terror of it. It had become part of his being. It had destroyed his old life and he had built a new life upon it – a life founded on a lie. *This* was the story he could write, and this story would never be written. All his life he had been dominated by the ambition to succeed as a writer, but now the pen fell from him and he knew definitely that no manuscript of his would ever go to the printer again.

A strange thought came to him – it flashed into his mind just as he woke one morning. He had saved his life, but his life was over. A man's life is his ruling desire – and Rutherford's ambition had been his horizon. It had died and, therefore, he was dead. The future was no longer a map on which Hope could trace its frontiers. Once, Time had seemed an invitation, a track which wound steeply upwards towards the peaks of Achievement. Now, it was a menace – a barren, flat, interminable plain. He had not saved his life: he had made the world safe for his ghost.

He that findeth his life shall lose it. The sentence wrote itself across his brain. It existed starkly in its own right, divested of familiarity, and divorced from all normal associations. It related to *him*, and he examined it for the first time. Was it simply a sentence like any other, or was it a statement so fundamental that it possessed an individual application to every man? Could it be possible that a sentence which he had known for nearly twenty years could make him tremble? He had triumphed over physical fear, but was there a psychic fear of which he knew nothing?

Such questions as these, however, only tortured him when he attempted to write. So long as he concentrated on his studies, the past was forgotten. But directly he entered the imaginative realm it claimed him and he experienced a type of fear different in kind from that he had known during the weeks following Feversham's death. He had saved his life at the expense of that which gave it purpose and perspective. He had found it and lost it.

Early in 1913 Rutherford left Paris and visited Germany and Italy. He had become an adept in the art of living economically and as he was now able to obtain a certain amount of translation work, the financial problem was mitigated to some extent. Although he now knew several languages intimately, he continued to work systematically and with great application, hoping that his studies would prove a permanent substitute for his ambition. He had severed every link with England and had no desire to return. He wrote to his mother at long intervals but with this exception he was as removed from his old life in London as if he had died.

But for Rutherford – as for millions of others – an event was approaching which was destined to set aside all his calculations and transform the whole structure of his life. That event was the war. He returned to Paris early in 1914 and witnessed the delirium which swept the French capital at the end of July. Possibly nothing could indicate Rutherford's state at this time more clearly than the fact that the frenzy by which he was surrounded left him entirely unmoved. Not for a single second was he a victim of that hysteria with which Europe greeted its apostasy. He watched the seething, yelling crowds; he read the fanatical newspapers; he heard the ridiculous rumours; and it all seemed nothing whatever to do with him – a pandemonium of fear and hatred masquerading as patriotism. It almost frightened him to discover the extent to which his isolation had removed him from the arena of humanity. He smiled grimly at the facile French enthusiasm which had already visualized a victorious army marching triumphantly on Berlin. He knew nothing of military affairs but he had seen enough during his recent visit to Germany to know that the Germans were equipped for a long and bitter struggle. He watched people in the cafés winning victories by moving gay little flags, attached to pins, hither and thither with remarkable celerity over small scale maps. He listened to all the excellent reasons why the war must terminate almost immediately and he gathered that a German collapse was imminent. It amused him to note that Russia was suddenly regarded as a vast military machine of unprecedented efficiency, quite capable of dealing with the Germans single-handed. Apparently every French civilian was aware of innumerable traps which were deceiving the German Staff with monotonous regularity.

Then, gradually, this easy optimism passed. People began to ask what was happening, and when the English were going to send the German fleet to the bottom. Meanwhile the relentless German advance through Belgium continued. Soon rumours of an entirely different kind began to circulate: there were whispers of incompetence in high places, hints of treachery, prophecies of disaster. The firework display was over and people began to realize the darkness of the night surrounding them.

Rutherford began to receive a series of letters from his mother. The first letter informed him that they had had to postpone their holiday because of the war, although his father – and all his friends at the club – was quite certain that it would be over by Christmas. The sixth letter he received from her, a few weeks later, informed him that his brother, Philip, had obtained a commission and had gone into training, but that his father thought that it was extremely unlikely that he would see any active service, as it was quite certain that the Germans had shot their bolt and that revolution in Germany was probable at any moment. In fact, Sir George Fagg – who would certainly be Lord Mayor in a year or two – had told his father this in absolute confidence. But, very soon after, another letter arrived in which she asked whether he thought it *quite wise* to remain in Paris. Not that she thought that there was the slightest chance of those horrid Germans reaching there, and that her husband said it did not matter in the least if they did – in fact it would be all the worse for them – but, still, did he think it *quite wise*.

Rutherford replied that Paris was as safe as anywhere else; that only one thing was certain in the whole situation and that was that if the war were a short one, the Germans would win it. He went on to say that he was busy and that he did not propose to return to England, or to take any part in the war. The result of this communication was a letter from his father, written in patriotic journalese, which pointed out (*a*) that so many recruits were flocking to the colours that the authorities were overwhelmed and did not want any more, (*b*) that it was the duty of every young Englishman to join immediately, (*c*) that the war would certainly be over by Easter, and (*d*) that he only wished that he were young enough to go.

Rutherford noted that the duration of the war had been

extended from Christmas to Easter and that – despite Sir George Fagg's inside information – there was no reference to a revolution in Germany. He tore the letter up and returned to his studies, having decided finally that whether the war lasted for a month or a year it was no concern of his.

Then, soon, the menace which crept nearer and nearer to Paris ... the dark nights ... the stream of wounded ... the mutter of distant guns ... women in mourning ... rumour ... panic ... and gradually the leaden realization that all these were the beginning – that no one knew when the end would come, or what the end would be.

The weeks became months and the months crawled away. Early in 1915 he heard from his mother that Philip had gone to the front. He read the letter one night in a café and when he had finished it he sat staring in front of him with the eyes of a man who is watching his memories. He saw a boy with very fair hair and deep-set blue eyes. It was Philip and they were playing together in a garden. Philip was laughing while he performed with ease some schoolboy feat Gordon had failed to accomplish. How perfectly he remembered that autumn afternoon! How proud he had been of his brother – how he had loved him at that moment! His affection had been so intense that it had seemed like a physical pain: he had longed to do something which would prove to Philip for ever and ever how he loved and admired him. But he could only watch with devouring eyes while Philip did the feat again and again as he shouted: "Look, silly! It's easy – a girl could do it." ... What had happened since then? How had he come to hate him? And now – to-night – Philip was in the trenches and he was alone, an outcast, in Paris.

He rose and began to walk automatically in the direction of his studio. Somewhere, out there in the darkness, men were killing each other, and Philip was among them. Why was it that he could not visualize him as a man? He could only see a fair-haired boy who laughed at him across the years. He was out there in the darkness, ringed by danger – he might be dead or dying now, at this actual moment, *now*.

He stopped and stood motionless. Why had Philip gone? Why was he here? Life held so much for Philip: it held nothing for him. Why had he decided so definitely that in no circumstances would he take any part in the war? Why was he so determined to live when life had sunk to the level of mere duration? He summoned logic to his aid in order to answer these questions and it informed him that Philip had gone to the war because he possessed a number of instinctive beliefs which could never belong to him. Paradoxical though it might seem, only those who loved life with a blind passion could serve a cause and die for it. For Philip, death at the front would be heroism; for him, it would be suicide. Philip would give his life; he would only end his.

He walked on slowly. Logic could provide answers to his questions but it had no effect on his emotions. The great love he had had for his brother when they were children emerged from the depths and possessed him. It seemed to him that they were still children together. The sundering years had vanished, they had found each other again. Yes, everything was clear now: he would go to the war because Philip had gone. It was ridiculous, illogical, sentimental – and because it was all these he would go. A fierce exultant joy leapt in him, a sudden sense of freedom. For over four years every detail of his life had been the result of scrupulous calculation; now he was acting on impulse. The fact that he was behaving like a fool was conclusive evidence that he had become human again. Besides, he might be killed, and, to his surprise, the thought of death did not dismay him – yet only a few years ago he had acted as a murderer in order to save his life. That was curious – but he had not time to think about it now.

When he reached his studio, he had definitely decided to finish the translation job he had on hand, then he would return to England and enlist.

II

Ten days later he received a letter from his mother telling

him that Philip had been wounded and that he was in a hospital in Paris. She enclosed the address and begged him to go and see him immediately.

He walked rapidly through the streets on his way to the hospital. Rutherford, in common with most people during the war, had now reached that state in which nothing was so fantastic as facts. He watched things happen to himself and others. For instance: Philip was wounded and was lying in a hospital in Paris: that woman in mourning crossing the road had lost son, husband, or lover in the war: he, Rutherford, was about to join the army. All these were facts, but he realized none of them. He discovered that the essential quality of horror is its unreality. In an instant of time, life had become as unstable as a nightmare – anything could happen at any moment to him or anyone. It was quite conceivable that London would be destroyed to-morrow – or the Germans enter Paris – anything was possible. Perhaps when he reached the hospital he would be told that Philip was dead, but if so, he would not be able to realize it. Something in him would say: "Don't take any notice. This is all a dream. It will end soon – you must be patient."

He inquired as to whether Captain Rutherford could be seen and after a considerable delay he was informed that Captain Rutherford was in Ward No. 10 and a few minutes later he was conducted to his bedside. A sheet was stretched over the bed next to Philip's as its occupant had just died. Rutherford noted the fact, then said:

"Hullo, Phil!"

His brother looked up at him. The action suggested immense weariness.

"Gordon!"

One word, but the tone in which it was uttered told Rutherford everything which his brother would never say. He glanced at the pale, drawn face with the deep circles under the eyes and suddenly Pity became a pulse which throbbed painfully through his whole being. He heard himself ask:

"Are you better? I mean, it's not serious, is it?"

"No – not serious. Through the leg, and I was hit in the shoulder. They'll patch me up."

His voice was faint and he was staring at something with a puzzled expression – something which was happening miles away but which he could see quite clearly. A man in a bed a few yards away began to cry. A moment later Rutherford said:

"Will they send you home?"

"Probably. I don't know – no one knows anything. Light a cigarette for me, will you?"

He lit a cigarette and handed it to him. There was a long silence. Rutherford had imagined that to meet Philip in circumstances such as these would enable him to express what he had been feeling, but he discovered that only the most commonplace remarks were possible. The image which had haunted his memory had been that of a boy, but now he was confronted by a wounded man whom he only just recognized. At last he said jerkily:

"I'm going home to enlist. This show will go on a long time, don't you think?"

"Yes, a long time. Long enough for me to get fit and go out again. The papers are full of lies. Don't join the infantry."

"I hadn't thought about which unit. I was going home next Tuesday."

"Stay till they move me. What's the hurry? There's plenty to go – and plenty of time."

This was their first meeting. Rutherford visited the hospital every day but on each occasion the conversation consisted of small talk. Neither made any reference to the past, or the future, and the war was seldom mentioned. Often they smoked in silence: Philip gazing with puzzled eyes into the distance, while Rutherford watched him furtively, trying to think of some topic with which to distract him. At first he found these silences embarrassing but gradually he recognized that there was nothing which could be said and that they were more intimate when they were silent.

One afternoon he found a visitor with his brother, a Staff Officer, Colonel Sharpe. His son had been a great friend of

Philip's at the university and as the colonel was stationed in Paris he had come to the hospital directly he heard that Philip was there. The three of them talked for an hour, then Rutherford left with the colonel.

"Come and have a drink," the latter said directly they reached the street. He was a typical English officer of the better type: lithe, very erect, and obviously in perfect condition. He was over fifty but looked forty.

They went to a café and talked on general subjects for some time, then the colonel said:

"Your brother tells me you're going home to enlist. You were abroad when the war broke out, weren't you?"

"Yes, I've been studying languages pretty fiercely for some years. I discovered that they interested me more than anything else. I once thought it was writing, but I found I was wrong!"

"Languages!" exclaimed the colonel. "Which do you know?"

"I know French, German, and Italian really well – a certain amount of Spanish and my Russian isn't too bad."

"Then what in hell do you want to enlist for? Good God, my dear fellow, we can't afford to stop bullets with linguists! I want a man like you on my staff desperately. They can get all the men they want for the trenches but knowledge and brains are rare and they're needed, I give you my word. Look here, I'm going to London in a few days. Leave yourself in my hands and I'll fix everything. It's just damned stupid to go into the line and get killed when you can do much more good here. Now, which is it to be?"

Rutherford took a pull at his drink then looked at his companion with a smile.

"I'll be frank with you," he began. "I don't care a damn what I do. I'd decided to cut out the war till I heard that Philip was in it. Then, for no logical reason whatever, I decided to join up. It's all one to me what I do, or where I go. So I'll leave it to you."

The colonel ordered more drinks.

"I'm damned glad I ran into you," he said with emphasis. "I can keep you at it day and night. Between ourselves, we're in a hell of a mess. Still, I've got some influence and I can fix you up in no time, but I'm not going to put it up on paper. I'll take it up personally when I'm in London. Otherwise, it will go on for months and then some ruddy fool will lose the papers and I'll have to begin all over again. My God! I tell you——"

He told Rutherford his opinion on a number of subjects with considerable candour, revealing many interesting details concerning inter-departmental jealousies and certain remarkable instances of futility in high places. Such outbursts usually feature only the sensational and therefore omit any reference to that anonymous army of unpretentious people who render the best service of which they are capable. Colonel Sharpe's outburst was of this type. It was an interesting indictment and when it was ended Rutherford said:

"I see how it is. I felt it was all something like that, although we're told nothing but lies."

"I'm all for lies," said the colonel. "Lies are a type of projectile designed to destroy the enemy's morale and to influence neutrals. You'll discover that. But lies are to deceive the enemy, not ourselves. For instance, put in the papers – if you like – that the Germans are cracking up, but for the love of heaven don't believe it! The war has only just started. I know the Germans pretty well – we'll have to have conscription before long. We're going to need every ounce we've got. But never mind all that. You stay here with Philip till I return and if I don't get things fixed up there'll be the devil to pay."

It was left like that. Rutherford was indifferent as to the result of the colonel's negotiations. If he succeeded, he would join his staff: if he failed, he would return to England and enlist. In the meantime he remained in Paris and visited Philip every day.

A fortnight passed, then definite information was received that Philip was to be sent home. It was only when they said good-bye that Rutherford found it possible to express his affection.

"I'm sorry you were hit, Phil, but my God I was glad to see you again!"

"It's meant no end to me your being here."

Their eyes met. A swift instinctive knowledge warned Rutherford that they would not meet again. This handshake in a Paris hospital was their last. Tears came into his eyes.

"Whatever happens," he muttered, "God bless you!"

"You too, old man. So long. I'll write you when I get back."

A week later the colonel returned highly elated. He had not only got his own way, he had got it quickly, and consequently was very jubilant. Almost before Rutherford had had time to think, he found himself an officer and one completely inundated by work. He worked the whole of his waking life and in a few weeks he discovered that liaison duties involve much more than a knowledge of languages. Jealousy, rivalry, distrust were everywhere, and to be a success it was essential to become a diplomat. He flung himself into this frenzied activity with fierce enthusiasm, deriving a deep satisfaction from constant contact with his fellows after years of isolation. The past was dead. No thought of Feversham ever crossed his mind. The amount of work he managed to get through was prodigious and very soon he was regarded as a star turn by his superiors. He remained in Paris for some months, then went to Italy on a confidential mission which he negotiated successfully. Early in 1916 he visited St. Petersburg but was back in Paris by June. On several occasions he visited the line and sometimes speculated as to the number of men who would remain in the trenches if they had even his knowledge of what was going on behind the scenes. He had no illusions of any kind. He worked because he had discovered that work was the best dope in the world, but he did not deceive himself as to the value of his activities.

In the autumn of 1916 he heard that Philip had returned to the front. A month later he was dead. The news came in the morning but he worked with his customary concentration through the whole of the day. In the evening Colonel Sharpe came into his room.

"Is this true about Philip, Rutherford?"

"Yes, sir, it's true."

"What a damned shame! He was the best centre England

has had for years. He'd be certain to go, though. He was the type."

"Yes, he was the type,"

That was all. He slept soundly that night and the next day he worked like a slave. He could neither think nor feel about personal affairs – he was a cog in a vast machine and had no life apart from it. He must go on blindly, an automaton, till the end. The war was no longer a horror which had suddenly emerged, it had become life itself, and everyone lived in its terms. You subordinated yourself to it, and it did what it liked to you. You watched yourself doing unimaginable things, or enduring unbelievable sufferings, in precisely the same way as you watch yourself act in a dream.

A few months later, just before his second visit to Italy, he had a letter from his father which informed him that ever since Philip's death his mother had been ill and that her present condition gave cause for the gravest anxiety. His father explained that he did not wish to alarm him but, in his opinion, it was necessary to state quite openly that unless there were an immediate change for the better she could not possibly live much longer. Rutherford wrote a line in reply and enclosed a letter for his mother. Two days afterwards he left for Italy and six weeks later he heard that she was dead.

Grimly, relentlessly, the war went on. Conscription was introduced in England and in due course the German submarine campaign was launched. Before very long the utterly paradoxical position was reached in which England – the greatest naval power in the world – was trying to win the war on land: while Germany – the greatest military power in the world – was trying to win it under the sea. Air raids over London became frequent, and every day the papers contained such news that they might have been written and printed in hell. But everyone still said that the war must go on – so it went on.

It went on till every nation engaged in it had lost it – though this fact was not appreciated for some years. It went on till Europe was tottering on the brink of complete collapse, and then it ended. And its ending was greeted with the hysteria which had welcomed its birth. Once again easy optimism became the fashion: there was going to be a trade boom; great prosperity was imminent; the Kaiser was about to be hanged; and Germany was going to pay.

The end of hostilities made little difference to Rutherford. There was still an enormous amount to be done and he worked for several years after the Armistice quite as strenuously as he had done during the war. Even after he ceased to hold a commission he was employed in various capacities in different parts of Europe.

In 1923 an event occurred which severed Rutherford's last link with the past. His father's business had flourished during the war and would probably have survived the post-war depression if his father had not been deceived by the prophecies of prosperity and had not embarked on a series of extensions which converted his war profits into bricks and mortar. It is probable that the deaths of his wife and son had rendered his judgment less reliable than formerly, but in any event the slump came and he was unable to weather it. The business was top-heavy and it collapsed. He survived this catastrophe by only a few months, leaving the meagre remains of his fortune to his son who was in Germany. His death left Rutherford alone in the world, with the exception of certain relatives in the north of England whom he had not seen since he was a child. He wrote to the family lawyer and instructed him to sell the house near Notting Hill Gate in which Philip and he had been born.

Till the middle of 1929 Rutherford continued to do a considerable amount of work, official and otherwise, then he recognized the futility of continuing these activities which made great mental demands and in which he had no real interest. He threw up everything, went away for a holiday, and returned to Paris at the end of 1929 – to find himself alone again with nothing to do.

One day in a mood of idle curiosity he walked to Montmartre to look at the studio to which he had fled after Feversham's death. It was vacant. He stared at it for some minutes, his mind active with a new idea. After all, it was the best substitute for a home which was open to him. He was sick to death of hotels. He decided to take it and a week later he moved in.

CHAPTER IX

I

Before he had been in the studio many days Rutherford was aware of a change in himself and one which he would have found impossible to define. The place received him so completely, claimed him so absolutely, that it annihilated all memories in which it had no share. A room possesses psychic as well as material furniture, for it is haunted by the thoughts and emotions which we have experienced within its four walls, and it is the intensity of these which determines the degree of its influence over us. It was extremity which had originally driven Rutherford to this studio – in it he had endured crisis after crisis – and consequently for him it was haunted. Frequently we become helplessly subject to a vibration we have created.

But at first he was only vaguely surprised by a feeling of familiarity. Instinctively he arranged the sitting-room as it had been formerly, and gradually in a hundred minor ways he subconsciously adopted all his old habits and customs. He frequented obscure cafés and often wandered about Paris late at night. By imperceptible degrees he slipped back into a life of isolation, only realizing that he had done so when the process was complete. It is true that his days were no longer spent in the study of languages, but reading became the substitute for that activity. He had been cut off from books for years and he began to read with insatiable hunger, racing through volume after volume till his room resembled a second-hand bookshop.

In a few weeks the whole of his work during the war and afterwards seemed simply an episode, and it was difficult not to believe that he had only been absent from the studio for a few months. Yet, strangely enough, no thought of Feversham disturbed him – in fact, it is probable that this period was the happiest Rutherford had known since childhood.

But Change was at hand – dramatic, devastating Change – unheralded and unimaginable. . . .

One night Rutherford woke in the early hours. He had gone to bed much earlier than usual and was, therefore, unable to sleep again. He lit the candle by the side of his bed, took a volume at random from a shelf within reach of his hand, propped up the pillows behind him, and opened the book. It was *Moby Dick*. He had read it a dozen times and was about to replace it when his eye fell on the opening sentence.

"Call me Ishmael."

Only three words, but they evoked the whole of the spectral narrative which follows them. How often had he tried to discover the essential theme of the book! Was Ahab's quest that of Don Quixote? – although the Don's adventures took place on this earth, among men and women, whereas Ahab's occurred in an astral world inhabited by principalities and powers? Had each – in his degree, on his plane, and in submission to his own madness – set forth to conquer Evil with its own weapons?

For over an hour he dipped into different parts of the book, taking these liberties with that justification which enables friends to dispense with those formalities which are necessary between strangers. At last he replaced it on the shelf and feeling somewhat drowsy decided to go to sleep. He was about to put out the candle when – suddenly – the memory of the terror he had felt when he had tried to extinguish that last candle in Feversham's cottage swept through him. In an instant the whole scene became actual. Again he stood in the cottage: he could hear the silence; he could feel the awful emptiness of the room; he could see the flame of the last candle like an eye watching him.

Rutherford became rigid with fear as he lay in bed, staring in front of him with eyes which saw, not his bedroom in Paris, but an empty room in a cottage in Cornwall. But this was madness! It was impossible, unbelievable! Anger stirred in him and with a rapid gesture he extinguished the candle. . . . Immediately he saw the glimmer of that fire which Feversham had lit.

He lit the candle again hastily, then fumbled for a cigarette, amazed to discover that he was trembling. He inhaled the smoke deeply and exerted all his will to gain control of his nerves, but it was useless. One by one the incidents of that desperate visit to Cornwall passed like a moving picture across his brain. First the fog, then the unexpected meeting and reconciliation. The lunch in that restaurant; the journey down; their conversation; the eager vibrant tone of Feversham's voice. Then the deserted station; the long walk through the darkness. Again he heard their footsteps ring out on the iron ground. Their arrival; the way in which the room had come to life as Feversham lit the candles, then kindled the fire. He listened again to the argument they had had; saw the struggle between them; heard the report of the revolver; then looked down at Feversham motionless at his feet. Then – then – but he could bear it no longer! He leapt out of bed, struggled into a dressing-gown, and fumbled feverishly for a drink. Useless! He stood like a man hypnotized by the horrors of memory. With fearful clarity he saw himself drag Feversham's body out into the cold darkness. He heard a dull splash rise to him from the invisible abyss of the well. Then – the empty room . . . the silence . . . the last candle. . . .

He flung his cigarette away, then lit another. He began to reason with himself – that frenzied type of reasoning in which argument after argument leaps into the arena of the mind, hoping to overwhelm the Adversary by sheer force of numbers. He must be ill, that was the only explanation. A man does not suddenly become the slave of a fear he had known nineteen years ago. He had triumphed over that fear, trampled it under foot, forgotten it. It was only in books that the ghosts of vanished things came through the darkness to haunt their victims. He had been a writer and he knew that authors had to make such things happen, otherwise they would not have a plot to offer – and the public demands a plot. Still, he must think. He had a dim recollection of a book he had once read in which the memories of a guilty man and woman had destroyed them. Yes, he remembered! It was Zola's *Thérèse Raquin*. But the circumstances had been entirely different. Laurent had murdered Camille; Thérèse had known that he was going to murder him, had witnessed the murder, and had remained silent. There was nothing in common between them and him. They were murderers and he——

The cigarette fell from his hand and he rose slowly to his feet, the light of a new and terrible idea blazing in his eyes.

Had he murdered Feversham?

At that actual moment, when they were struggling together, had a wave of hatred surged through him and had he pulled that trigger, realizing in a second of time how all the circumstances rendered it possible for him to kill Feversham with impunity?

He tried to brush the question aside, but it was not to be denied. A torrent of new ideas rushed through his brain. Had hatred so possessed him at that actual second that he had obeyed its command and shot Feversham deliberately? Was *that* the reason why he had immediately decided that the truth was powerless to save him? Had he decided to act as if he were a murderer because – in the darkest abyss of his own heart – he had known that he was one?

Against his will an advocate rose in his mind to condemn him, marshalling all the old facts in the terms of a new and pitiless logic. He seemed to hear the cold, precise voice of this advocate, who asked questions then proceeded to answer them himself:

"You say you are innocent, that you never intended to kill Feversham? What was your *immediate* reaction when he lay dead at your feet? It was Fear – nothing else, only fear for yourself. You proceeded to review all those circumstances which would condemn you. You dismissed, in a few seconds, the case you could advance in support of your innocence. Why? You were *not* innocent – that is why. Feversham had only been dead for a few minutes before you were certain that the truth could not save you. It is significant how rapidly you were convinced on that point. Then – do you remember? – how eagerly you reviewed all the circumstances which shielded you: – the fog; you had been alone in the carriage on the journey down; the deserted local station; the lonely walk to the cottage through the darkness. You remember how gladly you enumerated all these and how swiftly you came to the conclusion that you had only to get rid of the body in order to be safe."

Rutherford flung himself into a chair, and buried his head in his hands. But the advocate who had risen in his brain continued his pitiless indictment:

"You say you are innocent? When – precisely – did you suffer any regret that Feversham was dead? Not for a single second. You knew that he had great possibilities – that he might have done anything – yet never once were you racked by a sense of loss. You had one thought, one only, always – to save yourself. That is the supreme objective of every murderer. Yes, I know what you are thinking! You are thinking that, after you crept away from the cottage into the night, you reviewed those points concerning which the truth would have supported you – if you had trusted to it. Naturally! You were then subject to a different type of fear. You knew that if anything *were* detected, you had condemned yourself by hiding the body in the well. So you became sentimental about the power of Truth – people are often sentimental about Truth who rigorously banish it from what they call practical affairs. People who give their souls to the devil continue to touch their hats to God. It looks well."

The voice ceased. Rutherford remained huddled in his chair, his fingers working convulsively. Outside in the darkness he could hear a taxi; it came nearer and nearer and for one impossible moment he believed that someone was coming for him. He heard it pass the house, nearly stop on the hill, and a moment later everything was silent again.

A few minutes elapsed then he was forced to listen again to the relentless logic of this advocate who forgot nothing and revealed everything in a new and terrible perspective:

"You always hated Feversham. That is the supreme fact. You were jealous of him because he was what he was; because he revealed you to yourself; and because of Sondra. Long before you quarrelled, your whole heart was often black with hatred for him. Your hatred for him was stronger even than your ambition, and that is why you quarrelled with him about the play. Your hatred triumphed even over your own literary interests. But never mind that. Do you remember when you were alone in the darkness, after you had crept away from the cottage, how easily the word *murderer* slipped into your thoughts? That word is not usually found in the thoughts of innocent people. Then – when you were back in your rooms in Bloomsbury – once again you reviewed all the points which made discovery unlikely. You had a new fear then – you remember – that Feversham might have lied when he said that no one knew of his ownership of the cottage. You spent two days alone in your rooms before you came to Paris. Not once, for a single second, did you suffer regret for Feversham's death. You believe you can account for that by the argument that you were naturally concerned about your own safety. But in all the years which have passed since then – when you *knew* you were safe – did you once regret his death? Did you suffer for a second because he was dead? Never – not for an instant. And you *dared* not write to Sondra because you knew you were guilty – and you were afraid that she would see the lie lurking behind every word you wrote."

A quarter of an hour passed but Rutherford still remained motionless. He had no answer to the ruthless indictment to which he had been forced to listen. Two facts were paramount: he *had* been certain almost immediately after Feversham's death that the truth could not save him; and he *had* acted as a murderer. It was possible that he had pulled the trigger of the revolver deliberately. He remembered, quite definitely, that a spasm of hatred had possessed him while they were struggling together. And it was idle to deny that he had hated Feversham long before their quarrel – just as it was useless to pretend that he had ever suffered because Feversham had died. He had felt resentful against him even since his death because he had believed that Feversham, by dying, had separated him from Sondra permanently. The more he considered his actions from the moment that Feversham lay dead at his feet, the more he was forced to admit the *possibility* that he had yielded to a sudden access of hatred and had murdered him deliberately.

He rose and began to wander about the room wearily, then paused by the window and drew the curtains. The first faint flush of dawn trembled in the sky. But he saw that other dawn in Cornwall: the wood made musical by an unseen waterfall; the song of a bird; and the beauty of earth re-born from the womb of night.

Gradually, however, the coming of day comforted him. During the night the world is inhabited only by our own thoughts but, by day, it is thronged by men and women and we can stupefy ourselves with the belief that the ordinary is the understood. Rutherford hurried into his clothes, then went out to a café to get some coffee. It was essential not to remain alone.

He decided to confront this doubt which had emerged so dramatically. He was tired of arguments and counter-arguments – he would admit the worst with which he could be charged. Assume that he *had* murdered Feversham, what then? What was the death of one man years ago in Cornwall? From 1914 to 1918 murder had been fashionable – nine million men had died. It did not alter the fact that murder had been nicknamed glory. Was it not also true that the pestilence which had swept the world during 1918 to 1919, destroying many more millions even than the war, had been nicknamed influenza? The main issue was that human life was cheap enough. Only money was sacred. The State could conscript men's lives, but it could not conscript money. People "gave" their sons; but they wanted five per cent on their money – and the best security in the world. Why should he bother about the death of one man? If he had gone to the war and killed a dozen complete strangers, he would have been a hero – until he returned to civil life and was unable to get a job.

Rutherford clenched his fists angrily. By God! Hadn't he seen enough humbug, and heard enough lies, during his "war-service" to deliver him from subservience to that conventional and hypocritical code which cowards call morality? To hell with all that – where it came from! We were all murderers – every man Jack of us who lived through the war, or went to it physically, or supported it financially! Why, in 1916, D.O.R.A. would not tolerate quotations from the Sermon on the Mount in pacifist propaganda! Rutherford laughed at the memory of the ironic joy he had experienced on discovering that fact. What more could Anti-Christ do than suppress Christ's words? Well, in any event, he would not become tainted by the leprosy of subterfuge and evasion. If he *had* murdered Fever-sham, he was no worse than anyone else.

He returned to his studio and tried to read, but each book in turn failed to hold him. It was evident that he would have to probe this problem to its foundation. After all, it did not illumi-nate anything to include his own crime in a general indictment of Europe. As he saw it, there was one fact of profound impor-tance. It was this: his real life had ended with Feversham's. It was fantastic – but it was true. He had made a decision in that cottage – he had trusted to a lie to save him. He had failed to trust the power of the truth in the supreme crisis of his life. And, therefore, his life had become a lie. It was no accident that writing, which had been his god, had deserted him – just as it was not accidental that he had become an outcast. He had had one thought and only one – to save himself. He had suc-ceeded and his ghost had survived.

He reviewed his life since his arrival in Paris at the end of 1910. If it had not been for the war, he would probably have been a madman long ago. For years he had been so immersed in duties, official and otherwise, that he had become only a brain. For years he had drugged himself with work. Other-wise this doubt concerning Feversham would have emerged years ago. Within a few weeks of his return to isolation, it had risen to challenge him and he knew, deep in him, that no matter which argument eventually prevailed in the forum of his brain, he was confronted by a greater crisis than any he had yet experienced.

The days passed but he remained obsessed by this new problem, and somewhat to his surprise he found that he concentrated more and more on that period of his relations with Feversham which extended from the date of their first meeting to that of their quarrel. *Why* had he hated him? He had never asked himself this question before and he discovered that to answer it truthfully wounded his pride where it was most sensitive. He had hated him because, in his presence, he became aware of his own inferiority; he had hated him because Feversham had been a challenge to him – had made him aware of a new possibility. Somehow Feversham, by the mere act of *being*, dwarfed Rutherford's achievements in his own eyes and made his ambitions seem slightly tawdry. What had been gold was recognized as tinsel – it was no more than that, and no less. It had annoyed him to see how lightly Feversham regarded his own gifts. If his attitude had been the result of inverted pride, Rutherford would have detected it, and would have known how to deal with it, but it was genuine and consequently it had disturbed him.

It seemed to him that his hatred of Feversham had been the real murder, and one which had involved his own suicide – just as Feversham's physical death had involved his own on a different level. Feversham had been not only a man to him, but also a symbol of a mode of being which he had rejected, and his hatred had been the sign of that rejection. Rutherford was convinced of this. He was *certain* that if all the tragic circumstances had been the same, with the exception that the man he had shot had been Ashley Alston, not Feversham, he would not be in his present predicament. It was not the fact that he had killed a man, accidentally or otherwise, which tormented him – it was because that man had been *Feversham*. Feversham represented a supreme opportunity for Rutherford and it was for this reason that his death had destroyed all that was potential in him. There was tragic significance in the fact that it was over *Feversham's* dead body that he had had to decide whether he would trust to the power of the truth, or that of a lie.

He recognized that it would be totally impossible ever to explain this to another but he knew finally, and with unshakable certainty, that it was true.

But he had to go on living and it was out of the question to remain in the studio any longer. It had been madness to return to it, and his sanity depended on leaving it. Where should he go? Only those who have travelled widely, alone and lonely, can know the weariness that that question holds. It was impossible for him to create new memories: he had reached the age at which the average man ceases to rely on hope and begins to look behind him for sustenance. Was there any place in which he had ever been happy? If so. he would go there without delay. . . .

He found that he was thinking of that night when he had read the letter from his mother which had told him that Philip had gone to the front. He had read it in a café, then a vision of those days when they had been children together had come to him, and his heart had grown big at the memory of the love he had once had for his brother. He had seen the garden in which they used to play, the garden in the house near Notting Hill Gate, which he had sold after his father's death.

England! The word was like a trumpet call. He had not set foot in England for nineteen years. Several times, when he was an officer, it had seemed certain that he would have to go to London but always, in the end, someone less in demand had been sent. When his mother died he had been in Italy; at the time of his father's death he had been in Germany, and on each occasion it had been impossible to return. Every attempt he had made since the Armistice to return to London in order to visit his father had been frustrated.

But now he was going! A quiver of excitement passed through him. He would take rooms near his old home and avoid all those places which held memories of Feversham. He would go as soon as possible. He *must* go. . . .

Two days later he looked round the studio for the last time. He had sold everything. It was stripped and bare, and he would never see it again. The first time he had entered it, he had been nearly dead with fear and exhaustion. Now, he was leaving it – a ghost in search of memories.

He noticed that his shaving mirror was still on the wall. It had evidently been forgotten. He crossed the room and gazed at his reflection. Usually when we consult a mirror we see only that for which we are looking, but there are occasions when we see with the eyes of a stranger the face it reflects. Rutherford did so in this instance. He saw a pale, heavily-lined face with rugged features; deep-set, very dark eyes with a fixed concentrated expression; a mouth and chin indicative of obstinacy and will-power; and dark hair plentifully streaked with grey. He was nearly fifty, and he realized dispassionately that he looked every day of it.

II

Rutherford naturally expected to find a different London from the one he had left but, nevertheless, he was surprised by the transformation which awaited him. The intimate, peaceful London of 1910 had disappeared entirely and two visits to the West End were sufficient to prove that pleasure had now become the city's chief industry. Every huge building was a shop, a picture palace, or a restaurant. Everywhere was crowded and he was interested to note that the well-dressed Englishman had vanished. In fact, it was not too easy to see any men who were characteristically and indisputably English. The populace had become a mob – a restless, worried, impatient mob – seeking distraction. Rutherford soon recognized that he need not fear that the West End would provoke memories of Feversham – the places they used to visit were no more. He passed the Regal Café, but only the name remained. A vast ornate building had replaced the old one. Its exterior defied you to drop in for a drink. It succeeded in being both vulgar and exclusive in appearance. The only concession the marble monster made to the relatively poor was a Robot table d'hôte luncheon or dinner. If that didn't please you – you could go to hell. It was flanked on either side by buildings of a similar type – the whole street had been rebuilt since Feversham's time – and you felt that if these edifices stood for a thousand years even the caress of Time would fail to make them beautiful.

Rutherford went to a small hotel in Kensington and spent two days wandering about looking for his old haunts. *The Dive* had disappeared, a block of offices stood on its site. He went, a trifle nervously, to see what had happened to *The Goya*. A large imposing restaurant awaited him. The one-room affair which he remembered had gone and now *The Goya* boasted a pretentious entrance, having spread round the corner for some considerable distance. A commissionaire with a row of shining medals stood in a triangular and highly artistic foyer.

Rutherford approached this functionary:

"I haven't been here for some years," he began. "Do Adolphe and Thérèse still run this show?"

"They do, sir. You notice a change, I reckon."

"I do indeed," he replied.

At this moment a smart car pulled up and the commissionaire hastened to open the door. Thérèse alighted, looking like a *Vogue* fashion plate.

Rutherford hurried off in quest of his youth and, in all innocence, went to see if the house in which he had lodged still stood in Bloomsbury. Ten minutes later he emerged into Oxford Street, having found it difficult to breathe in the highly abstract and consequently rarefied atmosphere of modern Bloomsbury. He returned to Kensington, having seen enough of the West End, and having realized finally that the London he had known no longer existed. He recognized, however, that the change was not simply a material one. It was not merely a question of new buildings and impossible blocks of traffic – the atmosphere was entirely different. It quivered with a new vibration: people were worried, listless, apathetic, or hysterically excited.

Four days after his arrival he went to look at the house near Notting Hill Gate in which he had been born. He had decided to take rooms in this locality and wanted to obtain them as near to his old home as possible. The house had evidently been painted recently for it looked very spick and span. He stood and stared at it, wondering what sort of family now lived in it, when a sudden desire came to him to see again the garden in which he used to play with Philip. But at this point the contrast between the present and the past presented itself vividly. Philip – dead; his father and mother – dead. Somehow it was unbelievable, but there the house stood – *their* house – the house to which his father and mother had come on their return from their honeymoon. . . .

He would ring the bell and ask if they had any objection to his seeing the garden – he could explain that he had been born in the house and had just returned to London after a long absence. There was nothing very unusual in such a request. He went slowly up the well-remembered steps, pausing at the top to look at the trees in the square. There was not much change here, anyhow. The silver birch still stood in the small front garden. How many hours had he spent at the nursery window, at the top of the house, watching its branches sway in the wind!

He rang the bell. The door was opened almost immediately by a smart-looking maid.

"I was wondering," he began, then paused.

"If there was a room vacant?" she inquired. Then half-turning, and so not seeing Rutherford's look of amazement, she went on: "If you'll come in, sir, I'll ask the secretary."

He followed her into the hall. A room vacant! Well, anything was possible. He tried to imagine what the businesslike little office could possibly be doing at the end of the hall. It was a glimpse of this innovation which had caused him to pause in the middle of his question to the maid.

At this moment, however, a masculine-looking woman with a hook nose and short iron-grey hair emerged from this office and came to greet him.

"Good-morning," she said in a light, careless, well-bred tone which implied: "of-course-you-know-that-ladies-work-for-a-living-nowadays-but-it's-great-fun-all-the-same."

"Good-morning," Rutherford replied. "I was wondering—"

"If there's a room? Well, oddly enough, there *is*. But it is at the top. I hope you don't mind that."

She spoke in short, crisp sentences, her voice rising to a little crescendo at the end of each.

"No . . . I don't think so," he said weakly. The whole episode had become such an adventure in unreality that he found conversation a matter of some difficulty.

"Perhaps the best way would be for you to *see* the room, don't you think?" she inquired in a tone of dignified badinage.

He followed her towards the stairs. That room had been his father's study – not that he had ever studied anything. They began to mount the stairs. The same broad banister, down which they used to slide! But his meditations were interrupted by the secretary:

"Most of our guests are permanent," she announced. "We rather *like* permanent people, don't you know." A pause, then diplomatically: "Were you thinking of making a long stay in London, Mr. ——?"

"Rutherford is my name."

"Thank you. Mine is Mrs. Winchester. I'm the secretary here. It's quite amusing in its way."

"I shall probably be in London for several months," said Rutherford. "I've been abroad for a long time." They paused on the second floor, outside the room that had been his parents' bedroom. "It's a good-sized house," he added.

"Oh, yes," Mrs. Winchester replied patronizingly. "We have another the other side of the square. Of course, it required a good deal of capital to furnish the rooms, put in gas fires and so on. We're a private limited company, you know. Oh, by the way, you understand that we only serve breakfasts?"

"That would suit me," Rutherford murmured.

They had reached the top floor. Mrs. Winchester opened a door which boasted a little plate with 21 neatly inscribed on it. He followed her into the room which had been his nursery. It was low and broad, with walls which sloped towards the ceiling; the windows were long and narrow and had bars across the lower part. Such a rush of memories came to him that he almost started when his companion announced with conscious pride:

"We had an *idea* behind this place when we arranged things. I wonder if you know what I mean. The average bed-sitter is *too* squalid, don't you think? So we decided to do something on the one-room-flat idea. Why have a hideous bed, when you might just as well have a divan, which looks quite an attractive couch by day? Then there's hot and cold water in every room. Do you see? Discreetly hidden, isn't it? Bare walls – why inflict others with one's prejudices in Art? Of course, guests can hang any pictures they like. Then we really rather let ourselves *go* about the carpets. They had to be thick and, therefore, expensive to muffle sound. And each room has a good big screen. Gas fires, each with an independent meter, of course. Good idea, don't you think?"

Rutherford said he thought it an excellent idea.

"Quite! One must use this dreadful mechanical age, don't you know. Electric light is included – and baths. There are plenty of bathrooms," she said spaciously, "and the water is always boiling."

"I like the room very much," said Rutherford. "It's really exactly what I've been looking for. I suppose a private family lived here before you took the house over?"

"Yes. A family that came down in the world, I believe. I'm glad you like the room – it's one of my favourites."

"And the rent?" Rutherford inquired.

"The rent is three-and-a-half guineas a week," she replied in a curt tone which suggested that money was such an unpleasant subject that any reference to it should be as brief as possible.

"That's rather more than I wanted to pay," he objected.

"It's awfully central – you save no end in taxis!" she countered in a Brighter London manner.

Three-and-a-half guineas a week to live in his old nursery! Possibly the rent of the whole house when his father came to it originally had been a hundred a year!

"Well, it's what I want," he announced.

"There's a telephone in the hall, you know. And you can always have an instrument in your room, if you like."

"I'll take it. I've a certain number of books. Do you mind if I bring some bookcases with me?"

"Not in the least." Her voice rose to a little scream on the last word. "Bring anything you like – except animals. No pets, I'm afraid! It's really part of our idea that each guest should mould the room to his or her personality. We provide necessities. That walnut writing-desk is the best in the house."

It was a good one and Rutherford said so, then added: "I'd like to come immediately."

"Do – *do*. Whenever you like." A pause. "Now, Mr. Rutherford, I'd like to be frank with you. We *do* like to know something about our guests."

"I have only just returned to England after a long absence, as I've explained to you. But I served under Colonel Sharpe in the war and I've no doubt that he——"

"Quite, *quite*!" she exclaimed lyrically – fortunately for Rutherford, who had not the slightest idea where Colonel Sharpe was. "We've had a number of service people here. *Please* don't think I wanted a reference. We just like to know something, that's all. Now, when will you come?"

"I'll come to-morrow."

That ended their interview.

During the whole of his stay in the house he scarcely saw Mrs. Winchester again. Although she had implied that she belonged to the company which ran the house, she was, in fact, only the secretary. The directors were three retired officers who owned several similar houses in the neighbourhood. Mrs. Winchester did not live on the premises but during the day was, presumably, hidden in her office on the ground floor – whence she emerged to do her song and dance to inquirers after rooms (as one of the lodgers expressed it to Rutherford subsequently). Otherwise, she prepared the bills in a highly characteristic handwriting, and doubtless supervised the servants. No one had ever heard of Mr. Winchester, and she never referred to him. . . .

The next day Rutherford moved in. He found the whole situation so fantastic that he spent the first few days trying to convince himself that he was actually a lodger in his old nursery at a weekly rent of three-and-a-half guineas, but he succeeded only partially as his mind began to play odd tricks with him. He kept remembering incidents from the past – incidents which leapt into vivid life from the darkness. They claimed him and the present dissolved into the past.

A night, ages ago, came back to him when his mother had been dangerously ill. There had been a heavy fall of snow and the house and the world were silent. Although he was only a child some fool of a servant had told him that his mother might die and, going to bed that night, he had stood by the window on the landing and looked down into the garden, all ghostly white beneath the moon, and wondered what it was like to die. He had repeated the word to himself – "die" . . . "die" – and for years afterwards, whenever he heard it, he saw a white motionless garden shimmering in the moonlight.

The memory of certain incidents would have remained buried for ever if he had not returned to live in this house – incidents which belonged to his early childhood, to an age which had vanished as if it had never been, and he recaptured something of the curious highly-coloured world in which he had then lived. In particular, he remembered what a strange enigmatic person his father was – an independent almighty sort of person, answerable to no one. The carriage used to take him each morning into some fairyland which he called the City, and punctually at six it brought him home again. Often the child would hover about the hall awaiting his return and directly he appeared a breath of another world seemed to enter the house with him, but you knew now that nothing could go wrong, that you were secure, although there were shadows lurking in corners when you went upstairs, and sometimes the weather-cock above the house squeaked in rather a ghostly way.

Then, on winter evenings, he used to stand at the nursery window and look down into the gathering darkness, waiting for that magician – the lamplighter. Soon he appeared, carrying a fairy wand which had a twinkling light hidden in the top of it, like a captive star. Round the square he went, pausing at intervals to create a jewel of golden light. Then, when he had performed this miracle several times, he disappeared – leaving you to marvel at his sorcery and to watch the new shadows which flickered far below.

What a curious, intimate, intense life he had known till the age of seven! – strangely independent of others for its interior satisfactions. It was as if he had dwelt on the threshold of some other world, the existence of which was known only to him, yet one which he could enter only by most mysterious processes – such as gazing for a long time at the colours in his glass marbles; or waking soon after he had gone to sleep and hearing the sound of a piano rise up through the darkness outside; or listening while someone read aloud about Joseph and his coat of many colours.

All sorts of very different things created a bridge by which he could enter this region, which nobody ever mentioned and which could not therefore exist for them. He remembered one occasion when he had entered it and when it had been real for a very long time. They had been to a children's party in Portman Square. They had driven to it in the carriage through the darkness. There had been lights, fancy dresses, laughter, dances, presents – and marvellously coloured jellies and rich trifle for supper. The carriage had come at about nine o'clock and he had gone down the steps in front of Philip and the nurse, and had stood and gazed at the horses waiting to take him home. Their eyes looked enormous in the darkness and they tossed their heads impatiently. He wondered what they had been doing while he had been at the party. Then, when they reached home, he looked at them again with great curiosity. Later, in bed, he wondered what they were doing now – whether they could speak to each other in any way – and suddenly he found himself in that strange world of colour and beauty, where he was free and where everyone loved everybody and everything. A world in which it was unnecessary to ask questions because he understood all things in an inner intense queer sort of way. . . .

After he had been in the house for a week Rutherford came to the conclusion that he would have to be more discreet in his movements or the other lodgers might think he was a lunatic. He was always hovering about the landings, trying to obtain a glimpse of the rooms which were ghostly with memories for him. Often he stood for a long time at the window of the half-landing, looking down at the garden in which he and Philip used to play. He had expected to find it smaller than his mental image of it, but could that really be the same garden? It had been a world and now it was – that!

III

Rutherford lunched at a restaurant in Knightsbridge each day then wandered about studying this new London which seethed round him. He read a good deal and studied the faces of the people in the streets. He went to picture palaces, to try to discover the secret of their attraction, but he avoided the theatres. He had visited a theatre only once since the death of Feversham for, discovering that the stage reminded him vividly of the days when he had striven to appear as part author of Feversham's play, he never went to the theatre again. He read the newspapers eagerly, interested to note the world they presented and how different that world was from the one they had depicted in 1910. It was only too obvious that most people were nerve-racked, worried, or unhappy. Everywhere he detected a frantic eagerness to snatch at pleasure or excitement. Consequently there was a good deal of humbug in the papers about happiness – particularly the pictorial ones: "Happy Holiday Makers at ——" or "Smiles All The Way At ——" There were an enormous number of photographs revealing scantily-clothed girls. Legs were evidently regarded as a synonym for happiness. Also there were many prophetic articles on such subjects as: "Is A Good Time Coming?" or "What Will Men Wear In 1950?" or "When Women Reach The Limit." And – naturally – well-known writers frequently contributed their views on such subjects as "Should Men Push Prams?" Sport and amusements occupied a tremendous amount of space. And, at regular intervals, pompous leading articles appeared on the subject of Unemployment. They invariably started by announcing that this question was above party – and they invariably ended by advancing the panacea evolved by the party whose views the particular paper presented. The truth was that everyone was in despair over the question of Unemployment, but newspapers are largely dope, like almost everything else, so articles on Unemployment always finished with some such peroration as: – It is only by the recovery of our export trade, which involves the recapture of markets temporarily lost, that this crucial problem can be permanently solved, and we offer no apologies to our readers for stating again that this most desirable consummation can only be attained by a rigorous adoption of the policy of Protection; or Empire Free Trade; or Free Trade; or Empire Preference; or Rationalisation; or Nationalisation; or whichever dogma it was the particular editor's duty to boost.

The weeks went by. 1930 was duly ushered in to the accompaniment of numerous great gales and hints of grave disturbance in India. By this time Rutherford knew a number of the tenants in his old home by sight, but had not yet entirely accustomed himself to their presence in it. One or two of them were evidently willing to be friendly and this fact somewhat disconcerted Rutherford for he knew that intimacy between him and another was impossible, and that anything less was valueless. He made no attempt to evade the implications of his position: he was a man with a problem of such a unique nature that it set him apart from his fellows. His whole appearance proclaimed it, yet no one observed it.

After he had been in the house some time he discovered that there was a kind of common-room on the first floor where people could play cards. Mrs. Winchester had omitted to mention this in her list of amenities provided – had she done so Rutherford would probably not have taken the room. There was an old Civil Servant who asked him to have a game of chess with him and he repeated the request a week after, although Rutherford had informed him that he had never played in his life. The Civil Servant's next proposition was an offer to teach him the art. Rutherford refused, but spent a couple of hours with him one evening. His name was Montague. He was a queer, fragile creature, rather like a bird, with a squeaky voice and amazingly precise in his movements and habits. He was exceedingly disturbed by the knowledge that he would have to retire in six months. Rutherford asked him why.

"Why!" he exclaimed with an odd old-lady-like gesture. "Surely that's clear! You see, my official duties occupy me from ten till five. At five o'clock I go to the club and read the papers – or have a chat – till seven-thirty. Then I dine, and I get back here precisely at nine-fifteen. Well, then – as no one here plays chess – I put my clothes away, get out my clothes for the next day, read a little – just to keep up with the times – " he gave a nervous little giggle, "and go to bed at ten-thirty."

He put his head on one side and looked up at Rutherford with a queer little smile.

"I still don't see why you're afraid of retiring from the Service," Rutherford said in order to draw him out.

"Why! what *shall* I do when I have all the day to fill in! It's really too dreadful to think about. Just imagine! I finish breakfast by nine o'clock. All the day ahead of me! I tell you I daren't think of it."

It's a strange thing but few of us have the slightest pity for those who have to face a smaller edition of a problem we have known long and intimately. Rutherford, to whom Time had been an adversary for twenty years, found Montague's alarm only childish.

"I can tell you what you'll do," he announced.

"What? What?" the other exclaimed eagerly.

"You'll go to the club all day, every day, till you die in an armchair in the smoking-room. The alternative is to take up the study of some subject and work at it a damned sight harder than you've ever worked at your office."

"I couldn't do that. No, I couldn't do that," Montague replied petulantly. "That would involve being alone, and I must have people round me. Yes, after all, I could go to the club all day. Still, even the club shuts sometimes."

"You'll want to live as long as possible, I suppose, in order to draw your pension?" Rutherford inquired.

"Just so – just so," Montague answered in that reverent tone he always employed whenever his pension was mentioned.

When Rutherford left him he ran into a jovial, red-faced man on the landing, called Trotter. They had just spoken to each other on two occasions previously.

"Hullo!" Trotter exclaimed. "Lord! you been in there?" He indicated Montague's door with a jerk of his head.

"I have," said Rutherford.

"Well, then, you'll want a drink," Trotter asserted in the tone of one who announces the obvious. "Come into my room and have one. Now, I'll bet old Monty offered you tea."

"You're wrong," said Rutherford, "he offered me cocoa."

"Cocoa! 'Strewth! Oh, well! I always knew it. It's a case of bats in the belfry, old man. Come in. I've the best room in the house."

It was true. It used to be the drawing-room. Rutherford entered and looked round – seeing the room as it used to be, not as it was. How often when he was a child had he crept down to this room on his mother's at-home day, after the visitors had gone, and studied the contents of the three-tiered cake-stand to see what remained! How warm the room had been, and how fragrant with the perfumes of the departed visitors! Often his mother would play the piano and he would eat his cake and listen to the music, feeling melancholy and happy at the same time. Now, Mr. Trotter had adorned the walls with a number of illustrations revealing beauties clad and unclad in the fashions of about thirty years ago, and he mistook Rutherford's preoccupation with the room for admiration of these pictorial effects.

"Aha! Admiring my pictures, I see. No bad judge either. Women *were* women then. Those were the days. Don't breed 'em nowadays, my boy. We *can't*."

Trotter's emphasis was so marked that it was evident that he had tried and failed.

"Still, never mind," he went on. "They say curves are coming back. I can't stick these damned women who look like boys. Have a drink?"

Rutherford accepted a whisky and soda. It was quite obvious that he would not have to say much, which was a relief as he did not want to talk.

"Twelve and six for this stuff," Trotter went on, gazing ruefully at the bottle of whisky. "And eight bob of it goes to this damned Bolshie Government. Well, I get it at trade price, thank the Lord!"

"How do you manage that?"

"I haven't been a commercial traveller for thirty years – just on – for nothing. There's precious few things I buy at retail price. Yes, I'm damn near fifty. What do you think of me, eh?"

He drew himself to his full height, five feet five, and threw back his shoulders for Rutherford's inspection. He was very broad and had short muscular legs. He wore two or three rings and a very florid tie which made one think of the tropics.

"You're a good example of your type," was Rutherford's verdict.

"I believe you," his companion replied, greatly flattered, then rattled on: "Now, I'm only ten years younger than old Monty and look at *him*. That's what happens to a man if he coddles himself. No drink, no women, and in bed soon after ten – what the hell can you expect?"

Trotter selected a cigar with great deliberation, Rutherford having refused one.

"You said you were a commercial traveller," Rutherford began after a pause. "What is your line? That is, if you've no——"

"No offence," Trotter cut in briskly. "Cloth's my game – or was. I've practically retired. There's nothing doing, old man," he added confidentially. "I tell you, I get the fair hump some-times, Lord bless me, when I think of the old days!"

He stuck his thumbs into the openings of his waistcoat, extended the fingers of each hand fan-wise, threw back his head, and beamed blissfully at the ceiling.

"The old days," he repeated with a slightly tragic note in his voice. "Lor' love us! *Then*, when you called on a customer, in you went into the guvnor's room and it was 'Good morning, Mr. Trotter – always glad to see *you*.' Now——"

Mr. Trotter emitted such a mighty puff of smoke from the cigar which he held tightly between his stained teeth that he disappeared from Rutherford's view for some seconds.

"Now," he went on dramatically, "some damned counter-jumper is sent down with a 'nothing for you to-day.' I tell you it was driving me to drink, and I don't need much driving. You in business?" he added so sharply that Rutherford started.

"No, I'm not," he replied. "I'm a——"

"Well, you thank your stars you're not," Trotter inter-rupted. "I don't know what's going to happen – that's flat. Six months ago my directors sent for me – said they wanted my views on the situation. I told 'em – and it didn't go too well. They wanted me to say what *they* thought, not what I thought. See? Too many guinea-pig directors in this country. Didn't matter once – it's suicide now."

"Go on," Rutherford said, "it's interesting."

"Really! Didn't think it would interest you, not being in business yourself. I'm not a fool you know – little Harry keeps his eyes open. I was one of twelve, I was, born in a back street in Brixton. That opens your eyes pretty early. Here! Where was I? Forgotten what I was going to say."

"You had just mentioned guinea-pig directors——"

"I get you! This is how I see it. For a hundred years England was in the position to say 'take it or leave it.' And customers took it. She still says 'take it or leave it ' – and they're leaving it. We were without competitors for so long that we just can't believe that the whole world's full of 'em to-day – all keen as mustard and working like hell."

"I don't think you're far wrong."

"Wrong! Wish to God I was! It's a good thing for me that I saved a bit and was lucky speculating. No one's going to give little Harry a dole! Oh, dear no! The little Harrys of this world can go to hell – they've no union, their votes aren't enough to matter, and they're not Bolshies. So no one cares a damn about them."

He crossed his legs energetically. For the second time Rutherford discovered that Trotter could change the subject with remarkable rapidity, for he suddenly asked:

"Ever go to the pictures?"

"I used to, when I first returned to England, but I soon had enough of them."

"I go pretty often – go at twelve in the morning, when they're cheap. There's something in me which just won't let me pay the normal price for things. Lot of travellers are like that," he added philosophically. "Well, those damned places are a sight at midday. Sometimes crammed from floor to ceiling – and they hold plenty, you know. And – men! Hundreds of 'em! Where they come from? How they get the money? – well, don't ask me. I spend a lot of time in the West End, just wandering round looking at it. Money? – money to burn! Yet there's no business doing, and the budget will soon be a thousand millions. Perhaps you can explain it – you look like a scholar."

Rutherford smiled. "I'm a student of languages – that's my business. So I can't explain it. I suppose we're living on finance, on dividends from money invested abroad, and on the Past. Still, we can't go on like this for ever."

"Oh, yes, we can," said Trotter with heavy sarcasm. "You listen to 'em! Everyone is to have a dole till they're old enough to draw a pension. Unemployment is the only thriving industry. No one's going to work any more – and we're going to give the Empire away, because it's a trouble, and because foreigners don't like us having it. And *then* we'll all go to the pictures all day and every day; and we'll listen to the wireless all night and every night. That's modern England's idea of heaven."

He rose, pleased with this effort, and mixed more drinks.

"I must be off," Rutherford said.

"Don't go, for heaven's sake. I've got the hump proper – and I can't stand being alone. Didn't care a damn once, but I do now. But don't think I'll come worrying you. Not me! I know you're the sort who keeps himself to himself – and I can respect it, but damn me if I can do it nowadays――"

They smoked in silence for some minutes. Rutherford was glad to listen to Trotter. He was unlike anyone he had ever met and he thought that Trotter might provide a type of companionship hitherto unknown.

"Do you know the other people in the house?" he inquired.

"Very slightly," Trotter replied, mimicking an aristocratic voice quite effectively. "I'm not their class, old man. They're all very refined in this house. Old Ma Winchester sees to that – I slipped in when she was away. She's the sort that would rather be a duke's bastard than an honest woman's daughter. Well, here goes for the lodgers – old Ma Winchester calls 'em *guests*. Guests! 'Strewth! And I pay damn near a fiver a week for one room! Ground Floor – Mr. and Mrs. Latham. Oh, very modern, and so so. You know – big car, night clubs, theatres, Riviera, and no kids. Couple of rooms, and the rest goes on luxury. Next please! Small room at the back – Colonel Robson. Met him?"

"No, only seen him."

Trotter sniffed, flicked the ash from his cigar, then continued:

"Oh, you should meet the Colonel. He's one of the old school. Now he lives on his pension. He's a relic – that's what he is. His world's the Army List. Nothing else exists for him. He sort of clings on to the war, if you follow me, because he's afraid that if he allowed himself to forget it he wouldn't have a peg to hang his hat on – so to speak."

"I can understand that," said Rutherford quickly. "There must be lots like him."

"I hope you're wrong!" exclaimed Trotter. "He does it because he's not got a bean to buy a new rattle with, so he has to play with the old one. Do you know Miss Trentham?"

"I've just met her. I wish she hadn't that telephone in her room. I'm always answering it. She's a journalist, isn't she?"

"She's a social ferret, that's what *she* is. Knows all the nobs. I amuse her, I don't know why. She comes in sometimes to tell me about the bigwigs. She's pretty cute. Not my style though, too angular. The rest of 'em are duds. Old bachelor solicitors, you know the type. Then there's that aristocratic virgin on this floor – you know, she's about seventy – Miss Chelsey. Very erect and haughty – gives *me* the bird. Still, she had to speak last week because she'd left her key behind. I found her on the steps and she asked me to let her in. And, damn it – would you believe it? – her manner suggested that she'd done *me* a favour."

They talked on for an hour then Rutherford rose and said he really must go.

"Right ho, old man. Drop in when you feel like it. But just to finish off what I was saying, I'll tell you what's the matter with all of us. We're longing for the London of twenty or thirty years ago. I was at the pictures the other day and, in the interval, they played a selection of the old tunes. The audience nearly went mad with joy. You know the sort of thing."

Trotter began to sing:

> *It won't be a stylish marriage,*
> *We can't afford a carriage,*
> *But you look sweet*
> *Upon the seat*
> *Of a bicycle made for two.*

"There! *That's* melody – not Broadway Melody. That's music – you take it from me."

Rutherford started to walk towards the door but Trotter seized him by the arm:

"Here! Just before you go, I'll tell you what gets me." He paused dramatically, then added slowly: "Is the game up? That's what I keep asking myself. I'm no thinker – I know that – but this is how I see it. Old England became great under individualism. Is that the right word?"

Rutherford assured him that it was the right word, and Trotter continued:

"She became great under individualism. Well, individualism's over. It's *over*, old man. Everything to-day is mass production. That suits the Germans. Why, damn it, they fought in mass-formation! But it don't suit us. The way it's going, it strikes me the machines will put us all on the streets soon. If Old England cracks first, the rest will follow – quick! Machines!"

He uttered the final word in a sepulchral voice and stared at his companion. Then a new thought occurred to him. He beamed jovially and exclaimed:

"Still, it will last my time – thank the Lord! – and that's all little Harry cares about."

Rutherford escaped and went to his room. . . .

Two hours later, lying sleepless in bed, it seemed to Rutherford that in the same way as this house had once been a unity, so he too, long long ago, had been a unity. But now his soul – like this house – had many tenants and so it was divided against itself.

CHAPTER X

Rutherford's intention in returning to London had been to revive memories of his childhood and, by so doing, escape from the torturing perplexity of that doubt concerning the death of Feversham which had confronted him so overwhelmingly that night in his studio in Paris. By obtaining a room in his old home he had succeeded in evoking memories to an extent which, otherwise, would have been impossible, but perpetual indulgence robs a drug of its efficacy and after a few weeks the question as to whether he had shot Feversham deliberately occupied his thoughts to the exclusion of everything else.

Again and again he reviewed every detail of their relations from their first meeting till Feversham's death, analysing his emotions and motives during each stage, until fact and theory were so intermingled that he found it difficult to separate them. Notably this was so in regard to the ninety minutes he had spent in Feversham's cottage. Every detail, every incident, relating to that night of terror was re-lived and examined so frequently that he would have found it almost impossible to give a simple statement of the facts. The discovery that this was the case disturbed him so profoundly that he attempted to write the history of what had occurred from the date of his quarrel with Feversham to the latter's death. This manuscript took the form of a story – as a protection in case it should ever reach other hands – but even so he was extremely nervous concerning its safety and was always pulling the handle of the drawer in the cabinet which contained it in order to satisfy himself that the lock was secure.

He was more alone now than he had ever been. The hope that Trotter might provide a distraction proved illusory, for that gentleman – very shortly after their conversation – returned home intoxicated, hailed Colonel Robson as "Field Marshal of the Diehards" and capered round Miss Chelsey – when he encountered her returning from the bathroom – singing a song which had been exceedingly popular in certain circles in a grosser age. The result was that he was asked to leave – which he did, having revealed to Mrs. Winchester a number of remarkable facts concerning her ancestors, and after having cast the gravest possible doubt on the legality of the union between her parents.

"So long, old man," he said to Rutherford at their last interview. "I only came here because I wanted a decent address for a few weeks. I'm off to Blackpool – it's more my style. Why, damn it, you can't have a lady friend in here after ten! I have, mind you, on the q.t., but what's the good of that? Makes you feel a blinking criminal. Don't *you* stay here too long. Why, a parson couldn't stand it for more than a month."

So Trotter disappeared. Rutherford was alone, with nothing to do. He was accustomed to solitude, but he had always had either his studies or official work to occupy him. Now, he had nothing; and day after day the drama of Feversham was re-enacted on the stage of his mind.

His appearance altered considerably during this period. He became so much thinner that his clothes were too big for him; and his stoop seemed more pronounced. The lines in his face deepened and there was a haunted expression in the deep eyes under their shaggy brows. Hour after hour he sat in his room, afraid to look at his watch lest he should realize the extent of the loneliness ahead of him. Yet he was afraid to go out into the streets for – recently – on more than one occasion, it had seemed to him that he suddenly saw them, not as they were, but as they had been in Feversham's time. Only a week ago, idling outside the block of offices which stood where *The Dive* had once been, he had had a kind of vision. The building faded and instantly it was night: a dark night swept by a gusty wind, and the stars overhead were hard, clear, metallic points of light. A hansom emerged and two men and a woman alighted. He saw them quite clearly: Feversham, himself, and Sondra. They had dined at *The Goya* and he watched them go in to *The Dive*. They were laughing – and they vanished like phantoms.

A few days later a similar incident had occurred. He had been outside the new Regal Café one evening and suddenly he saw the *old* Regal Café. The illusion lasted only for a second but it was extraordinarily vivid. It made him tremble and the fear of remaining alone any longer had become unendurable. He had hastened into the great building and found his way to the café, half hoping that he would encounter Ashley Alston or someone – anyone – he had known in 1910. But the new café was utterly unlike the old one and its patrons belonged to an entirely different class. To enter the building was to realize conclusively that only the name remained as a link with the past.

These adventures frightened Rutherford. He felt his control slipping from him little by little, as a handful of dry sand diminishes no matter how tightly it is grasped. There was irony in the fact that this new type of fear urged him to do precisely what the old had made him avoid at all costs. When fear for his physical safety had dominated him during the weeks succeeding Feversham's death, he had evaded the possibility of encountering any of the friends they had had in common. But now that fear for his sanity possessed him, he sought them out in the desperate hope that they would provide companionship. To make new friends was impossible: he *must* discover the old ones.

To this end, he called at the house where Madame de Fontin had lived, but the present tenants had never heard of her. He visited several estate agents in the locality and eventually discovered that she had left England at the end of 1911 and had returned, it was believed, to the West Indies.

Whom else could he look up? Doubtless several of the men he had known had died in the war; others would have married and so become part of the social organism; while others would have gone to the devil quite effectively long ago. His quest was hopeless, as he had known from the beginning, but despair lends folly the mask of hope.

He was driven back to the solitude of his room but even there a new discovery awaited him. He found that the house held memories other than those of childhood. After all, he had quarrelled with his people and that quarrel had been so bitter – on his side – that he had not seen his father or his brother for years. When he had read the letter, in that café in Paris which told him that Philip had gone to the front, he had not only remembered his early affection for him but he had asked himself how he had grown to hate him. He had not answered that question then – he was forced to answer it now. The origin of that hatred had been jealousy, just as the origin of his hatred of Feversham had been jealousy.

In retrospect, how clear all his motives became! What he had believed to be righteous indignation had been self-glorification. His rebellion, which had seemed a crusade of the soul against the values of materialism, had been nothing more than vanity which refused to recognize itself. He had fallen into an abyss, imagining that he was scaling the heights. Now he realized why – although he had regarded his father and brother as symbols of everything he despised – he had hungered for their admiration and had known that any success he attained which did not compel their respect would be valueless.

There comes an occasion when a man reads the book of his life and sees, for the first time, what is written there. This knowledge came to Rutherford and humbled him to the dust.

Gradually, however, all his thoughts narrowed to one question: had he murdered Feversham? It must be answered truthfully – he had served lies long enough. He had built his life on a lie and everything which had once given life meaning and colour had been destroyed as a result. He had lived on substitutes: – study had been a substitute for ambition; affairs had been a substitute for love; duration had been a substitute for life. This question must be answered and nothing less than the truth would serve. His reason depended on the final answer to this question which oscillated like a pendulum in his brain, hour after hour, day after day.

Should he confess – give himself up to the police? He lay in the darkness considering this new possibility. Then, at any rate, he would not be alone with his spectral thoughts – others would share his secret, even if they were his judges. To tell someone – anyone – to tear his secret from its hiding-place! Surely that would be preferable to this succession of nights and days, on every one of which he was doomed to witness again the death of Feversham. Yet, if he gave himself up, who would believe his story? The cottage must have vanished long ago and if its ruin still stood, he could not say with any exactitude where it was. He had paid no heed to his whereabouts on the journey to Cornwall. He had been far too absorbed in their conversation, and his own thoughts, to notice anything. He did not even know the name of the local station. It was probable that no one in the vicinity had known that Feversham owned the cottage. But, apart from all that, who would believe a word of such a story. His history for the last few years would be examined. Several of his superiors during the war had warned him that he was overworking and would have to pay for it. People would think that he was a lunatic. And yet – was not anything better than a continuance of such days and nights as these, with the fear of madness like a deepening shadow in his brain?

It is probable that Rutherford would have reported the facts concerning Feversham to the police if an event had not occurred which changed the current of his thoughts and gave his life a new all-consuming interest. . . .

It was an afternoon in October, a day of golden mist and fluttering leaves. He had wandered about the park till nearly four, then, eager to delay the return to his room for as long as possible, he walked to Knightsbridge. It had become a favourite haunt of his, as it had no associations, and he lunched or dined frequently at a restaurant there. He paused to look into a shop window, then happened to glance at the entrance just as the doors opened and a woman came out.

It was Sondra.

He recognized her instantly with such certainty that the possibility of deception never crossed his mind. He stood motionless, frozen into immobility. But she was moving rapidly; to remain stationary was to lose her. He began to follow her, his heart beating violently, his mind a labyrinth where hopes, fears and plans emerged and vanished.

Sondra walked in the direction of Harrod's, stopping frequently to look into the shop windows. He was terrified lest she should turn and recognize him. He forgot that the years had changed him, for his mind was struggling with the problem as to what he should say if she asked him for news of Feversham. What was she doing in London? Was this her first visit? Was she married? The questions shot across his brain and died as quickly as they were born. One instinct dominated him – the instinct to follow her till she returned home and so discover her address, even if he had to follow her for hours.

Soon, however, they reached the Brompton Road where she turned off, walked for perhaps fifty yards, then entered a block of flats which had evidently been newly constructed. He followed her to the entrance. There was no one about. He pushed open the swing doors noiselessly. He could hear nothing. He glided in, crept into the hall, just as she disappeared round the curve of the thickly-carpeted stairs. A moment later he heard her key in a lock. She had a flat on the first floor! Somehow he must ascertain the number. He heard a door bang and a second later he slipped up the stairs, paused on the landing, and listened. He heard a movement behind one of the doors. He glanced at the number. It was number 12. He returned to the hall, went out on to the steps then paused irresolute.

Sondra!

He whispered the word to himself. This was no illusion – he had not seen a girl but a woman. Sondra – in London! Either this was deliverance, or there was none for him in this world. Yes, deliverance – whatever the difficulties! He *must* think that, he *must* believe it, for the alternative was madness.

"Were you looking for someone, sir?"

He started. A commissionaire was eyeing him critically. Rutherford knew instinctively that he must act promptly and with resolution if he were to obtain the information he required.

"Hullo, sergeant!" he said. "Yes! I was looking for you. I want some information, confidentially. Can you come outside for a minute?"

"Certainly, sir."

They went down the steps and strolled a few yards along the street.

"Of course," Rutherford began, "don't answer my questions if it's against your orders. I don't want to get you into trouble."

"I quite understand, sir."

Now, this remark of the sergeant's meant two things: one was that he had decided that Rutherford was a gentleman; and the other was that he was satisfied that he was good for a large tip.

"The lady in No. 12——"

"Miss Nesbitt, sir." The commissionaire filled in the pause smartly. It was policy to assume that the gentleman knew the name. Then there was clearly no harm in reminding him of it.

"Just so, Miss Nesbitt. I knew her in London before the war. I only want to know this: has she been here long? how much longer will she be staying? and is she alone?"

"She's been 'ere – what? – a matter of three months, and she took the flat for three years. She's on her own."

"I see. Thanks very much. You will not, of course, mention this conversation to anyone?" He slipped a ten shilling note into the man's hand.

"I quite understand, sir."

They parted and Rutherford returned to his room, with only one fear – that all this was a dream.

CHAPTER XI

I

Belief is usually a matter of feeling, not evidence, and Rutherford felt that Sondra's presence in London was destined not only to deliver him from the inferno of his thoughts regarding Feversham, but that it would also provide a future for him in some way that was at present unimaginable.

Nevertheless, his reason soon warned him that if he had found it impossible even to write to her, a much greater ordeal now confronted him. He would have to look her in the eyes and answer her questions. After all, what was the link between them? Feversham! Inevitably their conversation must centre in him. It was useless to try to deceive himself. Either he must find the courage to discuss Feversham, easily and lightly, or he must abandon the hope which the sight of Sondra had created, and continue to live alone with accusing thoughts and haunting memories for company.

He studied the problem for two days and discovered that although he feared meeting Sondra, he was more afraid of continuing to live with the threat of madness becoming more menacing each day. Fear, therefore, gave him the courage to do that of which he was afraid, and so he decided to call.

It was a Friday afternoon. It had rained all the morning but now a mellow sunlight made shimmering mirrors of the puddles and kindled the autumn glory of the trees. He walked through Kensington Gardens, thence into Hyde Park, unable to believe in the reality of his objective. But when he reached the block of flats in which Sondra was living, a sudden stab of realization made him pause. He looked at his watch – it was nearly four-thirty. A sense of utter inadequacy possessed him. He began to tremble slightly and felt that passers-by were looking at him. The alternative, however, was his room! – to stand for an hour at the window watching the branches of that silver birch sway in the wind, then to draw the curtains, pull up his chair to the fire, and surrender himself to those arguments which continued endlessly in his mind concerning his guilt or his innocence. He could not return to all that! Even if Sondra detected that there was something curious about him, what did it matter? Had he not practically decided to make a full statement to the police? Besides, she might have forgotten Feversham – it was twenty years ago. *She* had not the reason to remember him that he had.

He passed swiftly through the entrance, nodded to the commissionaire, ran up the stairs, and pressed the bell at number 12.

He had been certain that the door would be opened by a maid. It was opened by Sondra. For a few seconds they stared at each other.

"You don't remember me," he stammered in a low voice.

She did not reply immediately, then she said: "I know you are someone I knew a very long time ago."

The voice was the same, low and vibrant, and its tone seemed to steal through him like a subtle essence.

"I'm Rutherford – Gordon Rutherford."

"I can scarcely believe you," she said slowly.

"Naturally, you had forgotten me. Of course——"

But she interrupted.

"Please come in. I can't see you properly in this light."

He followed her into an attractive sitting-room. The curtains were drawn but although the room was softly lit he could see her quite clearly. They stood and studied each other with frank curiosity.

The change in her was slight, yet it riveted his attention. The powerfully moulded features were the same under the dark heavy hair. The hair was short now but that was not the cause of the alteration in her. The eyes too were the same – those curious enigmatic eyes with that slightly Eastern slant which had always fascinated him. He glanced at her clothes. They still possessed that individuality, the secret of which was quite beyond his guess. He was wrong, she had not altered. Unless – yes, perhaps that was it! – expectancy had left the face for ever. That was why she was a woman now, not a girl, and perhaps that also explained why the mouth was firmer, less receptive.

"Well?" she queried. "And your verdict?"

"You have not altered," he replied. There was a pause. "And yours?" he asked.

"You have worked hard since we met." Then with a little movement of her hand, which he had forgotten and which he recognized with a thrill, she added: "Do sit down. We'll have tea. I shall have to make it as the maid is out, but everything is ready."

He sat down and lit a cigarette, thankful that the first, if not the worst, was over. It was an immense relief not to be subjected to the scrutiny of her eyes. If only he could come here each day and sit silent with her! An atmosphere of peace caressed him and his surrender to it was in the nature of a wordless prayer.

"Why were you so certain that I should not remember you?"

Her words reminded him of the necessity for defence and he became alert immediately.

"Memories do not exist for modern people," he replied slowly.

"That's an interesting theory. Please develop it."

"I've thought about it a good deal," he went on. "Memories must possess organic sequence. They must be strung like beads on a rosary. Our lives before the war are unreal to us, and so our memories are unreal. They relate to someone who is dead. Recently, I've tried to remember my childhood. I've even visited the scenes which formed its background – but I found that the stage had been set for another drama, and one in which I can play no part."

She handed him a cup of tea, then sat on a low seat by the fire.

"I believe you're right," she said at last. "I can see that the war left its mark on you."

He hastened to explain that he had not seen active service, then described briefly his determination to enlist; his meeting with Philip; and the nature of those activities which had occupied him during the war and for some years afterwards.

There was a silence. She had watched him intently during his narrative and he felt certain that now she would ask the question which he dreaded but which was inevitable. It could not be delayed any longer – it was a miracle it had not emerged much earlier. She would ask about Feversham, and he would have to answer.

But the silence continued. She was still studying him with those strange eyes of hers and he began to feel embarrassed. God! if only she wouldn't watch him, then the silence could last for an hour! All he asked was to sit here with her; to glance at her from time to time; and to inhale the fragrance of the perfume she wore. But, day and night, for years, he had lived and slept with a sword in his hand – and it was there still, although he was now on the frontier of paradise.

"And you?" he managed to ask at last. "What has happened to you, and why are you in London? Is this your first visit since – since – " His voice trailed off, but after a pause she came to his aid.

"I came over just after the war, but only for a short visit. I haven't any very pleasant memories of the years since – since we met." She altered her attitude and looked down into the fire. "I married just before the war. It was a failure. If I told you all the details, I should only reveal the futilities which made it a failure. There was nothing very original about them. I divorced my husband a few years ago and I prefer to forget him, his name, and everything to do with our marriage. Thank God, there were no children!" She spoke with sudden passionate emphasis, then added: "My father is dead and my mother lives with her sister in Italy."

Except for her one outburst, she told her story as if it related to someone else – someone they had both known, who was dead – and when she ceased he could think of nothing to say. He recognized, however, that he could not continue to sit silent. In spite of the fear which made him tremble each time she spoke, it was heaven to be here. He must exert himself or she would find him dull, and would not let him come again.

"I see now why my theory concerning memories interested you," he said with an attempt at a lighter manner. "Will you be here long?"

She turned and looked at him. He was surprised by the calm resolution of her expression.

"Yes, a long time. London interests me more than any other city. I've no one to consider so I shall stay here. And you? Are you going abroad again?"

"No," he replied emphatically. "I've seen all I want to of Europe. I, like you, have no one to consider and I shall stay here."

Then he told her that Philip had died in the war, that his parents were dead, and explained the remarkable manner in which he had become the tenant of a room in his old home. She seemed interested. He seized the opportunity and tried to amuse her by describing Mrs. Winchester, Trotter, and the other tenants. She encouraged him, and he explained at length the sensations he had experienced through being a lodger in the house in which he had been born – the house which he had not entered for years till, acting on an impulse, he had rung the bell a few months ago.

When he paused in this narrative, she prompted him till – being assured of her interest – he told her incidents in his childhood which he had never confided to anyone. Three quarters of an hour slipped away. When at last he paused through lack of subject matter, she said:

"You've a good memory."

Again the necessity for caution stabbed him, and he replied hastily:

"Yes – for my childhood. Living in that house has stirred all its memories into life. That was only natural, of course. I wish you'd come and see my old nursery, which is now my home, if – if——"

"I'd love to," she cut in. "It seems providential that two such lonely people should have run into each other again, doesn't it? But what a strange person you are – you always were rather strange."

They had risen as he was about to go.

"Why, what do you mean?"

"Ever since you came I've been waiting for you to tell me something."

"What? Really! I'm afraid I'm – well, very dense – but I don't understand. What is it?"

"Why, how you discovered me, of course," she said in her low, deep voice. He looked at her quickly. She was smiling.

"Oh, yes! How stupid of me! The truth is that I was so glad to be with you that I forgot to explain how I had found you. I saw you in the street a few days ago and I must confess that I followed you."

"A few days ago!" she exclaimed. "But why on earth didn't you speak to me in the street? Why follow me? And – anyhow – why wait a few days before calling?"

She looked up into his eyes as if she expected to find the answers to her questions in their expression.

"I wasn't sure whether you'd want to see me," he muttered.

"Why not? Anyway, you might as well have taken that risk first as you had to run it eventually. No, the truth is that you were too busy with your writing. That always came first, didn't it? You see, I've a good memory too."

She held out her hand and he took it gratefully.

"I may come again?" he asked.

"Of course. Why not? And I must come to see your nursery." She took a sheet of note paper from her desk. "You'll find the telephone number here. Ring up some time – soon."

A moment later he had gone.

She closed the front door noiselessly, then stood so still in the hall that she seemed to be listening. A moment later she returned to the sitting-room, switched off the lights, then sat down near the blazing fire.

For over an hour she remained motionless, staring into the flames.

II

The world's our mood. There is a legend that a wise man once said to his son: "You will never encounter anything worse than yourself." And doubtless his son believed him so long as his experiences were pleasant. In any event, after his visit to Sondra, Rutherford's mood had changed, so London and the world had changed.

He ran down the stairs, flung open the doors, and began to walk rapidly down the street. A taxi was crawling along at the corner: he hailed it, told the man to drive to a café in the West End, then lit a cigarette, leant back and put his feet up on the little seat opposite. Plans for the evening chased each other across his mind. He would not go back to his room till it was time to sleep. He would dine at a good restaurant and drink to his fortune. Sondra! It was not a word – it was a magic wand which had transformed his world.

He reached the café and ordered a drink. He was alone no longer – he had thoughts, dreams, hopes for company. And, like a recurring motif, one sentence haunted his brain:

She had not mentioned Feversham.

How baseless his fears had been! He was amazed to remember how nearly he had not called through fear that her first thought on seeing him would be Feversham. How utterly unimaginative he had been! Why, all that was twenty years ago! She might have had a dozen such friendships in Paris when she was there in 1910. It was true that she had seemed pretty intimate with Feversham in London, but what did that signify? Heaps of men must have been attracted to her: Feversham had had his day and been forgotten, like a dozen others.

He sipped his drink meditatively. It was rather significant that she had remembered him. At any rate, she had recognized his name immediately. And – yes, of course! – she had remembered that he was a writer, and how much writing had meant to him. That was distinctly curious because he had been most careful not to refer to writing in anything he had said. So the position was this: she had forgotten Feversham and remembered him. This thought exhilarated him far more than the cocktail he was sipping, and he tried to work out its implications.

An idea came into his mind which he dismissed as fantastic, then recalled it, as it created such a deep satisfaction in him. Was it *possible* that she had cared for him more than he had thought in those old days? He closed his eyes and summoned his memories. He had certainly tried to make himself more agreeable to her than he had to any other woman. It was true that after his quarrel with Feversham she had ignored him, but it was equally true that he had made no attempt to see her. Besides, she *must* have known Alston's theory that she was the cause of the quarrel. If so, she had never contradicted it, or he would have heard quickly enough. It was interesting, too, that she had never objected to his presence. Evidently she had not been so devoted to Feversham that she wanted to be alone with him.

Why hadn't he thought of all this before? Was he deceiving himself? He reviewed the chain of reasoning, tried it link by link, and was satisfied with the test. What a fool he had been not to write to her! He should have written soon after his arrival in Paris; it would have been quite unnecessary to have mentioned Feversham. She knew they had quarrelled. He seemed to have had the will in those days to do the impossible, and to fail over the trivial. And he was no wiser now. Why, if he

had not discovered Sondra, he might even have made a statement to the police! He must have been nearly a lunatic – and
they would have been certain that he was wholly one. Well,
that nonsense was over, once and for ever. He was a man again:
he could feel the blood leaping through his veins. He had done
with Feversham at last. *Of course* it had been an accident. He
had worked too hard for years, with the result that directly he
gave it up and had a rest, he had had a breakdown and had
allowed a bad dream to master him. Colonel Sharpe had often
told him that he would have to pay for the way in which he had
stuck to his work year after year without leave. He had cracked
up and he ought to have recognized the fact that night in his
studio when he had been afraid to put out the candle, instead
of suffering the torments of the damned month after month,
wondering whether he was a murderer. A murderer! The idea
was ridiculous.

He left the café, and went to a quiet expensive restaurant
where he dined leisurely and in peace. He sat for a full hour
over his coffee, striving to recall every word that had been said
during his conversation with Sondra. . . . It was interesting that
she had asked why he was so certain that she would have forgotten him. Of course it was absurd to read too much into a
casual remark – all the same it did contain an implied reproach.
Then there was no doubt that she *had* been very interested in
all he had told her about his old home and the memories it had
awakened. There was no doubt whatever that she had encouraged him to confide in her, or he would never have told her all
those trifling incidents of his childhood. Also, she had been
disappointed that he had waited a few days before calling on
her. She had even asked why he had not spoken to her when he
saw her in the street.

The more he analysed their conversation, the more convinced he became that the only explanation of the welcome
she had given him was to be found in the fact that he had
impressed her more deeply than he had imagined during those
days in 1910. What other explanation was there? A girl of nineteen does not remember a man and his activities for twenty

years, unless she had been very interested in him. Particularly as their friendship had been restricted to a few weeks. Besides, how readily she had consented to see him again. She had said: "Ring me up some time – soon." She had even remembered to give him her telephone number. And, above all, she had not mentioned Feversham.

He was not deluding himself. He was certain of it. He rose, paid the bill, and went home.

That night, for the first time for months, Rutherford was asleep before twelve and did not stir till the maid knocked on his door.

CHAPTER XII

I

The extent of the world's suffering may be recognized by the alacrity with which most of us will pursue the veriest will o' the wisp which seems to promise happiness. It was only necessary for Rutherford to meet Sondra in order for him to deny the past and to create dreams for the future. Yesterday, his thoughts had been wholly occupied by one grim speculation: had he shot Feversham deliberately? To-day they revolved round one question: when could he see Sondra again?

By necessity, he had been a miser – not of gold, but of thoughts and emotions. He had not dared to spend the mintage of his imagination. He had lived alone, hoarded his thoughts, buried his emotions, because it had been impossible for him to possess a friend. His gift for writing had died with Feversham. For years he had been a miser who had longed to turn spendthrift, and now at last it seemed that his day had come. A passionate desire to invest Sondra with all the riches accumulated during his exile possessed him: to tear the mask from his features, to fling the sword from his hand, and – by surrendering himself – regain all that of which he had been cheated. It was intolerable to be forced to remain on the defensive! To know that at any moment a question of hers would necessitate the adoption of his mask and the tightening of his hand on the hilt of his sword! But he flung this knowledge from him, striving to believe that she had forgotten Feversham entirely and so would never mention his name.

It is necessary to appreciate Rutherford's state during this period, and possibly nothing could be more indicative of it than the fact that an event which would be simply an incident in another man's life was an epoch in his. His visit to Sondra was an example. To spend just over an hour with a cultured beautiful woman in the privacy of her flat, was a return to the land of the living for Rutherford. Simply to be in her presence – to note the reflection of her thoughts in her expression, the movements of her hands – seemed a miracle. For over twenty years he had known either the squalor of lodgings or the ornate vulgarity of hotels. The externals of his life had lacked intimacy, just as his relations with women had lacked refinement. Consequently his visit to Sondra was not simply a pleasant interlude – it was an intoxicating experience. His delight in it, and the intensity with which he anticipated its repetition, made him reckless regarding certain things and blind to others.

The day succeeding his visit was a Saturday and it was obviously ridiculous to imagine that he could see her two days in succession, although the idea did occur to him. He decided, however, that he would ring her up the next day, excusing his precipitancy somehow, and in the meantime he was delighted to find that the thought of her continued to deliver him from the memory of that night in the cottage.

He telephoned her at one o'clock the next day. She immediately asked him to tea and suggested that he should come early. The friendly note in her voice confirmed him in the validity of those theories he had evolved concerning her indifference to Feversham, and consequently he went to her flat in a state not far removed from elation.

"I'm glad you telephoned," she said as she welcomed him. "You are the only old friend I have in London."

"I hope we shall meet often," he replied eagerly.

"I'm sure we shall."

They talked on general subjects for half an hour. His mind was extraordinarily active and he expressed his ideas with a facility which was remarkable in a man to whom speech was the exception not the rule. But whatever the subject under discussion and however much it intrigued him mentally, he was consistently aware of her beauty as she sat listening with the glow of the firelight about her. To him her beauty was more remarkable now than it had been when she was a girl. It was more individual because character had sealed it indelibly. Once, it had suggested the probability of a unique destiny; now, it was the fulfilment of that prophecy. The power which had been potential was now actual – purpose, courage, resolution were unmistakable in every line of the face and in the deep glow of the dark eyes. The impression she created, now as in 1910, was independent of all superficiality. It owed nothing to speech or attitude. Her individuality pervaded every detail – her gestures, her clothes, her surroundings – but it depended on none of them.

During a pause in the conversation, she asked casually:

"What became of Madame de Fontin? You remember her?"

He started and looked up at her quickly. The subject they had been discussing bore no relevance whatever to Madame de Fontin.

"Oh, yes," he stammered. "You mean that odd woman who collected freaks. I just remember her."

There was a long pause, then she said:

"And that strange man who was so decorative. What was his name?"

But he was alert by now and so was prepared:

"I don't remember. I only remembered Madame de Fontin because it's such an odd name."

"Do try," she said with a smile. "I suddenly thought of him yesterday – I've no idea why. He wore side-whiskers and a fob and strapped trousers – and he managed to leave you with the impression that he was witty in spite of all the evidence you had endured to the contrary. You must remember him – you knew him quite well."

He pretended to think deeply. His heart was beating violently and he wondered why she had suddenly remembered these people. But her eyes were upon him and he had to act.

"I've got it!" he exclaimed triumphantly. "Alston – Ashley Alston!"

"Of course. How clever of you! What happened to him?"

"You saw him after I did," he replied quickly, and immediately regretted the remark. He went on hurriedly. "You see, I left England before you did and I never returned to it till I came back a few months ago."

"But how interesting!" she exclaimed as she drew her chair nearer to him. "You never explained that on Friday. I gathered you had been away a long time but do you mean that you were actually away from England for twenty years?"

"Yes, practically. I thought I'd explained that. You see it was like this."

He seized the opportunity to give a detailed account of his activities in Europe. He explained how he had been commissioned to write a book and that was why he had gone abroad originally. Then he described, in more detail than he had done formerly, his war service and the duties which had occupied him since the Armistice. He spoke rapidly, striving to make his narrative interesting in the hope that she would forget all about the 1910 days in London.

He did not know, however, that frequently a woman only listens to the first sentence, or the last, in a long statement. Consequently he was surprised that her only comment was:

"You said you were commissioned to write a book. That reminds me – I meant to ask you on Friday – I suppose you've written a whole row of books which I ought to know?"

"No, I'm afraid not." A long pause, which he ended by adding awkwardly: "The fact is – I gave up writing."

"You – gave up writing!" She repeated the words in amazement. "But, in the old days, it meant everything to you. Why, you used to tell me that you did not care what you suffered if it provided you with the material for a book."

He laughed, but it was not a great success.

"Well, it's a long story," he said at last, "and a dull one. I was let down over the book I was commissioned to write, and that didn't help my enthusiasm. Soon the war came and I worked so hard for so many years that when I was free again my imagination had atrophied. The war did not only destroy men – it destroyed faculties as well."

She said nothing and they spoke little during tea. Rutherford welcomed this silence as it enabled him to regain his sense of security. After all, it was inevitable that she should make some reference to the 1910 days. But, despite his logic, he discovered that it would be a relief to go. He was afraid of these reminiscences.

She rose and wandered over to the window, parted the curtains, then looked down into the street. A minute later, she crossed to a mirror and glanced critically at her reflection. He had just taken a cigarette from his case and was about to strike a match, when she said lightly:

"Oh, by the way, what happened to Feversham – Martin Feversham?"

The box of matches fell into the hearth. He had been so certain that the danger was passed that he was unprepared. In a second, however, the reply he had learnt by heart flashed into his mind.

"Extraordinary!" he exclaimed. "I was just going to ask you. It was talking of Madame de Fontin and Ashley Alston which reminded me of him. What happened to him?"

"But that's what I asked you," she pointed out.

"But you – surely *you* heard of him after I did?"

"Well, when – exactly – did you hear of him last?"

She crossed the room as she spoke, then sat down near him.

"Why – I don't understand, I'm afraid – you know that I didn't see him since——"

"You quarrelled," she interrupted. "I've just remembered

that you had a quarrel with him. And so you never saw him since then?"

"No, how could I?" he asked. "I went abroad directly afterwards."

"You went to Paris, and so did he – the day after I sailed for America."

"Paris is a big place. And, anyhow, I wasn't there very long."

"Oh, well, it doesn't matter," she said after a long pause. "I just thought you might have run into him again during your travels. He used to travel a lot. I wonder if I may have one of your cigarettes? Mine are in the next room. Thanks so much."

She lit her cigarette, then went on:

"I'm sorry to hear you gave up writing. Sometimes I used to think of you when I was in New York and I was certain you'd make a name for yourself."

Again she paused, but as he remained silent she continued:

"You know how you feel certain that some people will succeed – well, I always felt that way about you."

"I could have succeeded," he said in a low voice. "I'm certain of it, but success demanded time, and for years I was a slave. Do you imagine that I gave up my ambition easily? It was all I ever had. I surrendered everything for it which other men value."

"I recognize a note in your voice which reminds me of the old Gordon."

She was looking into the flames and he could not see her face, but her use of his Christian name was like a caress.

"I tried desperately to quicken my creative faculty," he said fiercely. "I had staked everything on making a name as a writer, and I knew that nothing else could hold me permanently. But it was useless."

He went on and on as if his pent-up emotions found relief in a torrent of words. Also, at all costs, he must dominate the conversation and so make further references to Feversham impossible. Directly she had mentioned his name, he had seen that room in the cottage with Feversham dead on the floor. It was essential to talk and it was providential that she had men-

tioned his writing. He derived an impetus from his old enthu-
siasm which made sentence after sentence leap into his mind.
When at last he was silent, he could see that she had forgotten
Feversham.

"You've suffered a good deal," she said softly. "I noticed that
when you came on Friday. It was what I really meant when I
said that I could see you had worked hard."

He rose to go and she crossed to the window in order to see
if it was raining. He watched her as she stood motionless looking down into the street. She seemed to tremble slightly.

"Are you cold?" he asked.

"No, not cold," she replied, "but it looks wintry down
there."

"Then come back to the fire. And now I must go."

"Oh, before you go," she exclaimed, "do give me your telephone number. You're on the 'phone, of course?"

"The house is," he replied. "I'll write it down for you."

"Thanks so much. And I'll call you in a day or two."

A moment later they shook hands and he left.

II

The manner in which we use our privacy, immediately after
leaving someone, is usually indicative of the effect the meeting has had upon us. For instance, if we stretch, yawn, look
at the clock and mutter: "Oh, hell!" it's probable that we are
convinced that we have wasted our time. On the other hand, if
we move about briskly, whistle, smile retrospectively, it is clear
that we think the meeting was well worth while.

Judged by this theory it was evident that Sondra and Rutherford regarded the interview which had just ended from very
different angles.

Directly the front door closed, Sondra returned swiftly to
the room in which she had received Rutherford, sat down at
the writing desk, and wrote rapidly for nearly half an hour.
When she had finished, she read over what she had written,
pausing occasionally to insert a word, or delete a sentence,

then she folded the sheets carefully and locked them in a drawer.

Whereas Rutherford, directly he was alone, ran down the stairs, paused in the hall, turned back as if he had decided to return, hesitated again, and finally went out into the street. He looked first in one direction, then the other, then at his watch, and generally exhibited all the unmistakable signs of irresolution. He could not decide whether to go home, or to go and drink in some café or——. He began to wander down the street, having left the problem unsolved. A few minutes later, however, as it began to rain heavily, he returned to his room.

"I couldn't stand much more of that," he said aloud, then stopped abruptly. This habit of talking to himself had increased recently and he was determined not to encourage it. Why the devil hadn't she referred to Feversham at their first meeting! He had been on his guard then, but to-day – relying on her former silence – he had been unprepared. Yet probably the explanation was simple enough. She had been so surprised by his sudden appearance on Friday that it had overwhelmed her. She had had time in the interval to fit him into his old background – hence her questions. Yes, he was a fool to worry. But still——

He mixed a drink, then pulled a chair up to the fire. Thoughts seemed to tumble into his mind from every direction. . . . Would she mention Feversham next time they met? She'd called him by his Christian name to-day – that was something, anyway. Also, she'd been pretty sympathetic about his writing. But what a strange person she was! Incalculable in many ways. Her husband must have been a damned fool! . . . Had his manner changed when they discussed Feversham? It had been clever of him to say that he was just going to ask her about him! What a good thing he had prepared that reply beforehand!

And so on, and so on. Thought after thought, flashing and fading, as if match after match were being struck in his brain. Then, at last, the emergence of a new idea which immediately became dominant. It was this:

Suppose he ran into Alston, or Madame de Fontin, or Wolheim, or several of the old crowd and they asked him about Feversham, what effect would it have on him? To his amazement, he discovered that it would not worry him in the least! He was certain of it. He would simply say: "Feversham? Oh, I know who you mean! No – never heard of him from that day to this." It seemed to him that he could hear the question, and his answer, and he knew, definitely, that he would be adequate to a discussion with them about Feversham. It was not a case of circumventing a difficulty imaginatively. The difficulty would not exist. So, then, it was because it was Sondra. But why? Why Sondra more than another?

Five minutes ticked themselves away, but he could find no solution. Then, dimly, he half-remembered that when Feversham and Sondra were dancing together on their first visit to *The Dive*, he had noticed how perfectly they seemed to belong to each other. But of course all that was nonsense! The idea had crossed his mind, it was true, but nevertheless he had spent most of his time on that occasion studying her figure. She was more beautiful now than she was then. No, it must simply be a coincidence that it was *her* references to Feversham which disturbed him so profoundly. It was a fact, and an unfortunate one, but it was no good bothering about it. He'd learn to deal with it somehow.

He forced himself to think of other things: to imagine how marvellous it would be if the menace of Feversham did not exist; if it were really true that she had cared about *him* in the past; if she could love him now! Yes, if *that* happened, he would still have a life to live. If only she were here now and the night were before them. . . .

Rutherford soon learnt that it did not rest with him to determine whether his fear of Sondra's references to Feversham was so intense that it would be better not to see her, for she now took the initiative in regard to their meetings and frequently telephoned him in order to make the necessary arrangements. In less than a week he was entirely dependent on her, and those days on which he did see her revealed to him

the extent of this servitude. They lunched or dined together
and went to an entertainment when they could find one. It was
not easy however. With one, or possibly two, exceptions, the
theatres offered: – musical comedies (two songs in each, and
the same dance) pyjama farces; comedies which were mental
tennis, at the best; intellectual contortionism; or an orgy of
slithering sentimentality. As to the pictures, you had a choice
between back-stage revelations – chiefly physical – and crook
detective drama. Sometimes there was a concert but you had
to be on the alert or you missed it, and then your chance was
gone for months.

On more than one occasion Sondra came to tea in Rutherford's rooms. His preparations for her arrival were so elaborate
that Mrs. Winchester and the whole of the staff were amazed
by them. Mrs. Winchester was even consulted as to the best
brand of China tea. These activities destroyed her favourite
theory, which was that Rutherford was a Trappist monk in
mufti. When the servants saw Sondra, however, they regarded
Rutherford as a dark horse and consequently he rose in their
estimation. Sondra made the acquaintance of Miss Trentham,
the journalist, who had the room below Rutherford's, and evidently liked her as they dined together on several occasions –
somewhat to Rutherford's surprise.

One condition imposed by Sondra during this period irritated Rutherford a good deal. She refused to allow him to pay
for their pleasures, pointing out that it was ridiculous, as she
was better off than he was, and she insisted that if he paid
to-day, then she would pay tomorrow. He was forced to acqui-
esce, as she was adamant, but it detracted from his enjoyment.

She still referred to Feversham at intervals but he noticed
with great satisfaction that allusions to him were not more
frequent or more marked than those relating to Alston, Wolheim, or Madame de Fontin. In fact he had almost accustomed
himself to them when a more dramatic example shook his
new-found assurance.

One morning Sondra telephoned and asked him the date.
He consulted the calendar and gave her the information.

"I thought it was," he heard her say. "Well, will you dine with me to-night?"

"I'd love to," he replied. "Where?"

"I'll think that over. Why not come for me here? Then we needn't decide now. I'll be ready at a quarter to eight, and we can sit on and talk over dinner."

"You've given the day a shape," he said. "I'll be with you at a quarter to eight."

As he changed for dinner that evening he congratulated himself on the progress he had made. It was no longer a question of distinguishing between hopes and actualities: they were meeting three times a week and usually as the result of her initiative. That was a fact, not a theory, and its implications were obvious.

He arrived a few minutes before his time and smoked a cigarette till she appeared. She looked magnificent in evening clothes and he allowed his glance to rest longer than usual on the beauty of her neck and shoulders. He felt a thrill of pride at the knowledge that she would be seen with him, and a sense of possession quickened in him.

"Well, where are you taking me?"

"All in good time," she replied. "It's a secret at present."

There was a ring at the bell.

"That's the taxi," she informed him. "I ordered it for ten to eight. Have you ever known another woman so punctual?"

He laughed, and they went down the stairs together.

"But where shall I tell the man to drive to?" he inquired.

"He knows," she answered.

"You're very mysterious."

She looked up at him with a smile. "I love mystery, don't you? The simplest thing becomes thrilling, if you keep it a secret."

He talked a good deal during the drive and as a result was unaware of the direction. In a quarter of an hour the taxi stopped. He got out and looked up at the restaurant. It was *The Goya*.

He glanced at her quickly as she got out of the taxi but she was evidently preoccupied, for she nearly left her bag, a slim, brightly-coloured affair which enhanced her whole appearance by some miracle quite outside male comprehension.

Adolphe advanced to greet them. He was less decorative than he had been in 1910 but he made up for this by being immensely immaculate. His evening dress was not a suit – it was a creation. Also, his manner was so distinguished that you wondered why he was not wearing his orders. The face was sterner, the mouth tightly closed. It was impossible to believe that this was the man who had once served a *table d'hôte* dinner at one-and-six, and had been eager to secure writers and painters for his patrons. Everything was now *à la carte* – artists could go to the devil – and there were rumours that he owned a château in France and a car the size of a cottage.

"I have the table for madame," he announced with a bow which did homage to his own dignity. "Good-evening, monsieur."

The other diners paused. They glanced at Sondra and presumed that her beauty was the cause of Adolphe's attentions, which were usually reserved for royalty alone.

"This way, madame, if you please."

They followed him till they reached the little room which had originally been the whole restaurant but now it contained only eight tables and the walls were a delicate pastel green.

Adolphe waved his hand gracefully indicating their table.

"The table in the corner, is it not?"

He smiled in recognition of the absurdity of the idea that in any circumstances he could make a mistake, then he adjusted Sondra's chair for her. A waiter approached and Adolphe gave him a number of instructions in his professional voice, after which he vanished elegantly.

Most of the other tables were occupied and Sondra glanced round the room. Rutherford said nothing. He had not entered *The Goya* since the three of them had dined there in 1910. By some unfortunate chance Adolphe had placed them in the identical corner in which they had dined that night.

"You don't say what you think of my surprise," Sondra remarked with simulated disappointment.

"It's a great success," he replied. "It's quiet and there aren't too many people."

"I thought you'd like it. I came and booked this table this morning, and ordered the dinner – so if you don't like it you must blame me, not Adolphe."

"Adolphe?" he inquired.

"Yes – you remember! The proprietor."

"Oh, yes, of course. I'd forgotten the place."

She chatted while they drank their cocktails and he welcomed her animation. Something always occurred to spoil his pleasure! Why on earth had she come to this cursed restaurant, and booked this actual table! The damned place had associations and consequently allusions to Feversham were inevitable! Perhaps it would be better for *him* to mention Feversham. Yes, he'd have to refer to him later on, otherwise he would be nervous every time she spoke.

He had a second cocktail and began to talk rapidly. He made a great effort to be amusing, and tried to present his views on current topics from an original angle. She seemed to listen with her eyes and only spoke in order to indicate her appreciation, or to furnish him with a new subject. He drank a good deal and felt more confident by the time dinner was over and coffee appeared. He knew that the moment for reminiscences had arrived but he felt more adequate to the ordeal.

He lit a cigarette and looked round the room.

"It's a pretty long time since I was here. Let me think." A pause. "The last time I dined here was——"

"With Feversham and me – twenty years ago to-night."

He started so violently that he shook the table. A moment later she laughed gaily.

"I told you that I loved mystery. So I do. And I've another surprise for you."

She opened her bag and produced a card which she handed him. He took it mechanically and glanced at it. But immediately an exclamation broke from him and he stared at the card with fascinated eyes.

It was the menu of the dinner they had had with Feversham

in 1910 – the menu on which he had sketched his prophecies concerning the three of them twenty years hence. He looked at the date – yes, twenty years ago to-night!

"*Now* you remember!" Sondra cried triumphantly. "I knew you would. He booked the table for to-night and made Adolphe make a note of it. I've a crazy idea that he'll turn up to keep the date."

He bent lower over the card pretending to study the drawings. He glanced at the one which depicted himself although it disturbed him. Nevertheless, he tried desperately to rivet his attention to it, for he was afraid to look at the drawing of Feversham. But it was useless, he could not control his actions, and the next second he was staring at Feversham's portrait of himself. The intensely blue eyes seemed to leap from the paper. The man rose before him. He could see his smile, he could hear his laugh——

"God!" he muttered involuntarily.

"What's the matter?" cried Sondra.

He steeled himself to meet her glance. "It's hell to think what twenty years can do," he said in a low voice.

"What an egotist you are!" she said lightly. "You've only studied your own portrait. What do you think of mine? Have I fulfilled his prophecy?"

He looked down at the card again and studied the sketch of Sondra. Fortunately it provided him with an obvious remark:

"He did not foresee that women would wear their hair short," he announced with an attempt at a smile.

"But apart from that?" she insisted.

"It might have been drawn to-day."

He handed her the card, but she did not take it.

"Why, you haven't studied Adolphe. Look – there he is and, underneath – what does it say?"

He read the words written below the portrait:

"Adolphe – when the dinner is three-and-six."

Sondra laughed. "I wish Martin would come. I always call him Feversham to you because I know you remember him better by that name, but I always think of him as Martin."

There was a long pause, then she added in a changed tone: "Just as I always think of you as Gordon."

He looked at her gratefully. He felt faint and hoped that his appearance did not betray him. He prayed that she would go on talking, for he could not speak.

At this moment, however, Adolphe appeared and scanned the room with the triumphant glance of a victorious general. Sondra beckoned to him and he smilingly obeyed the gesture.

"Madame?"

"Have you a good memory?" she inquired.

Adolphe gave an infinitesimal shrug of the shoulders as he curled up the corners of his mouth slightly:

"For some things – and for some people, madame," he replied as he glanced gallantly at her.

"Do you remember a gentleman who booked this table for to-night – twenty years ago?"

"Twenty *years* ago! *Mais non*, madame! The restaurant then – why, it was only this room."

"Exactly! I remember it! And there were paintings on the wall, and your patrons were artists."

"Ah! Madame remember! And the dinner was one-and-six. *Bon Dieu!* One-and-six!"

"I'm certain that this will interest you," said Sondra as she handed him the old menu card.

"*Mon Dieu!*" he murmured almost reverently. For a few seconds, however, his interest became wholly professional. "There is an omission here!" he exclaimed. "It should say at the bottom, in the left hand corner, *coffee extra*. Ah! the arguments there were as to whether coffee was included in the *prix fixe!*"

He began to fumble mechanically for a pencil, then evidently remembered that the necessity for remedying the omission no longer existed.

At this point he noticed Feversham's drawings – notably the one which related to him. Sondra explained the sense in which it was prophetic. Adolphe was delighted.

"Adolphe – when the dinner is three-and-six!" he exclaimed joyously, repeating the phrase again and again.

"Pardon, madame, but it is absolutely necessary that I show this to my wife. Forgive me – but it is *absolutely* necessary."

He disappeared and Sondra turned to Rutherford.

"Now I must explain. When I came over, I brought all my mementos of the old days. I had always kept them. Look! Here is another."

She produced the programme of an Artists' Ball which bore several signatures including Wolheim's and Feversham's.

"You did not come to that because you did not dance. There were other things, too. I happened to look through these things yesterday, and was amused by these sketches of Martin's. Then I looked at the date and remembered how he had said that we would all dine here twenty years hence. So I rang you up, and then booked this table."

Before he could reply Adolphe returned with Thérèse and an animated conversation ensued which attracted the attention of everyone in the room. Thérèse laughed, then cried, and assured Sondra that if it had not been for her the restaurant would still be one room and the dinner two-and-six at the most; that the sight of the old menu had reminded her of the days when they were so poor; and yet they were younger then; and life was very sad, was it not? and that the drawing of her husband made her laugh and yet it made her cry; and that madame must drink one little glass of Cognac with her, if she would do her that great *onerre*. And so on and so on. She and her husband remained chatting till it was time for Sondra and Rutherford to leave. . . .

When he reached his room, Rutherford collapsed into a chair. She *must* have noticed his behaviour to-night! He would have to tell her that he had been ill. God! When she had said that perhaps Feversham would turn up to-night! Could she have believed that to be possible? No – the whole evening was simply a whim of hers! The old menu card had no greater significance for her than the programme of the Artists' Ball. She had been through her mementos and planned a surprise for him. That was all.

But, later, when he was in bed, he could see Feversham's

face quite distinctly in the darkness. The blue eyes gazed at him with an unfathomable glance, and sometimes in the silence he heard his laugh.

CHAPTER XIII

The weeks went by, but Rutherford was unaware of their passing. His life possessed a new horizon. It glimmered in the far distance, turning his thoughts into spies.

He was in love with Sondra.

One result was that instead of continually glancing over his shoulder at the Past, he lived on tiptoe scanning the Future. What had been a menace had become a radiant possibility.

Love transforms all things, but especially the future. There was something almost luxurious in the passion with which he surrendered himself to this love for Sondra. It was a drug which deadened his memories, stilled his thoughts, and created visions of happiness. Most lives oscillate between opposites and, therefore, the hope of which we are capable is the measure of the despair we have known. Shipwrecked men, miraculously rescued, experience a rapture quite unknown to a Londoner whose greatest adventure was once getting lost in a fog.

So with Rutherford. A few weeks ago he had looked on life with the eyes of a man on his deathbed. Life was something which happened to others; a glory of which he had been cheated; an experience which he had never had, yet one which, paradoxically, was over. Then – Sondra appeared. A few weeks later, his love for her had raised him from the dead, and a fierce determination possessed him to wrest from the future all those joys which a niggard past had denied.

Did she love him? His thoughts foamed and seethed round this question like raging waves round a rock. His was not simply the concern of a lover: it was the agony of a condemned man about to hear whether a reprieve had been granted. Although he knew that the final answer could only come from her, it was

imperative correctly to anticipate it. As he saw it, if he asked
her to marry him and she refused, there was an end not only
to their present relations but also to the talisman which now
protected him from the spectres of the past. All his life he had
loved certainty, but never had he longed so passionately to possess it as in this instance. He *must* know, and with this end in
view he sifted the evidence again and again.

She had remembered him – that was the first great fact in
his favour. She had asked about his writing, used his Christian name, and had not mentioned Feversham at their first
interview. She had welcomed his visit, pressed him to come
again, then finally she had arranged their meetings. She was
beautiful, and, therefore, she could have any number of men
round her. She was alone, free, and consequently could do as
she chose. Yet week after week she continued to see him frequently, and so far as he could discover her only social activities
apart from him had been those occasions when she had dined
with Miss Trentham. Surely the inference was that she cared
for him. What other explanation could there be? Of course, it
was possible that after the failure of her first marriage she was
not eager to risk another attempt, but this possibility did not
discourage him.

Above all, she had shown him the type of attention which
greatly impressed such a man as Rutherford. She had visited
his room several times, rearranged it to greater advantage,
and generally shown solicitude for his comfort. For instance,
she had moved the screen from the door, and put it near the
window – having discovered a draught on her first visit, of
which Rutherford remained ignorant after a residence of several months. Now, most men imagine that they understand
their mothers – it's an illusion, but let it pass – and Rutherford
saw in this type of attention a quality which was associated in
his mind with the affection of a mother. Mere sentimentality,
of course, but he welcomed its contribution in favour of the
belief that Sondra cared for him. Eventually, he became certain that this was the case, but one obstacle still prevented him
from asking her to marry him. It was this:

Twenty years ago he had based his future on a lie, for he had denied the power of the truth to save him. Should he, now, base his marriage on a lie? That is, should he marry Sondra without telling her the facts concerning Feversham? And, if he did not tell her, would it not be because he had not sufficient faith in her love – just as, twenty years ago, he had lacked faith in the power of truth?

Suddenly he realized that it was the same problem which confronted him: a dramatic emergence of that dilemma which he had had to face in Cornwall. Then, he had solved it by acting as a murderer; and – now should he solve it by the lie of silence?

Would he never escape from Feversham! Again his shadow deepened across the path which led to freedom. How could he tell Sondra of that night in the cottage, explain his motives, justify himself! Would she believe it – would anyone believe a word of it? And, if he found the courage to tell her, should he also reveal how, last year – in Paris – a sudden doubt had been born in him which had suggested that he had *murdered* Feversham? If he did not confess this, he would still be hiding the darker half of his secret.

Anger flamed in him as he realized his predicament. What did it matter whether silence were the equivalent to a lie! Why was it essential that his marriage should be based on the truth? Which of all the myriad activities of man was founded on the truth? Was not "smart" a synonym for fraud in the business world? Were not politics intellectual warfare – with lies for weapons? What was law but an intricate device to protect the sacred rights of property, however acquired? What was finance but the tyranny of the strong? and what were governments but its lackeys? And were not reformers simply slaves of the will-to-power, who deceived themselves and their dupes with the vocabulary of altruism? And – religion! What was it but a chaos of conflicting sects? Which one of them had risen above the level of a recruiting office during the war? Why, all life was a lie! It was so inwardly corrupt that the only choice before the world was ruin or regeneration. Was *he* to wreck his chance of happiness through fear of basing it on a lie!

But when his anger cooled, Rutherford knew that, whether or not the world could continue to exist in the terms of falsity, he had once saved his life by a lie and the result had been that for twenty years he had haunted the world a ghost. He wanted to marry Sondra because he believed it would be deliverance, but if he remained silent concerning Feversham – and if that silence was a burden to him after marriage – then would he not still be in hell? The possibility was a grim one and it could not be ignored.

Just as his inner conflict had reached this stage, however, a conversation occurred which would have had a devastating effect on him if it had not been followed by an alteration in his relations with Sondra which occupied his thoughts exclusively.

The conversation took place in his room one afternoon. It was nearly six and Sondra had announced that she must go but he prevailed on her to stay a few minutes longer.

She lit a cigarette, then said to him rather abruptly:

"You're the oddest man! There's some mystery about you. Do tell me what it is. You know I love mystery."

"A mystery!" he exclaimed. "Nonsense!"

"I'll prove it to you. Do you know that all these weeks I've been waiting for you to explain something?"

"*Explain* something!"

"How you repeat my words! I wish you wouldn't. It makes me feel as if I've said everything twice. Yes – I've been waiting for you to explain something. Have a cigarette and follow this closely. You like logic so this will interest you."

He fumbled with the matches while he lit a cigarette.

"Now," she went on. "You saw me in the street. You followed me. You called. Since then you've seen me several times each week. So it's clear that you must care for me a little——"

"Sondra!" he interrupted.

"Wait! Yet, although you had my address in New York, you never wrote to me once. I wonder why that was."

He had only one reply and he had to use it although it involved a reference to Feversham.

"I meant to explain that," he said, speaking rapidly. "Well – you see, it was like this – I'd quarrelled with Feversham and I thought, perhaps, you wouldn't want to hear from me."

"I see," she replied. "You might have written to find out, don't you think? It never occurred to you that your silence might hurt me, I suppose?"

"Sondra! I – I was a fool!"

He rose impetuously and was about to go to her, but she had also risen and was looking for her gloves in a business-like manner.

"Oh, by the way," she said casually, "you mentioned Feversham just now. Do you think he's dead?"

"Dead!"

She stamped her foot with irritation.

"Don't repeat every word I say! Yes – dead – dead – dead!"

He felt his features become immovable, and heard himself say:

"It's quite possible that he was killed in the war."

The sudden involuntary control which enabled him to make this answer astonished him. It was as if great emergency had created a power in him adequate to his need.

"I shouldn't be surprised," she replied, as she adjusted her gloves. "Poor Ashley Alston too, possibly. But certainly not the famous Wolheim."

A moment later she left.

That night he decided finally that, whatever the effect on him, he would never tell her about Feversham

Two days after this conversation he telephoned her but could obtain no reply. The next day he called but she was out. Another day passed and still no sign came from her. Rutherford was seriously alarmed – the loneliness he now experienced made his former isolation seem quite attractive. True to his type, he reviewed mentally all the possible reasons for this desertion, but apart from the fact that she had shown unprecedented irritability at their last meeting, he could discover no cause which was logically satisfying. These days without her, however, proved conclusively not only the degree to which he

was dependent on her, but the extent to which he was relying on marriage as the solution of all his difficulties. It was the
door through which he would return to life.

He was afraid to go out in case she should ring up in his
absence. He wrote her half a dozen letters and destroyed
each in turn. He felt certain that he was concerned not with
Sondra but with some mysterious, anonymous, and invisible
Adversary. Either she had met someone who had revealed
something which had made her suspicious, or she had remembered some incident in the past which she was investigating.
It was useless to try to deceive himself with flattering hopes
which suggested that she was not seeing him in order to let
him discover the extent of his attachment to her. He was certain that there was a sinister motive behind her desertion and
consequently he did not know what action to take. Should he
remain entirely passive till she made some move? Recently, all
suggestions in regard to meetings had come from her, so that
passivity on his part would only be a continuation of his present policy. Or should he call at the flat repeatedly until he *did*
see her?

Fear makes all of us fools, and Rutherford was afraid. Fear
was no stranger to him but, formerly, it had been physical –
his skin had been threatened. Now – his soul was menaced.
He had proved that mere existence was not worth the having,
but the possibility of happiness had quickened the depths of
him. Life! Life! He had only a handful of years – so few, and
they owed him so much! He was frantic to grasp this happiness, to make it his own, to flaunt it like a victorious banner
over all the dark and desolate regions of his memory. And now
it seemed to be eluding him! An unknown Adversary was frus-
trating him. And he could only wait, racked by imaginings,
and shaken by impotent anger.

Then, desperate, he telephoned her repeatedly and at such
hours that the only explanation of the silence was that she had
left London. He went round to her flat and consulted the commissionaire.

"Is Miss Nesbitt away?" he asked.

"No. 12?" queried the sergeant. "No, sir, she went out not an hour ago."

"Oh, thanks very much." He gave the man a generous tip. "There's no need to mention that I asked the question."

"I quite understand, sir."

This conversation established definitely that she must have deliberately refrained from answering the telephone. He had rung her up two hours ago and had been unable to get a reply. She had guessed it was he and had let the bell ring! He must write to her! Anything was preferable to ignorance.

But while he was drafting a letter, he was summoned to the telephone. It was Sondra.

"I'm afraid you've not been able to get a reply," she began, but he interrupted her.

"I've rung again and again. What's happened? I've been dreadfully——"

"It's nothing," she cut in. "I've had to realize some investments unexpectedly. That's occupied some time. And I've had to give a great deal of attention to some things I thought were dead and buried."

"Well, can I see you to-day?"

"I'm afraid not. In fact, I have so much to do that it would be useless to arrange anything. I'd only have to put you off. Let's leave it like this: directly I can we'll dine and go to a theatre together."

"Yes, but when?"

"I tell you, I can't say yet. I'll 'phone directly I know."

He had to be content with that. This brief conversation only partially reassured him.

A fortnight passed before he heard from her again. Then she rang him and suggested that they should dine together and go to a theatre on the following Thursday. She added that she expected to be less occupied soon and hoped to see him frequently. His delight, however, on hearing this, and the affectionate note in her voice, was banished when at six o'clock on the Thursday evening a messenger came from her with a hurried note in which she explained that it was impossible for her to come, but begged him to use the tickets which she enclosed. The note ended with these sentences:

"You've *got* to go to the play, then you can tell me about it at lunch to-morrow. Call for me here just before one."

CHAPTER XIV

I

Rutherford had no desire to go to the theatre but there was no alternative in view of her letter. As he dressed he smiled grimly at the reflection that although two stalls were at his disposal, he did not know a single person in the whole of London whom he could invite to accompany him. In one sense, this was a final commentary on his life: in another, it defined the intensity of his hopes in Sondra.

He decided to dine at *The Goya*. He was no longer afraid of its associations. It was true that when he had been there with Sondra he had suffered damnably by reason of her references to Feversham, nevertheless, *she* had been with him and to-night he would visualize only her beauty and banish all other memories.

On arrival he made his way to the little room and selected a table next to the one Sondra and he had occupied. Adolphe appeared, inspected the room as if it were a mirror which reflected his perfection, and was about to leave when his glance met Rutherford's. He favoured him with a stereotyped professional bow, which proclaimed that he had forgotten him entirely. The latter was in that state in which every triviality assumes the dignity of a symbol, consequently he detected in Adolphe's forgetfulness another indication of the fact that without Sondra he was nothing.

The dinner bored him. The restaurant was crowded and the service was slow. All round him was a babel of conversation. He tried to divert himself by watching these men and women. It was useless – they, like everything else, only reminded him of his isolation. Then he thought of that dinner in 1910, and the irony of the sequel to Feversham's suggestion that the three of them should dine there twenty years hence emerged starkly for the first time. But was not the miracle that he and Sondra *had* dined there together on the actual date suggested?

He took his glass and was about to raise it when his glance fell on his hand. That hand had shot Feversham! It had helped to drag him to the well through the darkness. He gazed at it fascinated. He was not frightened, he was intrigued by the impossibility of believing the truth.

Speculations, normally foreign to him, flitted through his brain. . . . Did he believe that there was a life after death? Would he meet Feversham in some spirit world where the truth would be established beyond the possibility of doubt or denial? Why was it that he had no answer to these questions? They went deeper than any others, yet not only could he not answer them but he had no beliefs of any kind in regard to them. Philip was dead too. Then, was it *possible*, that in some world of the spirit Philip had encountered Feversham——?

The restaurant became dim and the conversation and laughter seemed ghostly echoes. He could not trust his thoughts: one moment they were his slaves, and the next they were his masters. He looked round quickly and seeing Adolphe he beckoned him to his table.

"Monsieur?"

I wondered, Adolphe, if that lady who dined with me here a few weeks ago had been in again. You remember that she showed you one of your old menus——"

"Ah! perfectly, monsieur! How could I forget? Yes, she have been in twice – three times – since then. She and my wife discuss all those people who come here years ago. But, as for me, monsieur, I do not care to remember how the years go. To-day – we are here. To-morrow?" He snapped his fingers and shrugged his shoulders eloquently. "To-morrow – we are gone. The women, monsieur, enjoy to cry over such things. But for me – *no!*"

Rutherford encouraged him to discuss the history of the

restaurant's evolution and as this theme was Adolphe's favourite one, the time slipped away. When Rutherford looked at his watch, it told him that it was twenty minutes past eight. As the play began at eight-thirty, he had no time to waste.

He rose hurriedly, paid the bill, and went out into the street where he hailed a taxi, as he was still a slave to the old-fashioned notion that it is quicker to drive through modern London than to walk. Needless to say, almost immediately, he joined an enormous motionless queue of cars – past which pedestrians seemed to rush like comets.

When he reached the theatre, he was late. He hurried in, noticing nothing, and accepted a programme, which was thrust into his hand – he was scarcely conscious of his surroundings – and then followed an attendant mechanically.

The curtain had risen and consequently the house was in darkness. Rutherford groped to his seat, asking forgiveness and receiving none. It was some minutes before he had recovered sufficiently to give his attention to the stage.

The star actor made his entrance and a ripple of applause greeted him. Instantly the audience became more expectant, and Rutherford heard a girl behind him whisper: "That's Robert Hillyer. He's marvellous!" Directly Hillyer appeared the action of the play became more defined, more dramatic, and consequently a new vibration was created.

As Rutherford watched and listened, he became aware of a feeling of familiarity which disturbed him. A moment later one of the actors said a line which woke unmistakable echoes in him. He stared at the scenery. Yes, he remembered the set perfectly! Suddenly recognition overwhelmed him. He felt feverishly for his programme, his heart beating like a drum. He tore it open and leant down to inspect it. His eyes were accustomed to the darkness by now and by the aid of a dim light near by he was able to read:

THE DEATH OF JOHN BRAND

By

MARTIN FEVERSHAM.

He began to tremble violently and a terrible desire to laugh possessed him. Not for one instant did he believe in the actuality of his surroundings. The dark theatre; the stage; the play in progress; the programme in his hand were a series of delusions. All he knew was that the fear which had haunted him for a year was a fear no longer. It was a fact. *He was a madman.* Yes, a madman, and everything which seemed to be happening round him was the proof of that madness.

But the supreme and abiding terror was that he was still sane enough to know that he was mad. Never, not even when his darkest fears had writhed in his mind like serpents, had he contemplated the possibility that a man could become insane and be conscious of the fact. He had clung to the belief that madness, at any rate, was oblivion. Even that gaunt hope was false and he wanted to laugh – to laugh terribly at this last deception.

As if hypnotized, he continued to stare at the stage, marvelling that his phantasm could be so vivid. Nevertheless, it could not deceive him. This belief woke a strange pride in him. He knew the utter impossibility of what apparently was taking place. Feversham's play in a London theatre! It was a monstrous illusion. There was one script of that play: it was the one he had picked up from the table in that empty room in the cottage. He had folded it up, put it in his breast pocket, and now it was locked in a drawer of the cabinet in his room. Yes, it was there, with the manuscript of the "story" he had written when he had tried to set down the truth of his visit to Cornwall. He *knew* it was locked in that drawer. He had seen it only yesterday. He would cling to this knowledge with the whole might of his will for while he could retain it, he would preserve a glimmer of sanity. It might even be that if he clung tenaciously enough to this knowledge, he would dispel this nightmare which surrounded him. He would not look at the stage, which seemed to boast its reality, he would close his eyes and repeat again and again: "There is only one manuscript of Feversham's play and it is locked in that drawer." He would make the sentence do service as an incantation. It would triumph over the necromancy of madness. It would——

Suddenly the whole house was illuminated. The audience was applauding vigorously. He started violently and looked round with haggard eyes. The curtain rose, revealing the situation on which it had just fallen, and the applause increased. Then people left their seats, produced cigarette cases, and made their way to the exits, talking excitedly.

He leapt to his feet convulsively. He must go! He must get away from all this. It didn't matter where – there was no need to think – he must go, immediately, out into the streets, back to his room, *anywhere. . . .*

He walked unsteadily and slowly to the exit, though it seemed to him that he was running. At the door he pushed past a man who regarded him with mild interest, then turned to his wife and said:

"That's the man next to me. The damned feller's drunk. Can't sit still to save his life. I wish he'd move up one, because the seat next to him is empty."

Rutherford paused when he reached the foyer. Men and women were dotted about in groups, smoking, and talking with great animation. He leant against the wall, watching them. Could *this* be delirium? Was all this the creation of his brain and was he in reality somewhere else? It was impossible to believe that now. In the darkness of the theatre, watching the mimic life of the stage, he had been certain of it. But now – when lights blazed down and he could hear the voices of men and women, note their expressions, and watch their movements – *now* could he believe that all this was a projection of madness? Why——

"Excuse me, sir."

Someone was speaking to him! He must control himself at all costs, he——

"I couldn't get a programme. Everyone seems to go mad on a first night. Might I have a look at yours?"

The programme was still in Rutherford's hand and he offered it mechanically.

"Thanks so much. Awfully good of you."

The man consulted it briefly and turned to a very smart woman near him:

"It's by Martin Feversham. What? Oh, yes, wait a minute. *Three* acts. That's right. The next is a study and the last is the same as the first."

He gave the programme back to Rutherford.

"I'm so much obliged, most kind of you."

Rutherford took the programme in silence and the man walked away with his companion.

Rutherford began to wander about among these men and women as if to convince himself that they were not apparitions. A bell sounded but its significance was lost on him. He only recognized vaguely that a general movement began to which instinctively he subordinated himself.

Most of the people had returned to their seats by the time Rutherford made his way to his. He was only able to locate it by seeing two unoccupied stalls. His neighbour, however, recognized him with no enthusiasm, and said to his wife:

"Good Heavens, that feller's coming back! He's certain to have had a couple of doubles, so mind your feet."

"Hush, Frank! He'll hear you."

"Never! Here he comes. Look out!"

A moment later the lights were lowered and the curtain rose. Two things flashed into his consciousness simultaneously. One was that all this *was* real; and the other was that in the act now to be performed occurred that struggle about which he had argued so often with Feversham – the struggle they had rehearsed in the cottage.

Every line spoken on the stage was familiar to him. He had analysed each one, argued about it, suggested alterations, till repetition had branded it on his memory.

Gradually, inevitably, the action drew nearer and nearer to the struggle between the two men. A premonition of tragedy held the audience. There was not a sound from the darkness, only the voices of the actors rang out as line by line the climax drew nearer. Rutherford watched the stage, scarcely daring to breathe. Then he saw again that struggle – the one he had witnessed a thousand times in his imagination. He saw one of the actors make precisely that sudden, unexpected movement which Feversham had made. A report rang out and the man fell to the ground.

He wanted to leap to his feet and shout: "Feversham's dead, you fools – he's dead! I shot him years ago in Cornwall and hid the body in a well." But by an immense effort he restrained himself.

He closed his eyes. His body seemed flame and his thoughts were chaos. Repeatedly, one question emerged – how had the play been produced? But instantly it was swept away by thick-coming fears and forebodings. He was no longer aware of the actors or the audience. He seemed to be wandering in some remote region where at any moment the impossible might become the actual, consequently he was unable to dismiss even the most fantastic of his thoughts. For instance, gradually the idea took shape in his mind that the seat next to him was *not* vacant. Someone had stolen in unobserved. If he stretched out his hand he would be able to touch this stranger. Then a new thought darted like forked lightning across his brain. *It was Feversham.* Useless to mutter "impossible" – *everything* was possible. Yes, he was sitting next to him, and would give no sign because he knew that his silent presence inflicted a more exquisite torture on his victim. This was the moment of his revenge and he would exploit it with subtle cruelty.

Again the lights went up but Rutherford remained motionless in his seat. He derived no assurance from the fact that the stall next to him was still vacant, for he was certain that directly the darkness returned Feversham would steal noiselessly to his side. Clamorous thoughts urged him to go, but he was unable to obey them. He could not formulate any policy and so he was impotent to act.

Where should he go? What should he do? And what should he say to Sondra? If he could find answers to these questions, his course would be clear.

But if Rutherford was entirely unaware of the play, it had

long since captured the audience. Probably this was due to the fact that many playgoers had become bored by the mechanical thriller in which someone is murdered – for an entirely banal reason – and the remainder of the action consists of disappearances through trap doors; masked figures threatening torture; impossible escapes; aeroplane pursuits; sorrows of dope fiends; underworld machinations; exploitation of the heroine's physical charms; noises off; till at last the stunt climax is revealed with Scotland Yard breathless but triumphant. In other words, audiences were becoming rather tired of thrillers in which situations were everything and characters were ciphers. Nevertheless, thrills they must have, for thrills are mental cocktails, but a new type was now demanded.

Feversham's play exactly supplied this new demand. He gave them a murder, and he gave them it soon. More, he took them into his confidence by showing them the murderer, so – for once – there was no doubt as to his identity. They forgave him this originality, however, as they became intrigued by the fact that all the other characters assumed that the dead man had committed suicide. The treatment here was brilliant, and the dialogue amusing, for each character had a different theory as to why the dead man had destroyed himself, and, in enunciating it, unconsciously revealed his or her own values and problems. Thus A. B. or C. in attempting to give abstract reasons for D's suicide, merely revealed the circumstances in which each one of them would do the same. In attempting a diagnosis they achieved a confession – the effect of which was rich in comedy, for it disturbed old relations and created new ones of an amusing order. The audience, however, forgave the introduction of psychology for two reasons: one, the treatment was witty and, two, there was that murder in the background. They'd seen it, and they knew who had done it, and the author would *have* to get back to it. Consequently, at any moment, they were expecting an authentic spinal thrill, for at present the murderer seemed perfectly safe and was entirely self-possessed. So, in the meantime, they did not mind laughing at human beings who were recognizable as such.

Then, at the end of the third act, came the thrill – swift, unexpected, yet inevitable. Through the agency of a most ingenious device, the murderer was suddenly revealed in such dramatic circumstances that the audience forgot that they knew of his crime. Before they had recovered from their surprise the curtain fell.

The applause was vigorous and increased as the curtain rose and fell several times in rapid succession. A man behind Rutherford, who had dined so well that he had slept through the last two acts, woke up with a start and finding himself surrounded by enthusiasm, he responded to it by shouting:

"Encore!"

Immediately realizing that this exclamation was not entirely appropriate, he hastened to regain prestige by yelling:

"Author! . . . Author!"

As it is easier to shout "Author" than to continue to clap, the cry was taken up by the house – although no one, quite rightly, really cared tuppence who had written the play. If he had been anybody, they would have known his name. Naturally!

Nevertheless, the demand for the author became so insistent that at length a well-known manager appeared on the stage. After it had been established that he was *not* the author – which took some time – he made a short speech which was characterized by the indecision and nervousness which is common to actors and managers when they are suddenly called upon to make a few simple remarks.

After two false starts, he managed to say, with a number of pauses and a lot of fidgeting:

"Ladies and gentlemen, I want – first of all – to thank you for your reception of this remarkable play. I only wish the author were present, but, unfortunately, he is not. You will be surprised to hear that I have never met him. The play was sent to me and I gather that it was written some years ago. I read it and venture to think that I realized its possibilities immediately. I am most anxious to meet Mr. Feversham, and as I believe that he was in London some considerable time ago, I should be grateful if anyone could inform me where he is now.

In the meantime, let me thank you in his name for your generous appreciation of his work."

The audience began to disperse. Rutherford found himself surrounded by a crowd of people talking excitedly and moving very slowly towards the exit. Then followed a slow procession through narrow winding corridors. Although he was nearly demented with the desire to escape, it was impossible to move more quickly than the others. Also, he had to obtain his things from the cloak-room, and as that convenience was about the size of a telephone box, the attendant kept disappearing for long intervals behind an arras of overcoats. When at length some favourite of fortune secured his coat, it was quite impossible to put it on owing to the crush. Nevertheless, each hero in turn put sixpence in a saucer, arrogantly displayed for that purpose, thereby proving that the English will gladly pay extra for any form of torture – always provided that it is sanctioned by tradition.

At last, Rutherford secured his overcoat and a few minutes later he was in the street.

II

It was a cold, clear night and the streets were thronged. Crowds were issuing from every theatre and picture palace: motor buses, taxis and cars hooted, electric signs flashed from the buildings; and at every corner a small army of pedestrians waited for the traffic to be held up. People were either discussing the entertainment they had just left, or the best means of getting home, while newspaper men shouted the tit-bit in the Late Night Finals.

Rutherford wandered aimlessly through the noisy streets, frequently colliding with people, and with no destination in view. During his slow progress from the theatre he had heard Feversham's name mentioned perhaps half a dozen times, but to his frenzied imagination it had seemed that everyone had been discussing him and now, in the streets, he believed that all these people had only one theme of conversation – Fever-

sham. The word rang in his ears. . . . "Feversham" . . . "Feversham". . . . The name which, for long years, had haunted only
the silence of his mind was now on everyone's lips. Within
a few hours, strenuous attempts would be made to discover
where Feversham was, or what had happened to him. The
manager's speech at the end of the play had made that a certainty. The papers were hard up for copy and it was inevitable that the mystery of the new dramatist's identity would
be exploited to the full. Naturally, the syndicate which had
produced the play would leap at this chance of publicity and
make as much capital as possible out of the fact that they had
produced a play by an author whom they had never seen and
of whose whereabouts they were entirely ignorant. The mystery of Feversham would be made the basis of every conceivable stunt. The result would be that some of those people who
had known Feversham twenty years ago, and had forgotten
him entirely, would remember him readily enough now that
he was famous. They would see a chance of getting into the
limelight and would leap at it – especially the highbrows. Very
soon every detail concerning Feversham would come to light.
Discussion would awaken memories, with the result that incidents long buried in oblivion would be resurrected.

Sondra! *She* would be able to supply the press with very definite information about Feversham. How could she guess that
by so doing she would menace him? Why had he not told her
the truth! If only she knew the truth! If he were to tell her the
facts now, it would be obvious that he only did so in order to
silence her and so make her his accomplice. Yet he would have
to tell her. It would be madness to let her reveal all that she
knew. Being ignorant of the facts, she would see no harm in
relating how Feversham had been his friend, and how they had
quarrelled. Why, good God! she might even tell people that he
had collaborated with Feversham in the play!

What was he going to *do*? It was terrible weakness to
wander about like this when immediate action was essential. He was threatened now far more critically than he had
ever been. Twenty years ago only a handful of people knew

Feversham's name and every one of them believed that he had gone to Paris. Now – soon – thousands would not only know his name but they would realize that there was a mystery concerning him. In 1910, there was not a single person interested in discovering where Feversham was; now, the vast resources of modern journalism would be utilized to discover him.

He must act, and he must act immediately. A crisis confronted him compared with which the dangers of the past were nothing. He must evolve a policy to cover a situation infinitely more complex than the one he had had to face when Feversham lay dead at his feet. *Then* he had fled to Paris, but if he were to vanish now, would not that act in itself create suspicion? There was only one thing to be done – he must tell Sondra. If she remained silent, he had little to fear. To allow her to remain in ignorance was madness. How easy it would have been to tell her a few weeks ago! Then, it would have seemed a voluntary act on his part; now, it would appear that circumstances had compelled him to confess. Nevertheless, no matter how he shrank from the ordeal, he must tell her everything, and trust his future to her. If she sheltered him, then he would know that she loved him. She had become his destiny – she ruled his past and his future.

He must go back to his room and nerve himself to his task. To-morrow, early, he must go to her. He would go to-night, but he must have some hours' solitude in order to recover his balance and to evolve the form of his confession.

Scarcely had he reached this decision, however, when the mystery of the play's production again overwhelmed him. Where had the manuscript been discovered? *He* had the only manuscript of the play locked up in his room. At least – yes – of course, it was in his room! It was ridiculous to doubt that for a moment. He had seen it there yesterday. He was certain he had seen it. Why did he torture himself like this when it was imperative to prepare calmly and coolly for his interview with Sondra? He could prove whether the manuscript was in its place by returning immediately to his room and so dispel the miasma of these haunting doubts and fears. He would get a taxi and drive home at once.

He looked round for a taxi but could not see a vacant one. Irritability flamed in him and he cursed the whole tribe of taxi-drivers to all eternity. If only he could hail a taxi, give the man his address———. The thread of his thoughts snapped. He could not remember his address! He stood motionless, certain that it would come to him instantly. A minute passed, but he could not remember it. The terrible desire to laugh, which he had experienced in the theatre, again possessed him. So it had come to this: he could not remember the address of the house in which he had been born, the house in which he had lived for twenty years, the house which had been his home for the last year! Then, with a swift transition of mood, he wanted to cry like a child, and at the same time a fever of impatience to return to his room raged in him.

An idea occurred to him and he began to fumble in his pockets, searching for a letter. He discovered one, and glanced at the envelope. A moment later a taxi appeared. He gave the man the address and told him to drive quickly.

CHAPTER XV

I

He opened the front door silently, then ran swiftly up the stairs. One desire had become paramount – to ascertain whether the manuscript of the play was still in its drawer in the cabinet. If it had been stolen, then it was obvious that someone knew of his connection with Feversham; but if it were still in its place he had nothing to fear except Sondra's ignorance. The production of the play would remain a mystery, but for the time being he could afford to ignore it.

He flung open the door of his room. With trembling hands he tore off his overcoat and searched his pockets for his keys. He was perspiring and his frantic eagerness to discover whether the manuscript was still in its place impeded his movements.

At last the drawer was unlocked and he began to turn over its contents with desperate haste. A cry of triumph broke from him – the manuscript was safe. He was not menaced by some unknown adversary. But, perhaps, it would be wiser to burn it and so destroy the only evidence of his intimacy with Feversham.

He was considering the desirability of this action when a movement in the room startled him. He turned swiftly, just as a hand appeared at the side of the screen. With a cry of fear he shut and locked the drawer, then turned and stared at the screen.

"Who is it?" he demanded in a low voice.

Slowly a section of the screen was bent back and he saw Sondra.

For a few seconds they stood motionless. Rutherford's head was bent and he looked up at her guiltily, amazed by her pallor and immobility, and by the glance of her dark eyes which was like a sword measuring the distance between them.

"You!" he muttered.

"What's in that drawer?"

He scarcely recognized her voice. Contempt, hatred, and passion had transformed it.

Silence.

She moved rapidly towards him. She seemed to tower above him, challenging him, threatening him. He bent his head still lower and made a quick staccato movement with his hands as if to push her away from him.

"What's in that drawer? Unlock it! I want to see!"

He heard the words but they conveyed nothing. Their literal meaning escaped him. He was only aware of the spirit behind them, but that told him that she was an enemy. The discovery stupefied him and he could not speak.

"You are going to tell me the truth about Feversham."

"Sondra!"

"*Feversham.*"

The word he had uttered had been a cry for mercy, but hers was a command. The issue was defined and the ensuing silence quivered with the antagonism between them.

"You have a secret. For years and years you have lived alone with it. You confided in no one because you dare not speak. You know the truth about Feversham. To-night, you are going to tell me what it is."

"Sondra – Sondra! – I know nothing."

"You are lying. You know *everything*. And only you know."

"I know nothing," he repeated mechanically.

"Then give me your keys and let me open that drawer."

"It's impossible – you don't understand——"

"I'm going to understand – you need have no doubt as to that. I am giving you one chance – the chance to tell me your secret. If you do not take it, I will force it from you. There is nothing I would not do to make you speak."

Instinctively, automatically, he pulled the handle of the drawer to convince himself that it was locked. Then he moved away from her and went to the fire. He was shivering. She followed, then stood looking down at him. The ticking of the clock on the mantelpiece seemed to fill the room.

"You are determined to remain silent," she said at last, "but I will make you speak. What was the title of the play you saw to-night and who wrote it?"

He said nothing and she continued:

"It was Feversham's play – the play you tried to get your name to in 1910. If you have no secret relating to Feversham, why did you rush into this room like a madman a few minutes ago and search the contents of that drawer with such feverish anxiety?"

"I cannot tell you," he replied almost in a whisper. "Why cannot you believe me, Sondra? There is nothing I would not do for you. Perhaps I have a secret but it has nothing to do with Feversham."

She made an impatient gesture, then said:

"Do you remember the first time you came to my flat a few weeks ago? Answer me. Do you remember?"

"Yes."

"You looked like a haunted man – you scarcely dared to look me in the eyes. I could see that you were afraid to meet me and yet something had forced you to come. I did not know what it was then. I know now."

"What was it?" he asked. He spoke lifelessly as if he were listening, not to her, but to the babel of his own thoughts.

"It was loneliness. You were so lonely that you were afraid of madness. That's why you came. And that is why you waited for days – after seeing me in the street – before you could find the courage to call. You came in, you began to talk, and I waited for you to mention Feversham. It was through him that we met, and yet you did not mention his name. Why – why?"

"There's an explanation, I tell you! But I cannot give it to you. Do believe that – you *must* believe that."

She went on as if he had not spoken:

"Again and again I was on the point of mentioning his name to you but I decided to wait to see if you would mention it before you left. I said to you: 'You've a good memory.' That was a hint, but you remained silent. After you had gone, I thought over every word you had said and I became suspicious. I decided that I would see you again and bring the conversation nearer and nearer to Feversham in order to *make* you speak."

"Why didn't you trust me, Sondra? Why don't you trust me now?"

"Trust you! I hate you as I have never hated anyone. I hated you from the first moment I ever saw you. I only continued to see you in 1910 because Feversham wanted me to. How blind and deaf you have been all these last few weeks. I'll tell you this now – and explain it later – I only came to London a few months ago because I was determined to discover what had happened to him."

He looked up at her quickly. Surprise and fear were evenly balanced in his expression.

"To discover what had happened to Feversham?" he repeated.

"You'll understand – later. Then you came to my flat a second time. I mentioned Madame de Fontin. Still you were silent. Then you pretended that you could not remember Ashley Alston's name. Then, when I was certain that you were determined not to refer to Feversham, *I* mentioned his name lightly. I had my back to you but I could see you in a mirror. Directly I said the word 'Feversham' your eyes blazed with fear and the box of matches you were holding fell into the hearth. And then – my God! – you pretended that *you* were about to ask me what had happened to him! You thought that clever. Why, guilt was written all over you. I pretended that my cigarettes were in the next room and asked you to give me one. Why did your hands tremble? Why did you begin to talk so rapidly and so vehemently about your writing? Because you wanted to make any further reference to Feversham impossible."

After a long silence she went on:

"Just before you left, I went over to the window. I dared not let you look into my eyes, for I was afraid you would see how certain I was that you knew some secret about Feversham. I shivered and you asked if I was cold. I shivered because I was certain – and because I hated you."

"Sondra!——"

"Wait! What a fool a clever man is! You suspected nothing, and you expected me to believe any rubbish you chose to tell me. Your vanity blinded you as it has always blinded you. You told me that by 1915 you were a master of several languages. You only knew French and German very tolerably in 1910 – so you had clearly studied languages exclusively during the interval. Why? You gave up writing. Why? You left England. Why?"

"I cannot answer you, Sondra. There is an answer but——"

"You dare not give it. You never wrote to me after I left London in 1910, yet you had made it only too clear that you were attracted by me. Then, during all these last few weeks, you never asked whether *Feversham* had written to me? Why not? You *knew* he had not – that's why."

She sat down in a chair by the fire and stared in front of her.

He watched her as if his life depended on her, but she seemed to have forgotten him and when she spoke again she might have been thinking aloud.

"I left London in 1910. Feversham came to see me off. He told me he was coming to New York in the spring and said he would write to me often from Paris. When I got back home I waited to hear from him. Weeks, months, went by – nothing. The spring came, but he did not arrive. I could not understand it – I did not know what to do. I wrote to Madame de Fontin and she replied saying that Feversham was in Paris and that you were there too. Then it crossed my mind that it was strange that you had not written. But I did not realize how strange till much later."

There was a long pause then she continued with a new note in her voice:

"My God! What I suffered through his silence. I was certain that he cared for me – almost certain that he loved me – and yet not a line from him. Nothing! A year passed, then another. I rebelled against my suffering. I told myself that he was not the only man in the world. Perhaps there were other men something like him. I thought that, then. I did not know the world as I know it now. My pride advised me to forget him and I, therefore, married. Years of futility followed and then – some years before my divorce – I came to London just after the war. I could only stay a few weeks but I tried to discover some trace of him. I found none. I went to Paris. Useless! He had vanished and I thought perhaps he had been killed in the war."

Rutherford sat with his face half buried in his hand listening to her, hearing each word, yet striving at the same time to evolve an appeal which would move her. He dare not lose her. He had forgotten all about the play and the inquiries which would be instigated to discover details about Feversham. All that had become vague and meaningless. He could ignore all that if only he could bind Sondra to him. She was the future – his last remaining chance of life – and he dare not surrender it. He would listen to her, and strive to find an appeal which would compel a response.

"I came to London again a few months ago determined to find some trace of him. I made inquiries at the War Office, here and in Paris, but could discover nothing. Then, when my task seemed utterly hopeless, you appeared, and very soon I was certain that you knew everything. I pretended that I cared for you. I flattered you – and I set trap after trap for you. I refused to let you pay for our entertainments because I hated you. It was agony to shake hands with you. I made notes of everything you had said immediately after each of our meetings. And then – we dined at *The Goya*! I planned that dinner. I had kept that old menu card, for I had kept everything he had ever given me. And, that night, *you* referred to him. Do you imagine that I did not see what it cost you to mention his name? I reminded you that twenty years ago the three of us had dined together. I gave you that old menu with those sketches on it, and you lowered your head for you dare not let me see the fear in your eyes. But I was afraid to frighten you too much, as I knew that if I did you would stop seeing me. That is why I brought the programme of that Artists' Ball with me. I wanted you to think I had been going through all my mementos of the old days. And you believed it because your vanity whispered to you that I loved you——"

"Sondra!"

"*Feversham!*"

Two words – two themes. In crying her name he was pleading desperately for his future. In breathing the name of her lover, she was calling her dead life from the past.

"Why do you imagine that I came so often to this room? Why did I become friends with Miss Trentham? To see if she knew anything about you, and because I knew I should need a friend in this house. She is away, and she thinks I am sleeping in her room to-night. That is why she left me a key. I moved that screen a few weeks ago because I was planning all that has happened to-night. Do you know when I discovered finally that you knew the truth about Feversham? It was when I was here and asked you suddenly whether you thought he was dead. *Then*, I was certain."

There was a long silence. When she spoke again she was calmer.

"Night after night I lay sleepless plotting against you – knowing that your vanity was my only ally. No woman could have been such a fool as you have been. It was because you were clever and proud that it was easy to deceive you. But how was I to force you to tell me the truth? *That* was the problem which haunted me. Then I thought of a way. It was surrounded by difficulties but it was the only one I could devise. When I left for America in 1910, Feversham gave me the first draft of his play. A few weeks ago I took it to a manager. He read it and said that it would not be a success because the public demands one thrill after another. I let him make love to me and then his opinion of the play's merits increased. When I told him that I was prepared to put money up for its production, he began to think it was a masterpiece. Directly I got him to agree to produce it I stopped seeing you."

"Why?" he muttered. "Why?"

"Because I knew that loneliness would break down all the defences your fear had erected. I wanted to see you when you thought you were alone, after you had seen Feversham's play. I risked your seeing the preliminary announcements of the production. I knew you took no interest of any kind in the theatre. At the last minute I sent you word that I could not come to the theatre, but I knew you would obey me when I said that you were to go. And you raced back here, half a madman, because you are guilty. You shall tell me what your crime is before I leave you to-night."

Rutherford rose and began to pace the room. She leant back wearily and for a moment she looked quite old. Her glance followed him as he went to and fro but he did not look at her. When a man has only one hope left, he does not surrender it easily. At last he paused by her chair and began to speak rapidly in a voice which she scarcely recognized:

"Listen, Sondra. Listen to me – you must listen to me. You say there is a mystery in my life. I admit it – but I cannot tell you what it is. No, wait, wait!" he exclaimed as she made an impatient gesture. "You wouldn't understand if I told you the truth. You wouldn't believe it – no one could believe it. Yet it *is* the truth. But all that doesn't matter. Listen! My life has been hell – it's been hell for years and it still is. I haven't lived at all. I've been cut off from the land of the living. If you knew everything you would pity me."

"*Pity* you?"

"Yes! You must believe that! Listen! In those old days, twenty years ago, I loved you. Now, to-day, you are life itself to me. Many men say that to a woman but, for me, those words are literally true. You are my future. More, you are my very chance of birth. You can't understand that, but it's true. Before God, it is true! I have lived on substitutes and so I have never lived. Wait – Wait! Years ago I made a decision – what does it matter what it was? – a decision which destroyed the basis of my life and made me an outcast. If I had not met you again, I should have been a madman by now."

"What is all this to do with me?"

"You have not suffered as I have, or you would not be merciless."

"What do you know of my suffering?" she asked bitterly. "I have suffered as you have never suffered. *You* can imagine a future. I died when Feversham disappeared."

"Forget the past, Sondra. Let us forget it together. You have no one in the world and neither have I. I love you – I depend on you. All these weeks I have whispered your name in the darkness. You must listen, Sondra———"

"Feversham! . . . You always hated him. You have always hated everyone whose stature compelled you to realize your own littleness. The first time I met you at *The Goya* I could see that. Every reference you made to him was an attempt to lessen him in my eyes. You hated him – and I hated you. But *he* had a belief in you. Although he saw all your littleness even more clearly than I did, still he believed that there was something in you which would one day emerge and transform you. He made me see you although he knew that I loathed you. Even after the quarrel, he would not hear one word against you. He told no one what the cause of that quarrel was, but he told me that it would probably make a real friendship possible between you. And all the time I knew that the extent to which he was your superior was the measure of your hatred for him. I could *see* hatred in your eyes when the three of us were together. You used to watch him, when you imagined you were unobserved, and then your thoughts were in your eyes for anyone to read."

"That was twenty years ago," he said slowly. "Do you imagine that since then I have not gazed long and often into the abyss of my own soul? What I have learned about myself has destroyed me. Only fools believe that to know oneself is wisdom. To know oneself is to destroy oneself. People evade the horror of this knowledge – they evade it by taking every conceivable precaution against loneliness. The real terror of solitary confinement is that it forces you to think. Thought is the modern equivalent to the rack. For years I have been in prison, and only you can release me."

Again there was silence. Something convinced her that the words he had just spoken were the truth and, for the first time, she forgot the issue between them. She, too, had known loneliness and, therefore, she recognized the authentic note of sincerity in his voice. She did not look at him. She was gazing into vacancy, seeing nothing, unmindful of her surroundings, aware only of the unfathomable mystery hidden in every human being.

Rutherford noticed the alteration in her expression and, seizing the opportunity, began to plead with her in short passionate sentences. But she only heard the voice, not the words. She realized that to-night she would learn the truth about Feversham and that this knowledge might crush her. For years she had drugged herself with hope – and she was afraid that, if she forced Rutherford to speak, this solace might be denied her for ever. She began to tremble: all her weakness urged her to leave him and never to see him again.

Rutherford mistook her silence for attention and, believing that she was wavering, his advocacy became more ardent.

"Let's forget the past, Sondra. Let's go away together – at once – to-morrow – and never return. We belong to each other. Our only hope is to be together."

"Feversham." Her voice was a whisper.

He made a convulsive movement with his hands.

"Why do you keep referring to him? Forget him! I tell you the past is dead. Feversham is dead——"

"Dead!"

In an instant she was on her feet, facing him.

"*Dead!* How do you know he is dead?"

"He must be dead," he muttered. "I——"

"You *know* he is dead."

He sank into a chair and buried his head in his hands.

"You murdered him."

"Sondra!"

"You murdered him. That is why you left England. That is why you gave up writing and began to study languages. That is why you did not write to me, and why you were afraid to call after you had seen me in the street. My God! It explains everything. It explains why you became an outcast. It explains why you rushed back to this room to-night like a murderer——"

"Sondra – *Sondra!*"

"Feversham! He stands between us. I will make you see him. I will make you confess that you killed him."

"I am innocent, I tell you. You must believe me – I am innocent."

"You are lying. You have lied to yourself all your life and now you are lying to me. I understand now why you dared not mention his name – why your eyes flashed with fear when I asked you what had become of him. You murdered him and, to-night, you were terrified because you knew that his name would be on everyone's lips and that to-morrow they will try to discover where he is."

He crouched lower into the chair as if her words were blows of a whip. She seized him by the shoulders, forced him to look at her, then started back with a cry.

"*You murdered him!*"

The phrase seemed to remain suspended like a weapon in the ensuing silence. She sank into a chair. She was so near to him that their knees were almost touching, yet each was unaware of the other's proximity. Although he had admitted nothing she knew his secret, and he realized at last that he had centred all his hopes in his bitterest enemy. To each an end had come.

Several minutes passed but they neither spoke nor stirred. The house was silent and no sound rose from the street. Feversham was the most vital presence in that room – and he had been dead for twenty years. To Rutherford, he was a motionless body on the floor of a candle-lit room in Cornwall. To Sondra, he was the supreme lover: a symbol of all the ascending possibilities of life. It was through Feversham that they had met: it was through him that each of them had been driven into the desert of loneliness. Sondra's love for him had made her world a wilderness: Rutherford's hatred had made his world a prison. Each had died a different death in him. There was not one ghost in the room – there were three.

The sound of a distant train threaded the silence. A moment later a clock boomed out. The reverberations had scarcely died away when a car stopped a few yards from the house and the sound of laughter and boisterous farewells broke the spell which bound them.

Sondra rose and he followed her example mechanically. They stood for a moment facing each other, then she said in a low voice,

"Lie to me – tell me that he is not dead. If he had lived, if he had loved me – married me – all things would have been possible. *All things*, do you understand? Had I been greater, I should not have needed him. I could have found power in myself to accomplish. But, in my weakness, he was essential to me. Only in his presence were certain things true. Lie to me, lie to me! For years my life has had only one purpose – to find him. If he is dead, *I* am dead. Forget all that I have said, forget all my bitterness and hatred. Tell me that he is alive or, if not that, tell me that you do not *know* that he is dead."

"It is useless, Sondra. Each of us in our different ways will have to face the truth. He is dead."

"You killed him!"

"Yes, twenty years ago."

He was terribly pale but his voice did not falter. He stood motionless and although his glance met hers he was not looking at her. She felt that he was staring at someone behind her and she was afraid to turn round.

"How – when——?"

"It was an accident," he whispered. "I am certain it was an accident——"

"You are lying again. I can see it in your eyes."

She gazed at him fascinated. Despite her horror, there was something in his whole attitude which held her against her will. The curious thought flashed across her mind that it was strange that he was still alive.

She flung on her cloak and turned to him fiercely.

"To-morrow, everyone will know that Gordon Rutherford killed Martin Feversham. I am going – and I shall never see you again."

"You are all that I have in the world. And I am all that you have. Perhaps you don't believe that. When you are alone, as I am alone, you will know that it is true."

He did not look at her as he spoke. A moment later she went, closing the door softly behind her.

II

He crossed to the window, opened it, and looked down into the square. By the light of a street lamp he saw Sondra go down the steps. She hesitated for a moment then began to walk away rapidly. He watched her disappear with no more emotion than if she had been a stranger. It seemed to him that he had crossed a frontier and entered a region in which hopes and fears became irrelevant. He was watching himself from a great distance, surprised to discover that he was wholly indifferent to past, present, and future.

He reviewed his circumstances dispassionately, almost amused by the plans which his brain elaborated in rapid succession for his safety. Should he leave England immediately, return to his studio in Paris, and await developments? Sondra could prove nothing – the authorities would be slow to extradite him and charge him with murder merely on the basis of her evidence. He played with the idea, knowing that he lacked the incentive necessary for action of any kind. Twenty years ago he had fled, for he had believed that he had a life to live; now, he knew that his life was over – it had ended to-night. The world has no power over a ghost.

Another idea occurred to him. How easy it would be to deceive them! to admit he had confessed to Sondra that he had killed Feversham, and then to explain that this was a delusion from which he had suffered as a result of overwork. He would point out that for weeks together he was free from this nightmare and then suddenly it captured him again. He would assert that, in reality, he had never seen Feversham since their quarrel and had no idea what had happened to him. He would tell them all this with a smile, completely indifferent as to whether they believed him or not. He had not said a syllable to Sondra concerning the cottage in Cornwall. What would any of them be able to prove?

The possibilities of his situation intrigued one part of his brain, whereas the remainder knew that all these speculations were nonsense. It did not matter in the least what happened to him. At last the curtain had fallen on that drama which had been enacted on the stage of his mind for the last twenty years. Yes, he would tell them the truth about Feversham. He would tell them of the doubt which had tortured him that night in his studio in Paris. He would explain that he had shot Feversham, but that he did not know whether he was a murderer or not. He would reveal to them every detail of the drama he had been forced to witness in solitude. He would show them how he had based his life on a lie, and that the result had been twenty years' servitude, all the more terrible because his prison had been as wide as the world. It would be amusing to see how many of them believed that their lives were based on the truth. . . .

He began to watch the topmost twig of the silver birch. It was swaying gently to and fro. He remembered how on winter evenings, when he was a child, he used to stand by this window and watch the slender branches submit to the rage of the storm. How perfectly they had yielded to each furious mood of the wind! Each sudden onslaught had been made an occasion for a new revelation of beauty, in the same way as the temptations of a saint provide opportunities for a mightier demonstration of the glory of God. Storm after storm in turn had lashed this silver birch, each had perished through the excess of its own fury, but the tree had survived. It had resisted not evil; it had been true to the principle of its being; it had had no will apart from that of its creator. Rutherford felt that the soul of the tree was whispering its secret to him.

It seemed to him that one by one the years fell from him. He was a child again; the room was his nursery; he had crept to the window in order to watch the flickering lights in the square below. His father and mother were downstairs and Philip was sleeping quite near to him. He had recaptured that curious, intimate, intense life he had once known – that life which was strangely independent of others for its interior satisfactions. A sense of deep peace possessed him and gradually he became aware of the proximity of that other mysterious world he had known in childhood: that world invisible yet near, the existence of which was known only to him. He stood on the frontier of that strange region of colour and beauty in which was freedom – that world where everyone loved everybody and everything, where it was unnecessary to ask questions because you understood all things in an inner, intense, queer sort of way. His heart became a holy of holies where Wonder, Awe, Mystery were invisible presences. The answer to all the questions he had never been able to ask invaded his being like the ever-lengthening rays of summer dawn. It seemed to him that his life had been a great circle and that he had arrived again at the point from which he had started. From peace he had passed to anarchy; from anarchy to suffering; from suffering to peace. He had died, and so he had been born again. . . .

He would challenge this spirit of peace which had descended so strangely upon him. He would confront it with the facts of his situation in order to test its validity. To-morrow, he was going to confess to the world that he had shot Feversham. It was probable that he would be tried for murder. It was certain that no one would believe his story. Sondra was lost to him for ever. These were the facts, and he repeated them again and again, but they failed to disturb this mysterious tranquillity which had been born in him. The drama which had haunted his mind for years was ended. And he knew that by confessing everything he would discover whether or not the death of Feversham had been an accident. He desired only the truth – nothing less interested him. He would discover it because he was prepared to accept it.

He turned from the window and crossed to the fire. By what miracle had he been delivered from fear? Judged by the evidence, his circumstances had never been so desperate, yet he was free. Freedom had come to him at that moment when his hopes in Sondra had collapsed.

Then suddenly, clearly, he realized that he feared nothing in the world because he hoped nothing from the world. He had died to it, and, therefore, he was delivered from the illusion of hope and the illusion of fear.

Lightning Source UK Ltd.
Milton Keynes UK
UKOW04f1833070118
315699UK00001B/152/P